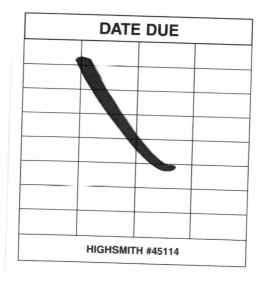

Angels
✃ IN A ✄
HARSH WORLD

Angels

◦8 IN A 8◦

HARSH WORLD

DON BRADLEY

G. P. Putnam's Sons

NEW YORK

G. P. Putnam's Sons

Publishers Since 1838

a member of

Penguin Putnam Inc.

200 Madison Avenue

New York, NY 10016

Library of Congress Cataloging-in-Publication Data

Bradley, Don.
Angels in a harsh world / Don Bradley.
p.   cm.
ISBN 0-399-14359-9 (alk. paper)
I. Title.
PS3552.R2264A8   1998   97-37358 CIP
813'.54—dc21

Printed in the United States of America

1   3   5   7   9   10   8   6   4   2

This book is printed on acid-free paper. ⊚

Book design by Lynne Amft

ACKNOWLEDGMENTS

The road was long and arduous, but those with vision and insight helped to put this book in your hands. Thank you, Susan Allison, for your priceless patience and acumen. My heart belongs to Trisha for being there through the dark nights and stormy seas. Richard Bach deserves special mention for his courage and inspiration while others dared not even dream. A nod of gratitude to Karin Pekarcik for her cherished devotion and labor. Finally, to everyone living from the heart and being part of the magic, may the One Life bless you and keep you in its loving embrace.

Don Bradley, Los Angeles, 1997

Violence has a great deal to do with shadow—the darker side of the world and the human heart—in particular, the shadow of power. For many people born and raised in modern America, innocence—the absence or rejection of shadow—is a strong obstacle to realizing the soul's power.

FOREWORD

I'm told that, after reading my books, readers will often ask themselves, "Are these stories real? Did they actually happen?"

It's apparent why we ask these questions when we find ourselves wishing to live the kind of lives that these books hold forth as a promise of things that can be. Making the story real requires striving from the reader.

When we read about Haley Olsten and her labors, we must realize we are meeting a woman who opened her heart and was willing to face any challenge, at any time, that the One Life placed in her path. Haley's perseverance brought her through the valley so that she, like others before her, could stand on the other side in the clear light of day.

Have you done that? Have you challenged your negative self-images, vanity, and ego to become a *living example* of truth, beauty, and goodness? Is your life an example of selfless service to humanity?

Why not?

That's what it requires to be of any use to Hierarchy, that supreme group of beings who stand ready to guide humanity. The spiritual kingdom is replete with advanced souls, living simply and forging ahead into realms of beingness the rest of the world can only imagine. These souls labor because their hearts are in tune with every single beating heart on this globe.

That's the entrance exam.

Are you narrow-minded, hating everything you don't approve of? Are you a constant critic of everything and everyone? Is your path empty and hollow?

If you look into your heart and find it selfish, vindictive, jealous, spiteful, and full of fear, then you can be assured that stories like this one will remain just that for you: *stories.*

If you look at your life and realize you are a hypocrite to your vision of beauty, truth, and goodness, it is never too late to live up to your own goal of betterment. *Don't be like everyone else: a spectator.* Live the path of wisdom and become someone stories can be written about.

To answer the original question, I have to say that these tales are factual. Many of the events that happened to these people as they struggled onward have been distilled into concise time frames; years became weeks, days an hour. The people in them lived or are living now in the world. Some readers recognize themselves in my books. Their names have been changed to protect their privacy and families, but their labors stand as beacons for those of us who follow. Watching their lives and learning of their great courage is a privilege for which my gratitude has no depth. My job is to tell their stories. How I tell them, and what parts of their lives I write about, is up to me.

If you find parallels in these stories with other teachings or tales, that is as it should be. The path of wisdom and becoming One's Self are universal realities, regardless of the age, Teacher, or medium used to educate.

The big question is: Is your life a story like this? Why not?

Don Bradley, Los Angeles

Angels
IN A
HARSH WORLD

Boston, 1918

His eyes never left her. She was the radiant center of any circle she entered. And she bore the mark. It was visible to those who had eyes to see, a heart to feel. But the danger was just beginning and it would hound her for all of her days, should she survive. The old man sighed, fingered the snow white beard that touched his chest, and straightened the folds of his spotless Temple robe.

Unless. Unless she should falter, the shield of the Brotherhood would always stand firm guard over her.

Therein lay the danger.

His face, careworn from a long lifetime spent watching, waiting, and serving, flashed a slight and momentary grimace. The others ... like wolves, they would be watchful for any mistake, any failure on the part of the Brotherhood. The dark ones would not stop, knowing the gravity of the situation. The clocks had struck their dreadful purpose and the time now brought all circumstances into the circle; that circle and destiny were the ever-present fate of mankind. The soulless would expend every resource, every weapon, every tool within their possession to block and destroy her.

His was a timeless battle, fought again and again in endless conflicts and eras. After a time, there seemed to be no end to it all, as there had been no beginning. The priest, ageless as the conflict that was in the process of engulfing the entire globe, smiled at the realization that the struggle between the two forces was beginning to take on a farcical element, like two maddened rhinos banging against each other until they tired, then resting, then banging away again.

Once again, the wheel was turning; the time for rest was over.

On the firing line of truth, beauty, and all that stood for what was good and pure in humanity, the priest was a front-line warrior in the truest sense of the word. The eyes that looked out over time and space, carefully observing the events that would bring the new century to a critical point, were eyes that had served the great Brotherhood for untold generations. Every step taken, every sacrifice made, all had been for this moment.

Easing into his chair that overlooked the great valley of Rishis, the priest watched and remembered. Remembered his friends, brothers, and sisters as they had been slaughtered by an ungrateful and ignorant humanity—as they willingly gave their lives to further the cause of freedom from a dark tyranny that continuously sought to enslave the human spirit. Though their bones were long since dust, their faces were still fresh in a memory as keen as a young boy's.

Each century the struggle emerged somewhere in the world: in a royal house, a new government, a civil war, or merely in some small town where seeds of intolerance boiled over into hatred,

2

allowing the forces of both sides to empower the tiny beings called men. And empower them they would, each side taking any opportunity given to them by the struggling human beings seeking their desires in prayer. Some asked for the healing embrace of renunciation, love, and an end to war. Others, as was more usually the case, begged in their secret thoughts to have the power of revenge over their enemies and to become victorious. The old man watched carefully for the slightest sign of a heart filled with compassion, grace, and love—ever eager to lift the weary soul from his trouble and pain into a clearer light. In each contest, those supplicant lights grew fewer and fewer until they could be counted with an effortless glance, as easily as one might notice a single torch lit in a valley at night.

Though every chance offered to aid and assist was taken, none of these events throughout history—either individually or in total—mattered when compared with what was coming. By the thousands, as each century passed, his warriors had struggled and died to make this moment in time possible.

How much time had passed since he had taken up the mantle of freedom? He recalled his own entrance into the realm of innocence as though it were yesterday. Julius Caesar had been ruler of all lands, a leader who had brought with him a new order and a new revelation of understanding that changed the world. Though not understood by many, that order was the beginning of organized civilization. But, in the end, no matter what course the Brotherhood had taken, their young Caesar went mad in an orgy of power and destruction. He had gone over to the other side. And so Caesar became their enemy, now an ancient foe growing more vicious with the passage of time.

Clearly, two thousand years ago, it had occurred to the two struggling elements of love or hate, unity or separation, that time was short—merely twenty centuries to succeed or fail, the victor able to rule for endless thousands of centuries on the face of the Earth. It was an endless war, with battles flaring into fever pitches: the Renaissance, the Inquisition, the Middle Ages, the Hundred Years Wars, the Industrial Age, the war to end all wars . . .

The crop of young ones grew each year and the ranks of both groups swelled; still, in spite of the numbers, only a trusted circle of Initiates remained in the Brotherhood who would not give up or give in.

A quiver. A quickening in his heart, a flicker of glee in his eye brought a deep smile to the old man's troubled visage. Suddenly, he was reminded of the *true* state of affairs. The One Life had foreseen all, its consciousness extending into his own, both to remind and as a reward for past service. Worry was folly, a lesson remembered and easily forgotten. Outwardly, in the confusion of a world gone mad, and inwardly, where a master design held all in order, there remained the *Watcher.* Because he held all in his hand, mortal days were as seconds to the Watcher's consciousness.

Seating himself, the old man let his smile become deeper. His joy swept out and away from him, as rays shooting through every part of the world.

All was looked after, cared for, and aided in each instance, no matter how insignificant or small. So it was as it had always been.

The drama existed outside his reason and consciousness to understand; it remained for him to play his part as best he could, never shirking, always serving.

Somehow, in some way, this cataclysm would be averted. It must be! Failure meant the end of humanity on this sphere. Didn't High Ones indicate as much?

And as he thought about the world and its troubles, he noted with satisfaction a turn of events. There was a chance—a chance in a thousand that this one would make it. But the laws of noninterference forbade him to help directly. He could only send her his love.

That would have to be enough.

Franklin Olsten looked out through the parlor windows, choosing to remain seated, knowing the effort his tired frame would have to make to rise at his age of fifty-seven. From there, he could see the maples that were scattered along the street, exploding colors and sheets of brown beneath them. They were beautiful this time of year, and yet he rarely seemed to notice that beauty, or take the time to drink in its gift. Finally, deciding any pain would be worth it, he got up from his chair and moved toward the glass, letting the coolness of it suffuse his face as he pressed against its hard, cold surface. The glass smelled musty, in an inviting fashion, bringing forth a shower of long-forgotten memories. When was the last time he had done that? He couldn't recall. Laughter. A child's laughter, ringing in his ears, caused him to turn. And as he turned, he remembered why he could see the beauty now.

Franklin could see everything now.

Little fingers poked and prodded around his watch pocket, and a sound of glee emerged when the wrapped candy treasures were found. Her eyes, buoyant blue pools of joy surrounded by a massive blond mane, reflected his eight-year-old daughter's endless spirit of mischief.

Haley stopped fussing with his pockets and stood rigidly in front of him, in a vain attempt to suppress her laughter. Franklin looked up at the ceiling—ignoring her eyes—and joined her in playing her favorite game.

Haley laughed. "Daddy's thinking of the curtain!"

Franklin turned his gaze slowly down toward a charming smile that said I-told-you-so. How did she *do* that? Every time, right on the button. Sighing, he retrieved another piece of candy from the pocket of his coat: the one place she hadn't looked.

Clasping her hands behind her, she barely held back her suppressed joy. "So that's where they are."

Franklin smiled, handing over the earned goods. "Yes. And that's quite enough before dinnertime, young lady."

Snatching the candy from his hands, she ran from the room—laughing and giggling the whole while—then stopped short and sauntered back near the door. Absently, as though she had entered a room all her own, she busied herself by the fireplace with her make-believe friends.

Franklin turned sad, watching her. He had told his wife a thousand times that Haley had been sent to save them. She agreed. But something was wrong now, even after all the years of joy his household had known since her birth. Haley was changing. Her joy was becoming cautious and thought-out, no longer spontaneous and explosive. Everyone noticed the shift, but said nothing. But behind their eyes, Franklin knew they were all thinking the same thing at the same time: What's happening to Haley?

The sound in his ears was his teeth grinding—a habit born out of anxiety, his doctor had told him. No one really cared more about Haley than any other family member. No. Their concern was selfish as was his own. If her joy left, what would become of them? No one, not a single person in the Olsten family had forgotten—could *ever forget*—what it was like before.

How could he explain to an innocent child about pain and suffering, about good and evil? These were concepts that he himself still struggled with. He had only hope: a hope born of desperation over a life not easily lived, or easily understood.

He had married late in life, at age forty-one, and his wife, Sarah, had borne him three children: Gary, the oldest, who was at Yale; John, the younger son; and Haley, his "Little Hope." Sarah understood his pain. She knew about Franklin's father and the severe trauma the American Civil War had inflicted upon him and his family.

His father, the colonel, had come to visit in 1897 and never left. The cable that spelled disaster came, as disasters are wont to do, during a simple Sunday dinner in the middle of an otherwise glorious spring. After recovering from the shattering news that his mother had passed away during a yellow fever epidemic in Charleston, Franklin barely noticed the postscript on the bottom informing him of his father's intended arrival the following Wednesday by rail.

Franklin winced at the memory. Their lives had never been the same after that.

"The Beast is loose." At least that's what Franklin's father always said. As a colonel in Hancock's II Corps, the Union Army of the Potomac, he knew. His father had seen the Beast devour men and states wholesale, leaving a trail of widows, orphans, and destruction in its wake. In the beginning, everything was fine, except on *those* days when the anniversaries of Malvern Hill, Gettysburg, and Antietam came around. The colonel spoke to no one, locking himself in the family study with ancient memories and friendships turned to dust by time and distance. Month after month, year after year, long after the cannons had grown silent, the war and its horrors took roost in Franklin's home.

In desperation, Sarah took him aside one evening to tell him that she could actually *hear* the colonel lost in antiquity—shouting hoarse orders to regiments being decimated by canister and grape. In tears, she described the bizarre scenes that flashed through her thoughts, as though some mystical and evil force linked her mind with Franklin's father's. Images of men and earth being shattered by shot and shell. Explosions rocking the horizon, followed by the screams of hundreds of wounded men.

Sometimes the screams—both real and imaginary—would force her out of that damned, dreadful house. Out . . . out and away, as far as running legs would carry her—away to the peace of soft leaves and the sweet song of birds. She told him these things because she loved him, that her love was being sorely tested and much more of this insanity could only end in one way. Franklin shuddered at the news. His face went white in disbelief that his home, once the garden of his life, was disintegrating into ashes. Glancing at her, his face etched with incredulity, Franklin shook his head.

Seeing that he didn't understand, Sarah explained how she had watched Franklin cringe in his room, crying with his father in consolation, the memories of his long-dead mother intertwined with his father's battlefield pain. She waited as their muffled weeping lingered in the house for hours, bringing a ghostlike presence to her once-bright and cheerful home.

Sarah wiped her eyes. "Please, send him away. I . . . I can't . . . much longer . . ." Sarah burst into tears again, unable to speak.

Franklin took her into his arms and lied to her, telling her that things would change. She accepted the lie, both to preserve hope and their once-wonderful home. Then her feelings flickered in her eyes. "But . . . how long can we go on like this?"

His answer came quickly. "It will change. I promise." Franklin moved to comfort her; her hands pushed him away.

Her weeping subsiding into a frankness such as he had never seen in her before, she told him that behind this treacherous pain lurked a deeper ugliness—she could feel it! A terrible, consuming form that stood behind the madness, the suffering, and the hollow life she and everyone else found themselves in. It stood like a distant lamppost, throwing its evil light into hidden places, affecting everything and everyone. The short joy of their marriage, the years before the colonel had come to stay, seemed like a memory that belonged to someone else.

"Have to protect the children from it, that's the thing," she began to blurt out, somewhat incoherently. "Protect the children . . . protect the children." She turned to Franklin, torn with rage and frustration. "Why can't the old bastard *just die* and take that . . . that thing with him!?"

Franklin shrank back, her words seeming more an accusation aimed at him than an indictment of his father. Sarah collapsed again into a chair, sobbing fitfully. He reached for her, extending a hand as to a wounded animal, checking to see if it would bite. This time, she didn't react to his touch. Relieved, he scooped his hysterical wife into his arms and carried her up to their bedroom. Unsteady on his feet, he fell with her onto the bed as he laid her down; he held her in his arms throughout that night, whispering his love and assurances whenever her sobbing grew loud.

The next morning did not recall the previous day's sorrow. The wisdom—everyone inwardly knew—was to let some time pass; and with its passage, the family resumed its quiet march toward annihilation.

Afterward, after the days of mourning, the colonel—now a hated figure representing every vile thing—assumed a post in the rocking chair facing the parlor window, oblivious to the destruction that billowed in his wake. Once there, he never left the room—as though he were waiting for someone to return from his invisible world: a world of marching armies and burning cities. Bringing him soup or sometimes coffee, Franklin noticed that his father anxiously watched the long slopes beyond the maples, his eye constantly scanning the horizon. Waiting.

Waiting. Then after a day or after a week, he would stand with rattling saber, brush off his sleeves, and say to his invisible captains, "Call the regiment to stand down arms."

Tears would quietly fall down the colonel's cheeks onto a frayed and tattered uniform he had never given up. Franklin realized that his father was deeply trapped by a death grip from the past that became an anchor to which his soul clung in its failure to find life and succor in the present. For weeks following the days of sorrow, Franklin would be with them and yet not there at all: lost, broken like his father, searching for a meaning to it all he was sure would always escape him.

As Franklin watched this tragedy year after year, his emotions ranged from deep compassion for the obvious suffering the poor man was going through to outright hatred and resentment that his own life was now a veritable nightmare. His friends made polite excuses to turn down his dinner invitations; his family was on the brink of hysteria. His Boston world was a shambles.

The gloom engulfed them—family, servants, everything that once brightened his life—darkening them, bearing down on them. At first, one at a time: the colonel, Franklin, Sarah, then Gary—until it seemed that their whole world was consumed with hopelessness and despair.

And so it went, a family in a modern age, linked with a past of slavery, freedom, and sacrifice. A family—Franklin knew then as now—that was doomed as long as it remained as it was.

These were the dark memories, no longer spoken of or mentioned. Dismissed. Forgotten. Erased. It had been a time before Haley was born, before life blessed the Olstens with hope in the form of a child.

The sound of a lamp colliding against the floor brought Franklin back to the present, a smile forming over his worn face as the past years of darkness and pain disappeared into the light of the present. Haley was standing near the shattered lamp, looking at him with wide eyes. Innocent eyes. Eyes full of freedom. Franklin felt the depth of his love.

"Clean it up before your mother finds it."

Watching her scamper away to the dustbin for the sweeper, Franklin turned back to the window, letting the cool glass press once again to his face. He let out a deep sigh. It all seemed so long ago, as if it must've happened to someone else—like a book read or a play watched that was forgotten and then recollected. Haley returned, the broom clanking loudly in spite of her efforts at secrecy.

Was it possible that it had all been a dreadful dream? Had not the last eight years since her birth been such a joy and celebration of life as to make it impossible to believe that their world had ever been so dark, so utterly devoid of meaning, as to be comical in its horror?

"But hush, old demons," Franklin told himself, watching the ray of joy that was the beauty in front of him. "My light is with me now and you cannot touch me." And for Franklin, finally and forever, the dark past slipped away.

Looking at Haley's gold locks that cascaded about her shoulders as she picked up the broken pieces of glass in front of him, Franklin's mind flickered with thoughts of joy. Right then, he promised himself that these would be the only memories he would allow to enter his mind . . . or his heart. Having made the promise, it seemed to him as though he might turn back the clock and start anew. "Focus on the beauty, my man," he told himself. "Focus on the beauty of life."

Then he noticed the twinkle of the stars through the leaves of the trees outside the window. They seemed to be encouraging his new resolution. Yes. He would do that. He would focus on everything that was shining. And were not the stars endless and timeless—existing in their patient radiance, waiting for a simple soul to notice? Without realizing it, he recalled the first time he had really seen the stars. California . . . yes, that was it: the year he had visited Los Angeles—the year of Halley's Comet.

In an instant he saw the key. It had been a time when life chose the Olstens for redemption and salvation. It had come in the form of his daughter, though he hadn't seen it— *couldn't* have seen it—until now. Only time would allow the wisdom; and only then, if the future remained embraced and the past forgotten. He laughed—his laughter loud enough to cause Haley to look up from the pieces of glass she was gathering and smile with curiosity. Slipping into a memory often entertained, Franklin drifted from the present into the past.

The journey, over three weeks long by rail, was necessary in order to establish ownership rights of a client of the firm that employed Franklin as their corporate attorney. The man refused to come east, so Franklin was forced to go west.

It wasn't prudent to take Sarah when she was so far along in her third pregnancy; she never traveled well anyway and preferred the time alone, Franklin believed. So, he treated it as a vacation, eager to remove himself from the house and its insidious influence. For most business travelers, cross-country train rides were tedious affairs, but for Franklin they provided an opportunity to reflect and read, his two favorite pastimes.

The woman was an odd old thing, twisted by time and standing in the rain as if it didn't exist for her. He saw her, he was sure, before she saw him. A reflection of a person, surreal, standing on the station platform as the cars slowed down for the stop. It was then, as his car screeched to a halt directly opposite her, that he realized she had been watching him for some time. Her eyes, shallow in the darkening light of a full rain, pierced the fogged glass, startling him. She did not blink, did not move. Franklin looked away nervously, uncomfortable with the depth he could feel in her stare.

They were the eyes of a mirror. A mirror to something inside him, something very . . . dark. Finally, after a long, terrible minute, he looked up to find her gone. Only then did he realize that the hat he was holding in his hand—a beautiful white skimmer—was crushed beyond use.

"Glendale!" a voice boomed, far in some distant place, snapping him back to his senses. "One hour. Keep your tickets handy!"

Hungry after the ride from Bakersfield, Franklin decided to grab a quick bite in town. After putting on his long coat, he found himself hesitating at the door to his compartment. A curiosity and terror lay in the darkness, creating such feelings as he had never known before.

What could it mean? It meant he would get off the train from the opposite side and go around the back, hoping never to see those terribly honest eyes again. And in moving decisively according to his plan, he emerged out of the last car before the caboose and jumped the four feet down onto the tracks. She was not there. Peering up the platform, he discovered with relief that the old woman had vanished and with her vanishing, the pulsing, racing fear slowly slipped away from him.

"Such nonsense," he muttered under his breath, ashamed at his conduct. Then he laughed at the absurdity of a simple old woman having *any* kind of effect on him.

His dinner of roasted chicken was consumed without event. The meal tasted even better as he realized that the rain was slowing to a slight patter upon the wooden boards outside the eatery. Franklin laughed again when he realized that he was looking out the windows before leaving. And even if she was there, what would it matter?

Bidding the matron a cheerful "Good night—delightful repast!" he moved out into the cool evening air and toward the train station two blocks away. Everything had been cleansed by the hand of nature, all wet and slippery, leaving the little village of Glendale scrubbed and renewed.

"It's when we don't pay attention that accidents occur," Franklin had told his son Gary a hundred times. He knew it, even as it was happening. Too busy watching the blue sky behind the quickly disappearing clouds, he could feel his left foot attempt to balance on the slick pavement and then fail in the attempt. It remained now only to minimize the impact and brace himself for whatever those muddy streets had to offer. Amazingly, his eyes never left the beautiful evening sky, as he landed squarely on the flat of his back. But before he could raise himself, the sky was blotted out by the shrouded figure of an old woman gazing down upon him. Franklin froze.

Those eyes again. But in their depths was a kindness and humility that touched his heart, warming him instantly and chasing away his former fears.

"Help me, mother?" he ventured quietly, unable to remove his stare from her saintly visage. As he stared, he discovered a depth so magnificent that a part of him wished he could just sit near her for a time, drinking in the healing effect of eyes filled with a tenderness he never realized possible in anything human.

"Yes," her gentle voice replied, a hand of great strength lifting him as if he were a mere rag doll.

Not knowing what to say, Franklin remained silent. He nodded his gratitude, unable to shake the wonder that gripped him. The old woman laid a gentle hand upon his arm, a smile coming to her craggy features.

"A child is born to you this night," she said sweetly and with great joy.

Franklin blinked, feeling the shock of more than coincidence: *Sarah.*

"She is one of many who come to aid, heal, and uplift. Our people are going through a dark cycle, and the harbingers of freedom are now emerging from shadow to light. Guard her well with love and truth and see that no falsehood comes to her."

Franklin stood there, stunned as if hit on the head with a stick—a daughter! Her words rang with a purity that seemed to echo with an air of purpose. "How?" he stuttered, not completely understanding, ". . . What do—"

Her hand shot skyward; Franklin's eyes followed it. Then he saw it, a faint light blazing across the horizon in the distance. What happened next startled him, as her voice filled with such power and conviction that it seemed to come from someone else. "It has always been so, when much is at stake!"

Franklin looked up again to see the arc of Halley's Comet, a flash of beauty across the evening sky. It looked grand, wonderful, and mystical—a great scientific conundrum, causing fear and panic among the ignorant and unbridled curiosity among the educated.

It was simply beautiful.

"You say—" Franklin stopped. She was gone, nowhere to be seen up or down the street. But it didn't matter, as the comet again commanded his attention as he stood there, staring into an evening sky in a suburb of Los Angeles. The hoots of a train whistle urgently commanded all passengers to the station; that, too, didn't matter. Franklin felt held in some vise grip of wonder and mystery, unwilling to let such a moment pass from him. Finally, still unable to avert his gaze from the fiery ball, he absently walked back toward the station, oblivious to all around him.

He spent the rest of the night and the early-morning hours going over and over her words until they were chiseled into his memory; soon, the words began to blend and blur to the point where Franklin began to doubt whether he had the encounter at all, fatigue and shock taking their toll on his tired mind.

A telegraph from Boston confirmed the truth of the message. His wife had given birth; both mother and daughter were doing fine.

Franklin joined the crowds on Hill Street, all watching and talking about the beautiful/horrible comet. He did not see them, did not hear them. He was back in Boston, laughing with his family, holding his little girl. Before the night was done, he knew what he would name her.

A tug on his sleeve brought Franklin back to the present, the years washing instantly from his mind. Haley was looking into his eyes with a curious expression on her face. Franklin cleared his throat. "I'm sorry, dear. What is it you wanted?"

Franklin realized where it was he had seen an expression like the one that constantly radiated from Haley's face. He laughed aloud in the knowledge. Wondering as he had for years, he realized that the glow that seemed to envelop only Haley and no one else in the world was the same glow the ancient woman from his trip had. Somehow, they were akin to each other.

Searching Haley's eyes, he realized she was seeing inside him, as the woman had. Franklin was certain that a person's eyes were a mystical doorway into his or her heart; he believed that from his many studies of spiritual matters, in the years since his meeting with the old woman seer. What was inside Haley's soul that allowed her to perceive a person's inner nature, when others could not?

All at once he felt naked, exposed—as though his every thought were written in the air before him. A quick glance informed him that he was probably right; she was still gazing directly into his eyes, a feeling of telepathy racing between them.

Then Franklin felt ashamed, knowing that she saw him as he saw himself—the self as he was before she had come into their lives. But, if she could go there, if she could see what he saw, feel what he felt, she might understand. Maybe she was gifted with solutions as well as with joy and wonder. Maybe she was what that old woman said she was: a harbinger of freedom.

Without a doubt, she had freed *him*.

Franklin leaned toward his daughter, now standing only a few inches in front of him. She smiled and motioned for him to bend down to her. "Yes, pumpkin?" When he was in range, she wrapped her arms around him and kissed him on the cheek. No words, no giggling. Franklin could feel a wave of love pour through him, filling him with joy.

He held her at arm's length. "Who are you?"

Haley smiled at the question, obviously not aware of her effect on her father. Chuckling, Franklin scooped her up in his arms, looking for some clue. None could be found. He sighed, giving up; her expression gave no hint that could answer his question.

September 1932

Rustling, the leaves fall.
Woe betides me!

The sun would be up in a short time, Haley observed as she stepped onto the balcony that extended from the second-story french doors of her bedroom. The night air still held its moisture, cool to the skin and a refreshing contrast to her hot, stuffy room. The stars were gorgeous in the early-morning glow—twinkling points of light, dancing on a shimmering, translucent background. Haley sighed as she put her hands on the wet railing. "The heavens care not for what troubles a universe . . . or a girl."

Haley glanced around at the sleeping world and frowned. She was twenty-three years old, and ever since her twenty-first birthday she hadn't had a decent night's sleep. Every night was the same story: sleep, then the dream—then waking up terrified. Each sunrise brought relief, each twilight brought terror . . . and an ache in her heart.

In the early hours of the morning, Haley remembered *the dream*, as she began to call it. At first, only fragments came through. But as the months since her birthday wore on, the dream had become more coherent, and more terrifying. A man . . . old, white, and ancient. A temple in the sky. Tragedy. Joy. Somewhere behind it all was a sunset that held, she realized, meanings beyond any knowledge she possessed.

Two months ago, the fragments started to coalesce into a kind of freakish order. At about the same time, Haley realized she was conscious in her dreams—*while she was in the dream.* From that time on, each night became a ritual of determination to remember more the next morning. In spite of her hopes, the morning would end in the same fashion: frustration, a feeling of despair, and a freakish awareness that her dreams were more than dreams.

Her mother took her to Doc Brown in April. He examined her thoroughly, asking her to cough, to count backwards from ten to one as quickly as she could, and to touch her toes. After ten minutes, the doctor went outside with her mother on some pretense, leaving her alone in the examination room. Haley could hear everything through the glass door that separated the reception area and the room she was in. "It's just a woman thing; happens to some, not to others, Mrs. Olsten." The doctor handed her mother a blue bottle. "Give her this before she goes to bed. She'll sleep all right."

Haley winced at the memory. The first two nights the dreadful substance made her vomit. Happily though, the dreams went away. The medicine did work, but she found she had no stamina or strength, wanting instead to just lie around and sleep all day. One night, upon learning his daughter was taking opium, her father threw the potion into the furnace. Soon afterward, the dreams returned with a clarity and ferocity that ended with her awakening and screaming in terror. If something didn't change soon, Haley feared she would ultimately be sent to an asylum, though her heart told her that her father would never allow such a fate to befall her.

Feeling the rays of the rising sun on her face, Haley walked back into her room and put on an Eddie Cantor record. She wound up the handle on the player and waited a moment before putting a scarf over the speaker. Her father hated swing music.

The song was mournful, about a love that was desired but could never be. Haley didn't really hear it, the tune blending into the background of her thoughts. What was it that gnawed inside her, eating away at what little happiness there was to be found in dreary Bostonian society?

Haley looked up at the mirror in front of her. "Why can't you be happy?" The reflection looked sad, making no offer to explain, waiting for her to give what she herself could not. Haley shivered, the idea occurring to her that the woman in the mirror was not her, but a different woman from another dimension. Haley looked more closely at the stranger: her twin, lost in a world filled with pain.

"How is it over there?"

The eyes in the mirror would not say, as if some hidden terror just out of sight prevented it from speaking. Whoever she was, she was afraid. Haley imagined that the reflection wanted terribly to speak, but could not. Afraid of moving away from her mirror, in her world, Haley's friend remained rigid in the glass. Haley reached out and touched the hand of her image.

"Come over," they said to each other, "and we will run away together." Eyes locked upon eyes in hopeless sadness, unable to share their burden.

Haley closed her eyes. She would have to pass the mirror to reach the record player; this was easily done, the event having been practiced a thousand and one times. Passing the mirror, Haley made it a point to avoid that terrible reflection, unable to face that desolate girl trapped in that dimension of damnation.

Her hand touched the volume switch, slowly cranking up the sound. Eddie's plaintive wail became insistent with the life of new strength. Why couldn't she be like Ann, her friend? Stunning, a tall brunette, Ann was always gay, always glad to be rushing off from one dance to another, from one boy to another. What Haley would give to know Ann's happiness, if just for a day.

Ann Rolingford's father was the city's chief magistrate. And even though he ruled Boston with a firm hand, his daughter was quite outside his control. This being so, he was the butt of not a few jokes. At first he pleaded for her to check her behavior; then came punishments—all to no avail. Finally, it was obvious that he had resigned himself to the fact that Ann had stallions racing in her blood. From then on, Ann was uncontrollable.

Haley always admired her friend's courage, pluck, and sense of adventure, though they often seemed self-destructive. Ann wished to be married into wealth, the goal of every educated society girl. She would have that and no less. Haley smiled at the thought.

Was that it? Were sleeping, eating, doing chores, meeting friends, getting married, then providing the same endless and tedious routine for the next generation the answer to the mysteries of being alive? Couldn't there be just something more, here on this Earth and in this life? Must it all be so stale till that damn Heaven's rapture the parson went on and on about every Sunday?

Haley put her hand against the wall, holding herself up, letting her head droop. "Life! This can't be all there is."

The door creaked; Franklin knocked softly on it as he opened it a few inches. "Pumpkin?"

Haley turned and faced him, smiling and trying to brighten up. Waking father with swing and big band music was criminal—at the minimum she would be lectured. "Morning, Daddy. Didn't mean to wake you with the phono."

Franklin stepped into the room, gently closing the door behind him. "No, not in the least. Was up to making a pot."

Haley smiled, placing a kiss on her father's cheek, relieved. "Coffee sounds wonderful."

Franklin put his arms around her, returning the affection. "Dreams again, eh?"

Haley froze, realizing she was looking directly at her friend in the mirror, who was herself on the verge of tears. A single tear slid quickly down her friend's cheek; Haley decided to join her and broke down, unable to keep the tears in. "It's always the same, Daddy, always! Roses and snakes and that awful white building!"

"There, there." Franklin held her tightly. Seeing the greatest source of joy in his life suffer so and being unable to help was unbearable. "We'll lick this, don't you worry." Franklin fought back his own tears.

Haley nodded, pulled away, and smiled—unconvinced. "Sure, Daddy."

Franklin blinked at his own lie—strength was of no value without conviction. He decided to let it pass, there being nothing else to say. "Let's go get that coffee, dearest." Franklin opened the door for her and waited. As Haley entered the hallway, he remarked, "After breakfast, what do you say we all go into town and do some shopping!"

Haley turned and smiled an unspoken "Yes, sounds wonderful; thanks anyway for trying," then disappeared down the stairs.

Franklin stood in the hallway, watching her, lost in thought. What could he do? He had consulted everything and everyone: doctors, friends—even the library. His chums at the Society for Metaphysical Studies could only blather, "Might be some bad karma coming up there!" or "Aura is cracked. Could be the darks." Franklin listened to each explanation, some plausible, most bordering on the absurd; nothing seemed appropriate. Deep inside his heart, he knew his daughter was in no real danger from her dreams. How he knew this and where this assurance came from, he could not explain, even to himself.

His "little hope" was different. Sensitive and reserved, she seemed to beam a quality everyone noticed and felt. Haley brought solemnity to a room and joy to an outing. It was always the same. Whenever someone asked about him, in the same breath came "And how is Haley these days?"

But that joy was dimming. Once a great fiery light, now it sparked into life only occasionally. Sarah noticed it first: "Your daughter's one unhappy little girl." Once in the open, it became painfully obvious at dinners, piano recitals, and during family drives to the park. What was once buoyant cheer in any weather was now brooding silence and a forlorn—even grim—view of life.

Was this the prelude of things yet to be? As Haley's joy lessened, Franklin's memory of the old woman increased. She warned him—told him. What he would give to see that sour old face again, if only for a minute. Franklin could not get the ancient hag out of his mind, nor her words: *"Guard her well with love and truth and see that no falsehood comes to her."*

Some great force or destiny was behind whatever was happening to her. He had seen evidence of this providence on several occasions. The fall from a tree that would have killed anyone— Haley walked away without a scratch. The carriage incident, when the driver suffered a heart attack and lost control, the horses mysteriously stopping inches away from her and Ann as they crossed the street.

The Cantor record finished playing, bringing Franklin back to the present. He walked back into the room and lifted the arm on the phonograph, turning it off.

Then he froze. Out of nowhere came the thought that she would be leaving home soon. His eyes traveled over her room; each doll, painting, or knickknack reminded him of a birthday, a gift, or a long-forgotten Christmas. Soon, this room would become quiet and dusty from lack of use. He could see himself in the distant future, opening the door, wistfully remembering when she was "just a little girl." On rainy, lonely nights, Franklin and Sarah would tread softly to the door, as they would to some sacred altar, and peek inside. They would cry and laugh, then cry some more.

Yes. Haley would go—would go and find that destiny that was hers alone to discover and live. Franklin realized that his daughter would do whatever it was that made her so special, just as she had done for her family. A soul such as hers could never remain long in bondage; it would need freedom to fulfill its plan in the scheme of things beyond his understanding. Instantly, Franklin felt grateful to have been her father, grateful for having been able to impart what knowledge and wisdom were his to give, grateful to have learned from her the mystery and healing bliss of joy.

Reaching out and picking up her favorite scarf from her dressing table, Franklin muttered a quiet "I will always love you." After a moment he lifted the record from the turntable, gently dusted it, and put it in its sleeve.

∞

The next year was uneventful, except for one spring afternoon. Ann broke the news and made the invitation to Haley at Pippins' Emporium. Naturally, Ann had chosen the seat facing the street so any boys who might pass could see her, and she them. She was convincing in her argument that going to India to see the strange sights was an absolute must for any true society girl before marriage—a husband was sure to forbid such outrages once the marriage had taken place. What these strange sights were to be, Ann could only hint at: fakirs, dervishes, magic, mountaintop palaces, and of course those mysterious, wonderful men in fantastic gowns of silk.

Haley set down her cup of tea. Facing Ann, she said, "No. What do we know of India or anywhere else, for that matter? We've never been outside Massachusetts, for heaven's sake."

Ann didn't even react to her friend's rejection, coolly setting her own cup down. "Simply amazing. You constantly moan about how dreary it is here, and at the first chance to break free of this morgue you fold up like a lounge chair."

Haley didn't have a chance to reply. A boy from school was at the window and waving to Ann to come outside. Without a word Ann flew from the table, leaving Haley to her thoughts about the trip—and to pay the bill.

Every day, Ann phoned to discuss the trip, constant in her attempts to convince Haley that "you absolutely must go, dear, or you'll regret it for the rest of your life." After two weeks of pleading, haranguing, and outright begging, Haley remained unmoved in her decision.

Ann's motives ran deeper, Haley knew. Her fiancé, a man of standing in England and a captain in the British army, was stationed in Allahabad. He had forbidden her from making the journey unless escorted; the dangers in the East were still all too real, even in the twentieth century. India, like most of the East, was still beset by bandits, and an unescorted journey into the interior was a dangerous proposition indeed. A woman traveling alone was quite out of the question.

Finally, though, news came that gallant captain Reginald Long was ill, and, through the good offices of his superior, had wired for his future bride to come at once to be married. Ann was thrilled and brought the telegram over for Haley to see. "You would deny me this? Is this what friendship means to you?"

Haley noted Ann's blatant lack of feeling for the suffering Reginald must be going through. Haley hesitated to ask about him, the question improper under any circumstances. Then she noticed that old glint of mischief in Ann's eyes as she snapped a cigarette into her mouth. Haley's eyes narrowed. "I'm sorry to ask . . . what is dear Reginald ill from?"

Ann shot back a hard look, obviously peeved. "Well, it doesn't say now, does it? Does it matter?" Ann started to grow emotional, tears forming underneath her huge lashes.

Haley embraced her friend, fighting back her own tears. "No, dearest, no. I've been selfish and cross." Haley pulled away, dabbing at her eyes. "It's just that . . . I'm scared. . . . Yes, of course. We'll go at once."

Ann put her arms around Haley, glimmering with excitement over her triumph. "It will be all right. Don't worry!"

The idea of foreign travel, though at first repulsive, began to take root in Haley's mind until the thought of not going became more than she could bear. She laughed when she thought of the time when she had actually said no to the voyage. Haley found herself pushed along inexorably toward something quite outside her control, as though events and circumstances had conspired against her.

But as the date for departure came closer, more and more of *the dream* was becoming clear. Every time Haley thought of

India, the memory of the dream intruded itself upon her mind, until she became certain that the two were intertwined somehow.

Once convinced of the idea, Haley realized there was yet another hurdle to clear—her father. Her father's means allowed her an opportunity few others could ever hope to have. Haley knew this and was grateful. She had never known want or been refused a request her heart earnestly desired. But foreign travel—especially to the East—was something else again. She would just have to lay the whole thing out on the table and see what happened.

Haley decided that the next evening would be the best time, right after dinner. After fretting and waiting to be excused from dinner, she walked into the study and found her father reading by the fireplace. Franklin, now graying and bent with time, seemed older, resigned, even at peace. He must have known what was coming, even if unconsciously. Right then, as if for the first time, she realized how much she truly loved her father. He was her everything: love, source of direct honesty, and a wonderful example of a good man, ever faithful to the needs of his family.

From out of nowhere, the thought that she would never see him again once she left flashed through her mind. If she stopped right now and left the room, she could end this. And in so doing, she could spend more time with a man who thought more of her than of his own needs. All she had to do was to turn around. Turn around and forget everything.

"Daddy?"

Franklin set down the book he was reading and looked up, indicating for her to come closer. Haley stepped up to him and gave him a hug. "What are you reading?"

"Oh, an interesting little book about people who are sent to help other people. *Invisible Helpers*. Fascinating stuff."

Haley gave him the details, explained everything, then sat

back in silence. Franklin smiled for a moment, lost in thought. So, it had come to pass at last. His consternation over the whole affair notwithstanding, he could not find it within himself to refuse his "little hope." Mystically, he knew that enslaving Haley would injure her delicate spirit and that imprisonment was no way to teach his daughter about how men and women should treat each other.

"If you feel you must go, then go, pumpkin." Franklin reluctantly consented.

"I don't know," Haley replied, as though not even present in the room, "Ann is so insistent, and you know how she is."

Franklin looked at his angel. Haley was a grown woman of twenty-two; she had the striking features of a Greek statue, long billowing blond tresses flowing full about her shoulders, and bright blue pools for eyes that seemed to pierce the very soul. And always there was the glow around her, that glow that seemed to come from everywhere and nowhere, its own source of light. The young men had been flocking around her since she was fifteen, and to her credit, she only spoke to the noble ones.

"Why not take John with you," Franklin implored, "as an escort. India is so—"

Haley snapped back to reality and looked at him in horror. "Oh, Daddy! John is such a bore, and, really, he won't do at all."

They stared at each other: two wills vying for supremacy. Behind and through their disagreement ran an undying love and affection, each for the other. Haley realized that final permission would not be given without some form of male accompaniment. Reluctantly, she acquiesced in her brother's presence on the journey.

John had just turned nineteen and had graduated after four rebellious attempts at high school. His new pastimes of Nietzsche and D. H. Lawrence were in full swing, evident in his recent passion and personality, the third such adopted persona this year.

Getting up and moving toward the door, Franklin called John down into the study and listened intently as Haley explained her travel plans for the second time.

"Why should I go?" John demanded angrily. "So I can see how the elite ruling classes are suppressing my downtrodden brothers?"

Haley and Franklin thought the same thing at the same time: John had a lot of growing up to do. A boy in a man's body, his life was an endless jumping from one old idea to another, as though they were brand-new and he was just the man to tell everyone what was on his mind. John usually rattled on and on noisily, those around him nodding in agreement from time to time without really listening. Like any thin reed, it took little effort to sway him. Although he was initially resistant, John finally consented as his father put him in charge of the finances and suggested a sum of three thousand dollars for their journey. Once the idea had taken root, he became outright enthusiastic.

"Besides," he offered to anyone who would listen, "how could I say I'm a true artist without having spent some time abroad?"

It was decided that Haley, Ann, and John would travel by rail to New York and then on to Liverpool and points east by ship. Soon, both households fluttered with activity surrounding the trip—parties, long dinners, expensive shopping trips. Ann was never happier.

On the evening before departure, all was settled, the bags packed and stowed downstairs next to the pantry, her records neatly shelved, and most of her things arranged in the closet. Haley smiled at the realization that this was her last night in her own bed. She stepped up to the mirror and faced it for the first time in a very long while.

"Hi. I did it. I'm going away. I hope I can find the answers for the both of us. Please don't be sad, as it will hurt me if I think you're sad." Her mirror friend tried to smile, but the eyes, the eyes weren't sure—even suspicious. Haley reached out, as her friend did, and touched her hand. "I will save us, I promise. Somehow, I'll find a way." Her friend smiled; then the hope in her eyes flickered as she looked down, unwilling to believe that anything would change.

Haley stepped away from the mirror and walked out onto the balcony. "I will. You'll see."

Sitting on a small stool beside a campfire, the aged peasant wrapped his shawl over his shoulders against the cold, a brisk wind flapping hair across his face and around his arms. He didn't notice. His eyes were fixed on the vast canopy of stars above, shining from horizon to horizon in the open plain that was his camp for the evening.

Suddenly he sat up stiffly, as a deer might, listening to something far off in the distance. The old peasant relaxed and smiled, deciding to turn in for the night.

She was coming.

CHAPTER 2

Ceylon, 1933

Let the new spirit fill,
flowing like water;
giving sustenance to the weary
and to the hopeful, life.

The ship rolled gently as it steamed through the dark waters of the Indian Ocean. It was the *Elizabeth II*'s final leg of a very long journey from Liverpool. To Haley, the sky seemed different from the sky in New York or Liverpool, its colors a shifting jumble of shades that reflected the emotions of an ancient race. Tropical. Hot. Wet. It was as if the very spirit of the old ones could be felt. India, land of mystics and seers, seat of wisdom for the planet.

The first month of the journey had come and gone uneventfully: the predictable party life on a grand steamer much suited the playful and fun-seeking Ann and was equally resented by John. He claimed an artist's dislike for the bourgeois class, as he openly called the liner's passengers.

Haley had survived the years in Boston by moving through her life from one observation point to another. Nothing had ever seemed striking or of deep interest. Now she watched with curious disinterest as the ladies and gentlemen lived their lives obsessed with class and place. A hollow existence, at best. John was right, to some degree, Haley discovered. Somehow, though, she realized that hating others for their beliefs was just as wrong. When John finally understood that, he had every chance of becoming a wonderful person.

A natural beauty, she was eagerly sought out by that eligible class of men who could afford leisurely cruises while whole continents suffered in the grips of a global depression. But these suitors were of no lasting interest. She knew there would be only one man in her life, and she meant to maintain her virtue until he decided to present himself to her. Until then she would wait, knowing that somewhere in the world, someone else might be waiting.

Haley was at an age when the world and the future seemed to be waiting for her to strike out and make her mark, whatever it was to be. Her father had told her that intelligent people planned their futures and found contentment in being good husbands, wives, and positive contributors to the community.

When she asked Franklin about marriage and work, he simply answered, "Whatever presents itself to you with greater need, do it. But, if you choose family, it must come before all other ventures."

Haley absorbed the words, thinking them through. "What about love?"

Franklin looked at her. How little she realized that his salvation depended on her very existence. At her birth, the joy of a child in his home had been the leverage he had inwardly sought to break the spell of depression that had very nearly destroyed his life and family.

He knew that she looked up to him as the sole fountain of truth. No matter what his deep concerns for her, he had to tell her the truth: "Love must . . . *must* be held as the highest of all things that you can know or be. You must love to marry, to bear children, and to aid others in need. If you cannot find love in your heart for yourself, you will never be able to find it for your husband, or for anything else."

Haley looked at him as if his words were obvious. Franklin realized that she did not understand. "Sometimes, people marry out of fear, out of loneliness and insecurity, or for darker reasons. They tell themselves that this is love, but it is not. It is fear. Love—*true love*—is when the happiness, welfare, and prosperity of the object of your love mean more to you than your own happiness or well-being."

He could see her thinking. Finally, she nodded. Franklin decided to take the matter further. "When the power of love pours through you, everything you see, touch, feel, and relate to changes by the love you give forth." Franklin paused, then added, "Then you become a blessing to mankind and can say that each day lived has been lived to its fullest."

The conversation, etched perfectly in Haley's memory, was interrupted by a shout from the crow's nest.

"Ceylon! Ceylon!" Dark against an evening horizon lay the island of Ceylon, the first stopping point on their trip to India, and a place full of legends from the ancient past. There was a bustle about the ship as passengers emerged from cabins to see the first land in more than twenty-three days.

Haley joined the throng on deck, lost in her reflections. In her hand was her father's favorite book, given to her as a departure gift. Flipping through its pages, she was stopped short from destruction by the iron rail separating polished oak from frothy sea.

"What are you reading?" Ann asked playfully, spilling champagne from her glass as she emerged down a staircase. She looked striking in her black silk evening gown. Nevertheless, it was obvious that she was acquiring a taste for the bubbly.

Haley reluctantly set the book down, making a mental note of her place in chapter eight, and blurted out a reluctant "Leadbeater. *Invisible Helpers*."

Ann staggered a bit, then righted herself against the rail of the ship. "Him again?" Ann's tongue stuck out in comical repulsion. "I thought you gave him up."

"I did . . . kind of. But, now that we are going to India, his writings seem so—"

"*Weird,*" Ann rebuked. "Deary, those people are nuts! I mean, if all that stuff was true, wouldn't science have proven it by now?"

Haley moved toward the ocean, looking out at the endless sky. In the distance, a low brown shape was growing larger on the horizon. "I'm not so sure. I mean, it might be true." A star, clear in the blue night's sky, winked at her, bringing a smile to her face. "It has to be."

Ann looked at her innocent friend, shaking her head. The whole world was full of magic, nonsense her father pushed on her. A girl had to be practical, and there was nothing practical in *Invisible Helpers*.

"Haley." Ann took another sip, thought about it for a moment, then drank again, nearly emptying the glass. "No man in his right mind wants a woman who believes that invisible guides control the destinies of people. And"—she continued, pulling Haley back toward her—"if you keep on with that, you might lose your friends as well."

Haley froze at the words, looking Ann directly in the eye, trying to see where her heart was on the matter. Then she relaxed. It was advice given out of love. Ann loved Haley as her own sister, always finding that her presence cheered her up when letters from Reginald became infrequent or when the parties became too wearisome.

Haley smiled at her friend, unable to be moved from her shaky convictions but exuding endless buoyancy and charm. Each one sighed for the other, content that their friendship could survive even the taboo mysticism of the East.

But Haley still had some fight left in her. "Electricity would have been considered witchcraft two hundred years ago," she offered smugly, knowing that Ann never had a rebuttal against that statement. Ann stared at her—and Haley stared back, both of them narrowing their eyes and smiling simultaneously.

John appeared from around a corner, dressed in gray slacks and a shirt very much unbuttoned. His "artistic" rejection of society was reflected in his refusal to wear formal dinner attire.

"Let's eat," he called out. "The feed's on for the swine."

Ann grimaced at the remark, emptied her glass, and headed toward the dining room. She stopped a few feet away and turned back to Haley. "Aren't you coming?"

"In a minute."

Ann paused a second, then took John by the arm. "God, John! You look dreadful," Haley heard as they disappeared from sight. Each reaction of disdain, disgust, or rejection brought joy to John, who lived for the sensations of a rebellion he was never truly able to understand.

Haley glanced down at the small book and then out to the sky and sea. Lost in thought and imagination, she could feel the truth in the pages. Her father had given her the book and hinted that it might provide "a solution to some things." Racking her brain, Haley came to the conclusion that he had to be referring to her inner discontent. He must have known then, the whole while, what she was feeling. Eager for any relief from those damnable dreams and the endless melancholy she could not shake, she spent more time during the voyage reading than at any other pastime.

But reading could never be enough. It would provide a doorway and a direction, but inwardly she knew that she would have to labor toward the ideals and practices set forth by what she read. Her father called his books and philosophies the *"Teaching."* The men and women discussed in his books were very spiritual and wonderful people. She had never been anything but self-conscious, self-absorbed, and far too lost in the beauty of nature and her friendships.

Haley was sure these qualities would never be enough to admit her to the higher ways—if there *were* any higher ways. And as she thought about it, she doubted it; as she doubted it, she began to feel a weight of sadness come over her. Real Initiates were grand and self-sacrificing people, living in poverty and laboring unselfishly toward only the highest for humanity. And that she was not. The tears falling on the cover of the worn book, blending into and staining the print, were tears from her soul.

At length she composed herself, glanced again at the book, and let it fall from her hands into the quiet waters below.

It barely made a sound as it splashed into the Indian Ocean.

The bell that sounded midnight roused Haley from her dreamless sleep. It was a hot night. She picked up a pencil, her journal, a lamp, then headed outside. Two minutes later she was on the rear main deck, listening to the waves lapping against the ship, the soft sound of the engines idling through the clear, summer night.

The captain had informed them that they would be docking in the morning, so that there would be no danger of being boarded by the dangerous cutthroats that preyed upon the well-to-do in these harbors. Haley wrote down her thoughts: confusion, loneliness, a desire to be home. Her father wanted her to attend Exeter, but she resisted, hoping that life would spare her the agony of a strict college, filled with selfish, vain women.

Writing in the journal was relaxing. She felt sleep coming on, and with it the dream. This time Haley found herself standing on a path before an immense structure with beautiful pillars of white marble and an arched Grecian portico. There were words chiseled into the keystone that she could not quite see. The most intense and gorgeous roses lined the path, each one inviting and radiant, pulling her eyes away from the building.

But the dream refused to come near, something instead pulling at her, down into the sands of the Earth, down into the prison of matter and hopelessness, down into—

"What are you writing about?" A voice, distant, pulling her away from the temple, the door to it closing as she was about to draw near.

The sound of the ocean against the ship, a pencil in her fingers.

"I say there, what are you writing about?" It was a man's voice—gentle . . . warm . . . kind.

"What?" Haley moaned, coming to.

"I'm sorry, I didn't realize you were sleeping," the voice apologized. "I'll leave you be."

The voice became a shadow which turned and began moving away from her, the outline of a tuxedo, stepping into view and then vanishing.

"No, wait."

The tuxedo stopped and turned around.

Blurry with sleep at first, Haley's eyes began to focus on brown eyes, kind and deep, a firm jaw, and wavy black hair. He was young in body—maybe twenty-eight or -nine—but old in spirit, as his soul seemed easily visible in the sincerity and warmth of what must be a very large and generous heart. She could feel a thrill run through her and then a wonderful sense of joy from a source she could not place.

"My name is David," the kind face declared, "David Hampton."

Haley was surprised that she could not speak, finally blurting out "Haley Olsten." She could feel her cheeks redden in embarrassment.

"I know," he replied sheepishly. "I've watched you from the very first."

Haley just looked at him in amazement. How was it that she had never noticed him before? Had she been that self-absorbed?

"I didn't mean to disturb you. I'll go now."

Before she could answer, he had disappeared down a staircase. Haley felt flushed, her heart racing and pounding inside her. She began to gulp air, finally steadying herself and regaining her composure.

It had taken David four weeks to gain the courage to speak to Haley. He had noticed her from the very first day of boarding. Her soft blue eyes, gentle, as of an angel. Her endless smile that seemed to shower its blessings upon everything. She seemed to come from a dream, a beauty too splendid, a love too wonderful to be possible.

But she was not alone. Had he not seen her holding hands with that man? Was he her husband . . . or lover? They seemed very close, and it was obvious that there was love between them; the awareness of their union brought the dream—the hope—crashing down. It was just as well; he had work to do in India. But he could not get her out of his mind.

David was now furious at himself for choosing the most obviously idiotic time in the world to approach her. The poor dear had been sleeping, for goodness sake. Then, to top it off, he walked away from her!

He slammed his fist into his open palm and then buried his head in his hands, leaning against the wall of his stateroom. Now, she would consider him a buffoon . . . or worse.

His one chance. A chance at a love greater than he had ever hoped for. His whole manhood had been spent in searching for the angel of his dreams, and now he had *insulted* that angel. There had been others. Fun, witty, erotic, and charming. Some so beautiful as to seem unreal, as if they would break into a thousand pieces if not handled ever so delicately. But none had been *her.*

The heart knew. The heart always advised him whether each one was or was not to be.

David walked over to his dressing table and sat down. The man looking at him in the mirror looked older . . . and tired. No, that wasn't it. Resigned. Given up.

"Dammit."

At length, he stripped off his clothes and dragged himself into bed. It would be a hard sleep, with little hope of joy for the morrow. Maybe, if only for the sake of love, life would give him another chance at the enchanting Miss Olsten.

The busy port of Colombo was a jumble of every kind of humanity and enterprise. Hundreds, nay thousands, seemed to crowd every space: hawking wares, looking tired and worn, and exuding a continuous attitude of distrust. A great dust hung in the air, rising to an altitude of about twenty feet. It covered everything and everyone in minutes.

John, Ann, and Haley enlisted the services of escorts from the boat—insisted upon by the captain before he would allow them to leave the ship. Once safely girded with sailors, they set off.

Everywhere Haley's party went, there were stares—the stares of hunger, poverty, and unrest. Revolution swarmed as an undercurrent among the life of the Ceylonese people, along with a deep hatred for the ruling British Empire and all it represented. The great dichotomy of the East was that the land and its people needed foreign trade to prosper but resented the presence of that trade in their lives, as well as the presence of the traders.

As the group moved from the docks into the city itself, awaiting transportation, a crowd began to form around them. Curious fingers tugged here and there, at Ann's fine gown and the spotlessly clean clothes of the men.

Ann clung to John, fear racing behind her eyes at the overwhelming multitude. "Don't they have something to do?"

"This *is* what they do," John admonished her.

Behind, and blending with all the sounds of donkeys, carts, and merchants, was the constant murmur . . . rupees . . . rupees . . . rupees." Hundreds of eager hands, palms held upward, were constantly thrust into the faces of the group.

Haley's heart was in shreds at the sight. For the first time in her life, she felt ashamed of being alive. They spent more money in a day than any twenty of these poor wretches would see in a year. Without thinking, she dug into her purse and began pushing coins and bills into the outstretched hands.

"I wouldn't do that, mum," an old sailor advised, his face reflecting a mixture of horror and concern at her actions. "They'll tear you apart, if'n they know you got coin." Haley ignored the man, her heart on the verge of breaking.

Another sailor grabbed her arm. "Won't do no good at all," he declared, urgent and fearful. "There ain't enough money in the world to heal their ills." The two sailors glanced at each other at the same time—both had the same idea: get out of there.

True to the prediction, the crowd grew, as if the throng could smell the release of British and American banknotes in the air, pushing in from all sides until the group couldn't move, held in a vise grip of humanity.

The flash of a blade! It was held by a young man whose left eye had been shattered by some old catastrophe. The older sailor saw the knife and the man, heading straight for Haley. Instantly, the sailor saw he could not save her with so little time and so many people in the way. He had warned her, and now she was going to pay for her foolishness with her life. He tried to shout, but no one heard him; it was too late, the angry little man was already upon her, both his hatred and his knife poised for striking.

It would have been just another sound, a backfire from a Ford or a Packard, had not the young man's head exploded in a foam of scarlet and gray, showering nearby people with a pink spray. He sank to the ground, swallowed up by a mob grown silent. All became still and frozen, as if a thousand hearts knew at once what had happened. Haley was horrified, her white sweater flecked with brain matter. She pulled a piece of steaming cerebellum from her neck and stared at it, mesmerized. Ann pushed her face into John's coat, shutting out the scene.

It was a sergeant—the commander of a small group of soldiers standing on the veranda of a hotel, and grizzled from decades in the service of Her Majesty's Army—who first moved toward Haley. The throng melted away in front of him, as though some invisible knife were cutting a path for him.

The sergeant stopped in front of her, assessing the situation. Stupid damn tourists, never knowing how to handle themselves in the colonies. Wouldn't they never learn? The crowd began to murmur something.

Seeing that she was in shock, he took Haley by the arm. "Come with me, miss." The group from the ship moved with her toward the hotel, the crowd letting them pass without further incident, powerless against the several rifles aimed at them from thirty feet away.

Haley watched, strangely calm, as each face in the crowd came into view—angry, accusing—and then vanished to be replaced by another identical face. There must be some mistake. One moment she was putting a penny into a young boy's hand and the next moment she was being dragged into the hotel. Abruptly, the angry face of Sergeant Toddner appeared in front of her, waving his weapon.

"I don't likes killing a man, missy," he barked hoarsely, "but you've given me no choice, as you'd be dead for sure, otherwise."

"But—" Haley began to protest, images of eyes, skin, and some wet gray substance exploding, continuously flashing in her mind's eye.

"Don't you knows any better than that?" the sergeant bellowed. "This 'ere's Ceylon! You can't be goin' around given all yer money away!"

"But—" Haley tried again.

"Don't speak!"

Haley closed her mouth tightly, her mind racing to regain its balance. "Look at something, Haley," it urgently commanded, "anything—and focus. Think about what you are seeing, Haley. Do it. Do it." Haley kept seeing the look of disbelief on her assassin's face as his life ended instantly. Over and over. Haley screamed inside and silently.

The sergeant became animated with anger and regret, the death needless and of no purpose. It was one thing to kill in battle—for country and duty—it was quite another to kill the damned . . . the hopeless. His queen would understand—give him a medal—but would his God?

The hotel became silent, all eyes scornfully upon the group of foreigners, intruding themselves into their part of the world. Except for the soldier who had saved a stupid girl from death, it was very, very quiet.

At length, the sergeant regained some of his composure and holstered his revolver. The room was still silent, waiting. He continued his practiced glare and scowl. "Now, then, you be a nice little missy and get yerself back on board that ship that brought you."

Haley barely nodded her compliance, all life drained from her. This was not the India she had expected. They were liars, all of them, those treacherous books and movies about romantic sheiks in wonderful silks and all that damnable tripe about beautiful cities. She looked up to find the face of the sergeant still inches away. She started to tell him that, yes, she would be glad to leave. Right this minute. Then sleep for a long time. Yes. Take me back to the ship.

"My men will escort you and yer friends back and I don't want to hear another—"

"Now see here!" John admonished. "We can go wherever—"

The sergeant moved directly into John's face, the whiskers of his mustache almost brushing John's lapel, each word spoken slowly, distinctly, and with force. "I said, 'Not anotha' word.' "

The room waited. Haley's eyes were fixed upon the brilliant belt buckle worn by the soldier in front of her. How did they get the brass so shiny? She could see her dress in its reflection.

"Sergeant Major!" A voice called out from the other side of the room. Every eye in the lobby turned to a tall man in a well-tailored white linen suit. He moved forward, his hand out.

Sergeant Toddner turned away from John to see who had dared to interrupt him in the performance of his duty, ready to strike any blow he decided was necessary to establish who was in charge. The instant he saw who the intruder was,

43

however, the sergeant's attitude turned from harsh resilience to humble pie.

"Mister Hampton!" the sergeant announced with such graciousness and decorum that one would think the king himself had entered the room. "So good to see *you*, sir!" David took his hand warmly with one hand and his arm with the other. "On seeing about the comp'nies, Your Lordship?"

Haley looked up, blinking. It was obvious by his tone and deference that Mr. Hampton was a man of substance. It was he who had interrupted her nap on the ship. He had good eyes—eyes that kept glancing toward her, again and again.

"Now, Sergeant," David Hampton began, "these people are my guests here in Colombo and I don't want to see them hauled back to the ship just now."

There was not a trace of anger or pomp in his words. Haley realized she was staring at him, but she didn't care. Watching him, she realized she admired him. As did Ann, with a twinkle, checking to make sure her assets were visible to their savior. John loathed him on sight, hating what the British stood for.

The sergeant shrank at the realization of what would have been his fate. David Hampton's father was the governor of Ceylon and, indirectly, the commanding officer in charge of all British forces on the island.

"I 'ad no idea, sir—of course, of course." Sergeant Toddner turned back to Haley, removing his cap this time. "Forgive me, miss. I didn't know you were guests of 'is Lordship."

Haley merely nodded, not sure what the game was, but somehow relieved at not having to go back to the ship just then. This Mr. Hampton kept staring at her, and she continued to return his gaze. After a few moments, she glanced down, realizing that she was unnerving him.

The sergeant began to turn away, when Haley touched him on the arm. He stopped. "Yes, miss?"

"Sergeant." Haley began, her eyes beaming with sincerity. "Thank you for saving my life. I'm terribly sorry for all the harm and trouble I've caused you. I will try to be more careful in the future."

Toddner straightened, the words from her heart raising him an inch taller than he stood, a smile broadening across his weathered face. Becoming self-conscious, the sergeant regained some of his steel, gathered his men, then proceeded outside.

As the troops moved out into the hot sun, the affairs of a busy hotel began to come back to life. Haley turned to her benefactor. "Thank you."

Hampton smiled, having redeemed himself for the previous night's bungle. "Not at all, miss."

"Please. Call me Haley." She let Hampton take her by the arm. From a vest pocket, he produced a handkerchief and offered it to her.

Ann watched the whole thing with dismay. There was genuine magnetism between the two, that much she could see. This Mr. Hampton was something of a prince and not bad-looking, either. She had all but forgotten Reginald, sitting in some hot, dirty camp, no doubt, and suffering from malaria. Well, he could wait. This David fellow was too much of a chance at real happiness to let Haley ruin it. She pictured the largesse of servants, a title, and being treated like royalty. But this would take some work and a great deal of finesse and patience. There had been other women who had the same idea. Then of course, Haley would have to see how absolutely wrong he was for her. In that instant, Ann decided to make sure of that.

David Hampton offered to show them around Colombo and

the better parts of Ceylon, if they didn't mind. Ann and Haley agreed instantly; John mumbled something but didn't say no— true to form.

Delighted with his success, their new friend offered to put them up in the Excelsior Hotel, as his guests, in no less than the best rooms. John offered a stiff and unfriendly hand in return. "Thank you . . . for your kindness. But we have reservations there already." Hampton took the cool handshake, looking puzzled at the hostility.

Haley moved away from the group to the big lobby window that looked out onto the street. The street had returned to normal; someone had put over the spot of the young man's demise a wooden box that didn't quite cover the scarlet pool. A man leaped on top of the box, carefully avoiding the blood, and began selling loaves of bread. Haley shook her head. Seeing her alone, her brother moved toward her.

John glanced outside, then at her. "Hey sis, what's up?"

"I can't help but think about that poor boy," she replied, her heart aching.

John blinked, unable to believe his ears. "What's to think about? The beast was about to only kill you! Best thing for him."

The look of horror from Haley put a bolt of shame through her brother that even he couldn't brush off. "You're right. It's a sad affair." John's anger began to boil. "But it wouldn't be like this if the damn British weren't enslaving these godforsaken people!" His last words rose in volume so loud that everyone in the great hall of the hotel could hear it, which presently stopped its activity for the second time that afternoon.

Seeing an angry bell captain start for John and Haley, David Hampton moved over to them. "May I be of some assistance?"

"Oh sure, some assistance, indeed!" her brother roared. "Why don't you mind your own business? Just like a Limey, always sticking their nose in where it doesn't belong. Killing and putting these people under the boot, why—"

"John!" Haley reached out and grabbed her brother by the arm, stopping him. Remaining speechless over the outburst, David understood the attitude; it was something he had heard many times before.

It was the common complaint, fueling revolutions and hatred for the British by the colonies the Home Office had created in its quest for international power. European countries still hadn't learned that the colonial system was dead and those who would continue them, the damned. Born into wealth, he could not escape it, but his heart was with the people. He did everything he could for them, and for that he was loved as one of their own.

"I understand," Hampton offered, speaking to Haley's brother. "We are trying to give these people self-government. But if we were to turn over the keys now, so to speak, the warlords of the island would be killing off their own kind by the thousands."

John was truly upset; it was always the same old calculating nonsense. His anger began to rise again. "Every country has the right to self-rule, and—"

"I agree," Hampton interrupted with perfect diplomacy. "We must get them up to speed as quickly as possible. But civil war will surely break out unless the machinery of democracy and government is installed beforehand."

David Hampton's tact, sincerity, and diplomacy completely disarmed the hostile John Olsten. Haley's brother found himself agreeing with the very man he had only moments before hated as the symbol of repression in the world. This Mr. Hampton now seemed kind and noble.

"We should talk more about your important ideas over dinner," Hampton offered with his hand.

John hesitated, unsure if the offer was sincere. Then he

smiled and took the outstretched hand. "Um, okay." With that, John moved off with an impatient Ann, heading upstairs to their waiting rooms. Haley remained at the window, again gazing outside.

David stood next to her, looking out at the street life below, his mind lost in the problems of Ceylon's people.

"I have to do something," Haley finally said, "for his family or something . . ."

David nodded and moved away a few paces, snapping his fingers. Out of nowhere, two men appeared in modern Indian dress. He whispered to them in low tones. They both bowed stiffly and disappeared.

He returned to her side. "What would you do?"

"I don't know. But if I hadn't been throwing all that money around, maybe—"

David stopped her by putting his hand gently on her arm. "People decide for themselves what they do, regardless of the actions of others." Haley turned away from the window, amazed with wonder at the words. David had her complete attention.

"Your brother was right, Haley. I couldn't help but overhear what he said. The man was a robber and you were a target. It might have been another time or in another way, but his fate no doubt would have been the same. Except that today . . . you might have been killed. If we choose to live by violent acts, we shouldn't be too surprised when the effects of our violence come home to roost." Haley nodded. Hampton was right, she knew, but his wisdom didn't erase her pain.

Haley and David chatted for several minutes about the great island of Ceylon and its history. The two men returned and signaled to Hampton.

David motioned for them to wait. "Please excuse me for a moment." Haley nodded and smiled. He went to his two servants and listened intently to what they had to say. He gave each of them a gold coin and told them to wait again.

David joined her again at the window. "You still feel responsible for what happened, don't you?" She nodded that she did.

"The boy comes from a local family. His father died two years ago from illness, forcing the lad from school to work on the docks to help pay for his family's needs. He had nine brothers and sisters, and now the mother has no one to provide for them."

Haley broke into sobs, throwing herself on Hampton's shoulder. It was all he could do to hold back his own tears. He let her pour out her grief onto him. Two hours ago, he would have given up all his riches to hold the woman of his dreams in his arms, and now she was wrapped around him tighter than life itself. Hampton's thoughts strayed from Haley to the weight of the affairs that were of greater importance. A man was dead; his family, destitute; David's angel, shattered with guilt and grief. He slowly moved his hands up and embraced her.

"I have an idea." With that, he led her outside, escorted by no fewer than ten of his employees. Some of the men carried sidearms and scimitars—long, curved daggers. The party moved down the street for some distance, making several turns this way and that, finally coming to a filth-strewn row of mud dwellings unfit for cattle to live in. One of his men went to a door and spoke Sinhalese through it. After a few more words from the man, an old woman, bent by a harsh life, came to the door.

It was obvious the woman was suffering; she carried in her heart the pain only a mother could feel. There was blood on her dress, spilled from the body of her son. She looked at Lord Hampton, whose eyes reflected his own torn heart, and Haley, who was inconsolable. Finally, Haley pushed David away and went down on both knees in front of the woman.

"This is all my fault . . ." she sobbed over and over again. The old woman looked down at her, not understanding. After a minute of Haley's wailing, other family members came to the door, trying to separate the two. The woman shouted something to them and they stopped. Haley was still weeping; the mother took Haley and embraced her as one of her own. Every eye on the street was moist from that single magnificent act of compassion.

David Hampton spoke to his man, handing him a small leather bag. He then pulled Haley away from the woman, the street, and the ghetto.

"C'mon. All's well, now."

Haley looked at him as if he were mad. How could all be well? The woman's son was dead, and now she was penniless.

David put a gentle hand on her arm. "She will be cared for, the family fed and housed. And I will personally see to each of the young ones' education."

Haley was taken completely by surprise; it was reflected on her face. "Why are you doing this?"

Still moved by the day's events, David wiped his eyes. "I could not go through life thinking that you would blame yourself for that poor family." Seeing her in the same state, he started drying her eyes. "Though one day, I hope you learn that you cannot take on all the world's suffering, though you think you might."

"You're wrong, David. We must be responsible."

"Yes, for whatever is within our limits. And after that, we have to let it go, or we'll be miserable forever."

Haley looked at him. What wisdom. Where did he learn such things? Why had she not learned them? Where did it come from? The answers to those questions could wait. He was a gift from Heaven. And at exactly that moment—with the sun dipping past the three-o'clock point, the azure Ceylon sky spreading like a great canopy over them, the dust over his now stained jacket, the look of compassion in his eyes—she knew she was going to marry him.

"Thank you," she said tenderly, "for helping them."

"Glad to be of service."

Obscure in the throngs of Colombo, the old man in a simple robe moved quietly toward the wooden walkway beneath the store's awning. He seemed a simple beggar—kicked, laughed at, pitied. Unless one looked into his fiery eyes.

The day, like all days, was excessively hot, and the years were beginning to tell on him. He moved slowly, each step thought out and with purpose. His last assignment, this. If only he had more time to prepare and more energy. He began to doubt if he would survive.

Turning toward the Excelsior, he could see her standing in the window, her heart easily visible and broken. She had arrived safely, the old man noted with a smile. Then he shook his head in dismay. She had a great deal to learn, if she was going to be of any use.

The dark ones had already put their plans into effect, narrowly missing their target. He and his brothers would stand vigilant, lest any harm come to her. Even so, no matter how much they prevailed in their protective shielding, her own free will might be her undoing. He could not watch her *all* the time. Even so, the Brotherhood could not interefere with her own personal karma.

There was much to do. The world was on the verge of events of cataclysmic proportions. It had been almost two thousand years since he had had to watch over another, and in the end, the opposition had very nearly won.

He let out a sigh; concern filled his heart. This time it would be different. But he was not so sure. She was not trained for the mission, and untried in the heart. How could she have been chosen for such a task as this?

A man stepped to the window where she stood and put a gentle arm around her. The old man smiled, more at his own doubts than the joyous image of two bound suns. It would be all right. There was hope.

The two lights had found each other.

CHAPTER 3

The Race Begins

Each event touching another;
like threads that design in concert,
creating the fabric that is life.

The first week was a whirlwind of activity for the visitors from America. They traveled over the breadth of Ceylon, a magnificent and beautiful island, full of Buddhist monks and temples, with a great and grand heritage every bit as important as any country could claim. During the day they took small road trips and at night attended parties and dinners with the notables of villages and towns. Haley had suspected correctly. David Hampton *was* a man of substance. He was also very much loved.

Wherever they went, she discovered that David and his father, the governor, had put up a boy's school, or an orphanage, or in some way contributed to the welfare and well-being of the locals. Though the busiest person in the world, it seemed, David always had time to listen to some complaint or spend a few minutes with the children who constantly followed him wherever he went. He was a gift to the Ceylonese.

In spite of the wonderful time everyone seemed to be having,

Haley had to face the fact that nothing had really changed. The dream, once a source of terror and fear, became simply a nuisance that interfered with a good night's rest. Something else, however, inflated its presence as each day passed—a sense of fear, anxiety, and, as usual, a deep and abiding unhappiness that continuously fed her awareness that something was very wrong.

Each morning, no matter how splendid everything was or how joyful she felt in her heart, a subtle sadness crept into her mind, destroying what she was sure should have been a sublime, romantic day. After a few days, a mysterious thought started to come into her mind, quite outside of any volition of her own. It was as if someone knew her thoughts and feelings, intruding when moments were quiet, dropping something in to make her think. The one single thought, over and over, was like a detail of the dream, but more real. The dream, discontented with living only in the dark hours, now sought an existence beyond the limitations prescribed for nightmares.

One moment she would be talking with someone, and the next find an intense image burned into her mind's eye, forcing her to abandon whatever conversation she was involved in. The images clarified and took shape, as though once seen from a distance, but now up close. Something else now presented itself in the dream, a part that remained hidden and unanswerable. Always the temple, the path, and the roses that seemed to stretch into forever, and the open door, bidding her enter—but now there was the face of an old man, whose features were indistinguishable to her.

After the most recent episode the hallucination had faded, leaving her with her worst fears realized as she discovered an entire roomful of people staring at her with their mouths open in pity. "Dear girl, what seems to be the matter?" Or under someone's breath, but still audible, "Queer one, that."

Unable to look into either the eyes of pity or condemnation, Haley made her excuses and found some reason to leave the room, heading into the library where she usually escaped. Closing the door, she began to cry despairingly, shaking her head and pounding her fist on a table. An unfortunate lamp fell to the floor and exploded into pieces. The noise carried down the hall and into the main drawing room, freezing the conversation. David was on his feet and moving swiftly.

Easing the door open, he saw her alone, leaning over a leather chair, sobbing. He glanced down the hall behind him as he closed the door to make sure they wouldn't be disturbed, and then locked it. Hearing the lock turn, Haley stood stiffly and started to wipe her eyes.

Hampton, sensitive and concerned, waited a full minute before speaking. "I'm sorry. I'm sure you wanted to be alone, but I had to see you." He waited at the door for her to reject his company; when she made no such indication, he started for her, completely ignoring the glass that crunched underneath his feet.

Haley looked up at the warm and compassionate face that now approached with all the bearing and concern a man could exude. How could she tell him that she loved him? And would it matter now? Now that everything was ruined by this … this damnable curse? Hiding it would do no good, as he was sure to discover her affliction and flee. Haley cringed; he had to know already that something was wrong, and seriously wrong at that.

Yes. The gods had cursed her, just as they had cursed her grandfather. She had to spare him that agony; she had to spare herself, as well. She looked up at his innocent warm eyes, the dream of every woman, waiting for her to allow him to kiss and then love her. He would go as far as she allowed, as he had already evidenced by all his actions. He reminded her of a dog devoted to its master, endlessly waiting for the odd bone to be tossed its way—grateful for whatever came its way.

That's when she decided to lie.

"I get nauseated." What was it she had read somewhere? When you lie, you murder some part of the universe?

David nodded in understanding. "I see." He turned away from her for the first time since she had known him. He knew. After a long moment, David turned around and faced her, his eyes full of accusation and pain.

Unable to look up into his gaze because of the sadness that shone from his eyes, she made matters worse by laughing in a carefree and foolish manner as she glided to the door. "See. All better. Just a 'woman thing,' you know. Let's join the others." Placing her hand on the latch, she noticed he wasn't following her. Haley couldn't turn and face him and his loud thoughts that echoed through the silent room: "Why is she lying to me? She doesn't trust me." Presently, his footsteps confirmed that he had resigned himself to solving the enigma another time. Haley went out of the room without turning around.

Though he never spoke of it again, or asked for an explanation, the lie created a barrier someplace deep in both their hearts, establishing a rift. She convinced herself that she would make up for it by loving him and allowing him the only thing he obviously wanted: to care for, love, and protect her.

True to the promise she made to herself, Haley maintained a concerted effort at being honest, pleasant, and loving. Each day they were together, David and Haley drew deeper into each other's arms and lives. Everyone noticed what was happening and could see the effect each had on the other. They were radiant in the splendor of love, and everyone approved—except one person.

Ann followed in the wake of the couple, the usual center of attention, forgotten and uncared for. She became more distant in her friendship with Haley, as the two young hearts in bloom at Hampton Manor grew into a mature blossom. Although many of the officers and not a few dignitaries found her charming and delightful, these were of no real concern. The main prize was out of reach, and Haley remained the only obstacle to it.

David's attendants were happy that he had found a woman who, aside from her odd moments of withdrawal, was every bit as noble a person as their employer. After several weeks, there was an undercurrent of whispers by the staff about an impending wedding. The radiance of the couple was infectious to all, reigniting in older lovers passions once thought to be extinguished. Even the governor intimated his approval, referring to Haley as his "daughter," from time to time.

Though Ceylon was hot and humid, Haley did not notice nor was she affected by the climate. The only thing that attracted her attention was David's smile and endless compassion. He worked hard and put in long hours, but he never let the strain of responsibility show or in any way diminish his spirit.

The Senior Lord Hampton, as his British friends called him, was the director of no fewer than four companies doing business in Ceylon. Two were trading firms, one manufactured sorghum and the other made shoes. David's father had grown rich on the coattails of his government, and his son was trying to give something back to the population that had allowed so much wealth to come into one family.

Haley's brother had also fallen for the warmth of David Hampton—they became fast friends. John was eager to learn of all the goings-on of the Ceylonese and their problems. For the first time in memory, John Olsten wasn't angry at something.

It was as if he had found his purpose, whatever it was, and was at peace with himself and the world. Gone were the blatant and often drunken declarations of revolution and death to capitalists.

This fact alone stood as a miracle of sorts in Haley's eyes and increased her affection for the man who was responsible for that miracle. Yes, David Hampton was a knight of the realm: noble, kind, and courageous; able to change darker natures through some mysterious alchemy of heart magic.

After the fourth week, the group left the Excelsior Hotel and took up residence on the palatial grounds of David's Ceylonese home, Hampton Manor, occupying the east wing. As a host, none better could be found, as David always made his guests feel as if they were the center of all activity. Though he had to leave for hours at a time, there was always something interesting for his guests to see or do around the estate.

"This is such a grand life," Ann commented to Haley one afternoon while walking under a veritable canopy of jacarandas that blanketed the southern section of the estate.

She was right. Each day was full of joy and beauty. Haley thought about her friend in the mirror for the first time in months. How was she getting along? Would she approve?

"So, has he asked you yet?" Ann glanced at Haley, watching her eyes.

Haley started to reply that she didn't know what Ann could possibly mean, but her heart told her that it would be a lie and she thought better about her response. "No, he hasn't asked yet."

Ann laughed, pulling a bud from a nearby tree. "Has he kissed you?"

"Ann! Certainly not!"

"Oh, deary, don't be so coy." Ann smirked. "If you don't let the man know how you feel, how is he supposed to get the message? You know how dreadfully dense men are."

Haley remained quiet, lost in her thoughts. What would her friend, stuck back home in the looking glass, think about the turn of events? Would she laugh derisively or would she be glad to see hope return in their parallel lives? Haley could hear her voice of caution telling her that this might yet be another disappointment. As she gave the matter more thought, she knew that something would get in the way of things. That something would be herself and the continuous plague of intense despair and depression that was her constant companion. Hidden. Invisible. Locked up. Yet ever eager to rise to the surface in an orgy of destruction.

After a minute, Haley glanced at Ann, who was in the process of ripping the petals off the bloom and flicking them into the air. "I think he knows how I feel."

" 'I think he knows how I feel,' " Ann mocked dramatically, crushing the core of the blossom under her foot.

Haley scowled back at someone she was beginning to see for the first time, feeling the bite of her now-continuous ridicule. Ann couldn't possibly know what she was feeling. Ann had loved so many times, how could she remember or even know what real love felt like anymore? Did Ann resent her relationship with David?

More than anything, Haley needed a friend; a quick look at Ann's face informed her that she couldn't be sure Ann really wanted to be one. Why was she always short these days? Could that be hate behind those pretty eyes? Was that why Ann's mouth spewed constant anger?

The sound of a lunch bell ringing in the distance pulled them back toward the main house. Ann lit a cigarette. "I think we should push on next week."

"You mean to the mainland?"

"Yes, *to the mainland*," Ann retorted with heavy sarcasm. "After all, Reginald is waiting and we do have reservations that are waiting for us as well."

Haley recoiled at the bite in Ann's words, choosing to remain quiet. She had all but forgotten the purpose of their trip, lost as she was in the charm of Ceylon and David Hampton. She knew that Ann was right and, more important, that the answer to her problem of the dream was not here on the island, but elsewhere.

What would it be like to be kissed by him, to be held in his arms? He was such a source of strength for so many and yet so completely tender with children. She thought of a home here, with children of her own. It occurred to her that his interest in her might be in her imagination, as he was such a good host toward everyone. Every guest might think she was the special center of his universe.

Her spirits dipped at the thought. It could just be that: her imagination. Might be that he had no intentions at all toward her. Haley's heart broke at the thought, as she wondered if she had misread the signals of love.

Guests were arriving for the evening dinner, as they usually did at Hampton Manor, Haley noted as they walked up the steps to the main house. David's home was an oasis of sorts, which many visiting Europeans used as an escape from the dreariness of Colombo and its environs. Most of them would appear around four or five o'clock on the pretext of some official matter, then conveniently stay into the late hours, enjoying the lavishly poured brandy and imported cigars. She was sure Hampton knew their motives, but he showed no sign of resentment at the presence of his many uninvited guests.

The rest of the evening was filled with conversation about the economies of the world and, David would often point out, the growing global interdependence necessary for the well-being and security of the globe's advanced countries. As a diplomat's son and a graduate of Cambridge, David could comment intelligently upon almost any subject and seemed to have the absolute inside track on things. He was amazing to watch and listen to, as well as to daydream about. At dinner, Haley observed him closely, more than ever before. What were his intentions? Was he simply a kind and generous host?

Lost in the conversation about some person who had everyone upset—Hitler, yes, that's who it was—she noticed Ann watching her constantly at the dinner table, smiling knowingly. Ann nodded, as if aware of her every thought. Haley became uneasy all at once. Everyone seemed to be so sharp and quick, and she was always getting on the train last.

Was she stupid? She *felt* stupid. Ann was laughing behind those mean, cold eyes. Everyone was laughing at something someone said. Were they talking about her? Haley could no longer hear, could only see the mouths of people laughing: some holding up glasses, some looking right at her, others talking to someone else. Then, directly in front of her appeared a glowing field of roses. Didn't anyone see this!? Haley's hands went to her mouth in terror. Surely they saw the roses!

No. They were not paying the least bit of attention to them. Someone was tugging on her arm. A man, with a great mustache and holding a sherry glass, was asking her something. "What? I can't hear you?" He laughed and turned away from her. Yes. They were all laughing at her, laughing at her stupidity. Haley just wanted to melt away, right then, into the darkness of the floor beneath her. To end the maddening laughter. To end the joke. She was a stupid, silly girl with stupid dreams, with old men who taunted her in her dreams and roses that called out her name.

She felt like crying. So she did. Out loud and with pain, Haley cried. Someone was screaming. Yes. She was screaming. Accept it. Go ahead and release the pain. Haley *screamed* and *screamed* and *screamed* with all her power!

Instantly, all activity stopped. Someone cleared his throat. "Thank you, God," Haley wept in delirious joy, "I can hear again." Then she looked around the table. Every single person, including the waiters, was staring at her, their eyes wide in shock and disbelief.

No one moved. Someone knocked over a glass, providing a break in the tension. "Get a napkin, there, ol' boy." In spite of this, everyone continued to gape at Haley.

She couldn't move, frozen to the table by the penetrating horror of thirty pairs of eyes. After a few seconds of intense struggle, she ripped herself from the iron grip of the tablecloth and excused herself from the stunned table—running from the room and into the cool night air.

Someone cleared his throat. It was David—who made a quick excuse and left the room. He found her leaning against an ancient tree, its branches reaching low as though to protect and succor any and all who would seek shelter under it. She was crying inconsolably, tears pouring out in torrents. He stopped a few feet away. "Haley . . ."

"Haley . . . dear . . . what is the matter?"

Haley did not respond, hiding her face from him in shame. David looked at her, wondering what to do with this beautiful angel. A second later, he walked up to her and took her in his arms.

"Haley, whatever it is that is wrong, just tell me about it and we'll fix it together."

Haley continued to cry.

"Don't cry . . . please."

Haley finally turned and looked into the eyes of her beloved. David radiated compassion and strength, two qualities she desperately needed at the moment. The dam, a creation of society's conventions that neatly held back all emotion, could not hold any longer, the waters of love bursting forth. Instantly, he pulled her deep into his arms, kissing her with his heart, letting a lifetime of anxious love pour into her. Then he stopped.

She had fainted limp in his arms.

David hooked his arm under her and carried her back to the manor, where his guests gathered on the veranda. Asleep, Haley radiated a pure and soft glow that melted his heart; at least whatever tormented her could not do so while she slept. "That's the thing. Sleep, my princess—nothing can harm or worry you there."

Then he realized what was happening to him. He smiled, unable to contain his love. "Don't worry. I'll take care of you. I promise."

Somewhere in the universe, angels sang in a chorus of joy.

The path was covered with rose petals of the deepest red and vermilion. She found herself standing in the greatest field of roses that ever existed—they extended from horizon to horizon in rolling carpets of dark red petals. Down the path lay a white marbled temple, its pillars shining like beacons under a gentle sky. As Haley looked at the temple, the roses seemed to become more fragrant, until the powerful scent of the blooms seemed to dominate her senses, causing her to feel faint. . . . Finally, unable to resist, she turned away from the great edifice and leaned into an especially large bloom. Haley drank in its heady waft, the narcotic effects of the bloom stultifying her senses.

She found that the more she looked at the roses, the more distant the temple seemed, when only moments before the steps were near at hand. She discovered that she did not care, taking another deep breath from the flower. The feeling the rose produced was exhilarating, making her feel relaxed and, for the first time in her life, aroused.

Beneath and behind the glorious world of soft, dewy petals was a rising crescendo of deep sound. A word. A single word, over and over again. Calling her. Calling her name.

"Miss Haley?" a Sinhalese voice called. "Please to rise, Miss Haley, and come to breakfast."

Haley opened her eyes, snapped away from the dream. Her attendant, Zalub, was standing at the foot of her bed, wringing his hands. She moaned for him to go away as she pushed her face back into the soft pillow.

"Today is a most beautiful day, Miss Haley." Zalub began to chatter about anything and everything, as was his wont, laying out some clothes for her to wear and puttering about. Haley turned away from the pillow in the realization that sleep was not going to happen. Not with the exuberant Zalub about.

She liked the small, chubby man. He had pleasant, warm eyes that wanted to please just for the sake of pleasing. He wore an impeccably clean—though frayed at the cuffs—shirt that had lost some of its luster from having been worn long after it should have been. His coat was small—Zalub's advancing years and increasing weight straining every button—and fit for a man twenty pounds lighter. Neither his face nor his figure was that of a man who concerned himself with any issue beyond clean silver and prompt service; nevertheless, he was relied on for advice about any social grace or custom.

Like all the servants at Hampton Manor, Zalub lived on the estate in excellent quarters with his wife and seven boys. The children seemed to have more run of the house than its masters or staff. Their endless interruptions were welcome breaks as many conversations within the house turned more and more serious with talk of war in Europe.

"Please to come down, Miss Haley, as Master David wishes to speak to you most urgently."

Haley found the Ceylonese way of speaking utterly charming. Feeling groggy, she slowly raised her head from the pillow. "Thank you, Zalub." Then she let it fall back into the soft down. After a few more minutes, she sat up in bed and reached for the glass of water waiting for her on her nightstand.

Her hand froze over the glass. Her mouth fell open in terror and disbelief. Resting on the silver service was *Invisible Helpers*.

"Zalub!" she called out to him as he was leaving. "Come here, please."

He returned to the foot of the bed. "Yes, Miss Haley?"

"Did you put this here?" She pointed to the book, her hand trembling. Zalub looked on with genuine concern. "No, Miss Haley. I did not do so."

Regaining some composure, Haley dismissed him; unable to move or act, she simply stared at the tear-stained cover of the book. It couldn't be. John must have found a copy in the library and placed it there the day before. Haley had simply not noticed. She relaxed, rolled her eyes at her silliness, and grabbed the book.

The volume fell from her hands. A muffled gasp escaped through her hands clamped over her mouth. The book flopped open as it fell upon the bed.

Property of:
Haley Margaret Olsten
Boston, 1932

All at once, Haley felt faint, dizzy, and lost. This couldn't be possible. She had dropped the book into the ocean, at least fifty miles out at sea! Even if someone had picked it up, it would have been ruined by the saltwater. After a minute, she picked up the book and flipped through the pages.

It was hers, no mistaking it. The dog-eared corners, her notes in the margins here and there. A loving dedication from her father. She froze again. This book had tear stains on it, and she had wept over her book moments before she let it fall from her hands. *She had watched it disappear into the water!*

Blinking hysterically and shaking her head, Haley threw herself from the bed and rushed to the mirror to look at her face. Was this the face of someone losing her mind? Was she going insane, having imagined the whole episode on the ship? For the first time in her life, she felt deeply afraid—far beyond the terror of unknowing that her dreams produced. She knew what would happen if she were going mad. Haley had heard the stories of those locked up in asylums, living in filth and squalor, the women raped and treated like swine or worse.

Haley crumpled onto the seat of her dressing table, the tears of sorrow and resignation more than she could hold in. Was this the beginning of the end of her life? Happiness found so soon, just to be taken away. Was madness visible? It must be. Surely they saw it in her before she herself came to notice it.

Everything began to go in and out of focus: the temple; the roses; the book; a young man's head exploding into red petals; a voice from the mirror calling her name, again and again and again. The room grew dim and faint, and pleasantly, it faded entirely away into quiet nothingness.

The next image Haley saw was David's. He was saying to someone that things would be all right, and to just take it easy. She wondered who he was talking about. He looked troubled, and she didn't ever want to see him upset. She hoped everything was all right.

David rubbed her hand. "You had us worried there, angel." Ann, John, and several other people were standing in her room. They were all gaping at her, their faces reflecting a mixture of curiosity and pity.

"What happened?" Haley asked, returning to consciousness.

"Well," a man with an iron gray beard down to his chest and wearing a stethoscope, answered, "You must have bumped your head on something." The man was looking into her eyes with a light, then he clicked the device off. "She'll be fine. Some rest is what she needs. Girl looks exhausted."

David stood up and turned to the group. "You heard the doctor; Miss Olsten needs her rest. Liza, would you bring up some soup and tea directly?"

"Yes, Your Lordship." The maid Liza curtsied and left, her face splashed with the worry and concern in her heart. The staff and others began to break up, slowly filtering out into the hallway. They had all come to love Haley and were relieved to hear a positive prognosis. John and Ann had stayed behind, on the other side of the bed.

John reached out and took his sister's other hand. "How are you feeling?"

"Fine. I don't know what could have happened. One minute,

I'm up and about and the next . . . well . . . here you are!" It was a lie and she knew it. A feeling of shame flashed through her heart.

Liza returned with a tray and set it on the table by the window. David thanked her as she left the room. He turned back to Haley. "Try to drink a little something, won't you, dear?"

Haley nodded. She looked over at the nightstand. The book was back on the silver tray, just where she had originally found it. She shrank into the covers and turned her head away.

David turned to John and Ann. "Could I have a moment alone with her?"

Ann began to move—disappointed. John kissed his sister on the forehead. "We'll be downstairs if you need us." He closed the door behind him as they left.

David and Haley looked at each other, love glowing in their eyes—eyes that only the night before had been given to one another. He reached down and kissed her with a passion and depth that she returned in kind. After a moment, David stood, went over to the table, and poured the tea.

It was a pleasure watching him, knowing that the love she felt for him would be fulfilled. The more she gazed at him, the more she loved and admired him. Truly, David Hampton was a prince. Haley realized how fortunate she was to have met him.

He brought the tea over and she took it from him, sipping quietly. They did not speak for a minute, both content with gazing at each other. David took her hand again and gave it a gentle squeeze. "How are you now, darling?"

Smiling her answer, she squeezed his hand in return. He kissed her again. But with eyes full of love and affection as he approached her lips, he pulled away with . . .

Haley saw it in his eyes. "What's wrong?"

David turned sideways on the bed, struggling with himself. She gently put her hand on his hand. His smile returned.

"I have to go to Bombay," he started, "and I won't be back for at least three months."

She could see that the idea of separation was tearing him apart, as it was her. She surprised herself.

"As it turns out," she began, sitting up, "Ann says that we must be getting on or we'll lose our reservations. She's dying to see her Reginald."

David really began to smile. Haley's healing gifts were coming back to the surface and working their long-unused magic; all his apprehensions melted away. "You are going to Madras first?" He was transfixed by her beauty.

"Yes," she replied somewhat distantly. His cologne was intoxicating. She wanted to hold him as tightly as possible, never to let him go. Never to part or to be parted by anything.

"Maybe we could travel together?" Her lips were full, perfectly set against the softest skin he had ever felt. She was magnetic, pulling him in.

"Yes," she whispered. His hair fell just across his right eye, carelessly . . . sensuously.

"I'll see to it, then." Her breasts rose and fell evenly, a slight air of lilac coming from her, arousing him.

"All right."

It was a whirlwind of activity—people, butlers, handlers, valets, baggage, noise, children, someone calling for someone—perfect madness. Such was the atmosphere of Hampton Manor with David, his attendants, and the Americans, as they had become known during their stay, all attempting to get organized for the trip. Through it all, Haley and David touched, kissed, and made a regular spectacle of themselves.

And everyone loved them for it.

Except Ann. Ann became . . . cranky. Finding fault with everything and everyone, she found herself conspicuously alone a great deal of the time, her company unpleasant and unbearable. As joy remained the single greatest reason most people were attracted to Hampton Manor, Ann's short temper made her someone to avoid. She had lost the battle, but the war was hardly over. It was all in the timing; she now saw Haley not as her friend but as a rival to be destroyed.

Ann smiled to herself, watching from the stairs as they kissed. Such are the fortunes of war . . . and love, Haley was going to learn; and who better to teach that lesson than herself? That stupid girl had not the right to and would not properly appreciate a man like Hampton. "A perfect waste," Ann commented under her breath, watching Haley and David embrace.

John came bounding down the stairs, his arms filled with orchids. He slid the rest of the way, stopping a foot short of his sister.

Haley laughed at the spectacle and accepted the flowers. John looked . . . alive! A smile was always on his lips these days. There was an air about him—about everyone—that was indescribable. Truly, these were halcyon times. "Are you sure you are going to stay?"

"I have to," he replied with enthusiasm. "There is so much work to do here."

She reached over the flowers and planted a kiss on his cheek, then embraced him, happiness for his joy overcoming them both.

John straightened his tie: something that was new to his wardrobe these days. "Now that I am in charge of the school-restoration project in Tangalla while David is away, he asked if—" John smiled. There was something secret and enthusiastic waiting behind his lips.

"What? What, John?"

"I've got a job."

Haley couldn't believe her ears. Her eyes narrowed. "Of course you do," she said. "The project—"

"No," he replied, cutting her off. "A real job. Sis, you are looking at the Superintendent of Affairs, Department of Education, Ceylon."

This was too much, even for Haley. "But you *hate* school."

"I *used to* hate school," John corrected her. "Don't you see? This is a chance—a real chance—to do something important."

Looking at the new man who was her brother, Haley brimmed with pride. "I think it's wonderful." She hugged him again. "You go and help these poor souls as best you can."

"Thanks, sis."

After an hour, they managed to fill no fewer than six cars with baggage and bodies; each auto groaned under the heavy loads as they turned down the lane. Two hours later the caravan ground to a halt at the docks, impatient valets spilling out in a hurry to open doors, stretch cramped legs, and light cigarettes. After much travail, the group was securely aboard the *Verdad* and awaiting departure.

The old man stood on the dock next to the Greek liner. "These are monstrous things." Someday, he would have to travel in one, just to see what all the bother was about. That brought a smile to his face. He would never need to.

He could see Haley standing next to the ship's rail, looking out at Colombo and beyond. Then David joined her, making their radiance complete. Each held a portion of a rainbow's color—needing each other to fill it out.

He watched as the ship edged away from the dock, turning out and away from him, the ropes of the tugs straining to move the behemoth ocean liner. The old man likewise turned away, disappearing into the throngs of the busy port city.

CHAPTER 4

Allahabad

Wretched is he who ever takes,
never giving.
Poor is she who steals love,
and not returns it.

Miss Haley," Zalub called out from the open french doors of the verandah, "are you writing Master David?"

The second story of the hotel where Haley sat writing, over-looking a pond fifty meters square and surrounded by little cottages and gardens, had a sunset view that would have inspired Michelangelo himself. She was in the best room in the hotel—courtesy of Lord Hampton's grace and hospitality.

"Yes, I am writing Master David." Haley smiled. Zalub had brought some of the much-needed charm of Hampton Manor with him, erasing somewhat the dreariness and bleakness of Allahabad.

Zalub walked to the edge of the balcony, wringing his hands. "Tell him please," he continued with urgency, "I wish that all is most well and to hurry up and rescue us."

Haley attempted a smile, watching with sadness Zalub's obvious distress. If only she could do something to cheer him up . . .

Allahabad was dirty, hot, and totally under the thumb of the ruling Punjabis and the British military. She and Ann had only been there for three days, and Haley already wanted to leave. She hadn't seen David in two weeks, his business having taken him elsewhere in India, but she knew his destination and had promised him she would write often. Haley dutifully kept her part of the bargain to escort Ann—with Zalub in attendance—and meet the patient Reginald Long. All she could think about, though, was Lord David Hampton II.

The place was nothing like what she had imagined. The class and caste systems were stifling in the worst way. Everyone had his place—his order in the ranks—whether military or civilian. Mrs. Eve Gordon, the wife of General Gordon, headed the Allahabad Ladies' Society and so led the brigade of officers' wives. She was nice enough, providing one didn't violate her sacred rules of conduct. Every woman Haley met kowtowed to and placated "Old Bootstrap," as the others called her.

Hampton Manor and the British in Allahabad were perfect opposites. The "darkies," as the Indians here were called, were treated with the highest contempt and were regarded as foreigners in their own land. This was something that Zalub had never before experienced, and it made him sad. Ever cheerful and light on his feet, Zalub began to reflect in his own demeanor the attitude of his fellow citizens toward the British.

The aberrant side of it, Haley noticed, was that the Indians encouraged elitism through their own harsh treatment of the poorer classes: the pariahs. What Haley had witnessed in the few short days since their arrival had turned her stomach. Haley and Zalub found solace in each other's company; they were isolated lights in a sea of bigotry.

Upon arrival, Ann flung herself into the world of dances,

parties, and social occasions of every kind, finally enjoying herself on their journey. It seemed as though Ann had been biting her lip the whole trip, waiting to get to Allahabad. Her only comment when they got off the train was a sarcastic, "Thank *God*."

Haley discovered that Reginald's illness was not as bad as Ann had made it out to be, but she let the deception pass. She would never have met David if it hadn't been for the trip and Ann's gift of persuasion.

Captain Reginald Long was a perfect saint. Glad to show off his beautiful catch, and sincerely in love with Ann, the captain spent more time with Haley and Ann at parties than on duty with his regiment. Behind his facade of arrogance toward other races, Reginald was true to himself—a real human being. When an Indian boy's arm was crushed under the wheel of an oxcart outside a restaurant where they were eating one afternoon, Reginald rushed outside, carried the unconscious toddler three miles to a hospital, and paid for the care out of his own pocket. When the child awoke, there the captain was at his bedside with a smile and a sugar stick. Haley heard also that Reginald stayed with the boy until his parents were located.

As Reginald—the husband-to-be of her best friend—grew in her estimation as Haley came to know him, her respect for Ann was beginning to lessen.

Having dragged Haley eleven thousand miles to be with the man of her dreams, Ann appeared annoyed at his constant presence and devotion to her. She also seemed to have eyes for almost every single man in the regiment. Ultimately her irritation with Reginald extended to Haley, and to everyone unfortunate enough to have more than a few words with her.

Ann could be a charming angel of grace with some eligible young nobleman or a seething hotbed of anger with those who were once her closest friends. Haley was sickened at her behavior and a day never passed when she didn't feel ashamed, seeing Ann's dark side take over her personality. Haley wondered why it had taken her this long to see the ugliness in Ann.

"I miss him, too, Zalub," Haley said under her breath, her pen moving swiftly over paper.

Setting the pen down, Haley sat back and watched the sun begin its final descent behind distant hills. It seemed she was living a dream come true—romance in a distant, foreign land with a handsome prince—but her happiness was shattered by one single curse: the nightmares. She stood up and walked to the railing of her balcony, fighting back tears. She possessed within her reach what many could only imagine . . . and nothing had changed.

She was, in fact, completely miserable.

The dreams hadn't stopped. The restlessness hadn't stopped. The ache hadn't stopped. She knew without looking what her friend in the mirror would say. The hallucinations were constant now, appearing without warning at the oddest times of the day or night. Her inner sorrow, a part of her heart she had come to accept back home, now was mixed with new feelings of terror and dread.

For the first time in her life, twenty-four-year-old Haley Margaret Olsten seriously considered suicide.

She realized, perhaps for the first time, that maybe she had been trying the whole time to fall in love with David, merely in the hope of being cured. Did she really love him? Haley looked down at her hands. Finding David could be just a hoped-for escape from the unnatural pressure that haunted her without end. But no, she denied that. Whatever her original motive had been, she knew now beyond question that she did, in fact, completely love the man.

"I don't understand any of this!" she wailed to growing

twilight. A waiter carrying a tray stopped and looked up from the courtyard, smiled, then continued on his way.

Haley's head snapped up, fear racing in her eyes. Was she going mad? Would this . . . presence or unseen force inside her *ever* go away? Her thoughts ran to her grandfather. They said Grandpa was not well, and he was often the butt of jokes. Then she remembered Thoreau and something he had written. Was it in *Walden*? Something about if you have to ask something about yourself twice, then it is very likely to be true.

The sun was gone and, with it, light by which to finish the letter. She put the paper and pen away on the nightstand next to her bed. "Tomorrow, I promise."

Zalub appeared at the doorway. "Miss Haley? Miss Ann is telling me to remind you most urgently to be getting ready for the ball tonight."

She sighed. Three days—three dances. "Thanks, Zalub. Be ready in a minute."

Haley stopped in front of the mirror. "I can't finish the letter. I have to go with Ann." The woman in the reflection glared at her, seeing through the lie. Haley looked away, snatched a pillow from her bed, ripped off the case, and draped it over the mirror. "I can't talk to you tonight. I'm busy." Haley put her friend—and her reproaches—out of her mind.

The drive to the party was filled with Reginald's chatter about India, its natives, and his important role in local affairs. Ann listened and smiled politely, occasionally glancing sideways at Haley and raising her eyebrows. Forty-five minutes later, their taxi pulled up to an iron gate.

"I can't see the house," Ann complained, leaning forward over Reginald.

"Dearest," he replied taking her hand, "once in the gates, it's ten minutes farther." Ann looked at Haley, a quick smile coming to her lips.

The maharaja's estate was amazing. There were elephants, birds, and trees like Haley had never seen before—every animal roaming free. Every piece of ground was landscaped and tended; gardens wove about great trees and paths. What she saw next startled her.

"Is . . . is that a statue?" Haley asked, her face against the glass.

Reginald glanced out the window, then laughed. "Not a bit of it. He is one of His Majesty's guards."

The man stood as if made of stone, holding a rifle, his eyes forward as their car passed. He paid no more notice to their presence than if the car and its occupants had not been there at all.

Haley squinted, trying to get a clearer look. "Why doesn't he move . . . or blink?"

"Discipline," Reginald replied sharply. "Discipline's the thing. Why, if we had troops like that, imagine what we could do."

"He looks . . . soulless." Haley leaned back into the seat, the air becoming suddenly cold. "Who is this maharaja?"

Like snakes, Ann's arms wrapped around Reginald. "This is the house of the Great Maharaja Saling," she replied smugly. "It took Reggie all week to get us the invite." "House" was an understatement, Haley thought to herself. She tried to smile, but found it difficult.

As the taxi pulled up to the steps of the main building, two men in bright uniforms rushed toward it. In perfect precision, they opened both car doors, while extending a hand to each of the ladies. Moments later, Reginald, Ann, and Haley stood at the foot of the steps leading up to what was truly a palace. They took in full Ionic columns, grand archways, turreted parapets, and a huge double oak door at the top of the stairs with elephant tusks crossing at the center.

Haley had seen a great deal of wealth back home in Boston and in other parts of the world. This wasn't wealth. This was extravagance on the scale of emperors.

"Ladies, shall we go in?" Reginald offered politely.

Without a word, Ann grabbed Reginald by the arm and half dragged him up the steps. Haley followed, a shiver over her shoulders requiring her to pull up her stole. As they reached the top of the stairs, the two immense doors silently opened to reveal a crowd of several hundred people mingling and dancing; a full orchestra was playing a waltz, adding splendor to the shimmering chandeliers that hung as mighty suns above the gathering.

They were guided by a butler to the receiving line, where polite introductions were made to some of Allahabad's leading dignitaries. Each one graciously took Haley's hand and gave her their warm regards—some more than others, admiring her youth and beauty. Finally, she found herself standing in front of a tall dark man with striking brown eyes, wearing a simple white uniform with gold braid. His bearing was erect, like that of the statues in the garden, giving no hint of emotion or purpose. A turban, resting on his angular handsome head, held a violet/red sapphire the size of a walnut.

Haley curtsied, but she found she could not take her eyes off that beautiful stone. It shimmered in the light, and at times she felt sure it was glowing.

"It's been in my family since the days of the Prophet," the man said in perfect English.

"Hmm. What?" Haley responded absently; it occurred to her that she had been staring. The man with the turban smiled at her awkwardness.

"I'm terribly sorry," Haley apologized, her face turning red. "My name is Haley Olsten."

The gentleman clicked his heels, his head tipping toward her slightly. "Maharaja Damor Saling. At your service."

Ann looked back, wondering where Haley had gone off to, when she noticed the maharaja escorting her onto the dance floor. Her eyes narrowed. "Of course." She began to turn back toward Reginald, then she stopped, smiled, laughed to herself, and proceeded to join her fiancé with some of his friends. She glanced at the maharaja and Haley from time to time, hate and resentment burning in her eyes.

The strains of some familiar Bavarian waltz finally came to an end. Damor bowed to Haley. "You dance wonderfully, Miss Olsten."

"As do you, sir," she replied nervously. There was no sign of her friends, she observed. Wouldn't they be dears and liberate her?

"Please. Call me Damor, I insist upon it."

Haley blushed. "As you wish . . . Damor."

"Would you care for a refreshment, Miss Olsten?" Without a movement, word, or otherwise, a waiter appeared nearby.

"Oh," Haley replied, "yes, of course." She felt awkward and out of place. It was obvious that the maharaja had taken an interest in her, but she could not return that interest; Haley's heart had already found its one love.

Once again, she found herself drawn to the glow of the massive gem. Without realizing it, Haley took a step forward, pulled into the brilliance of the stone. It understood her. She could feel something soothing penetrate her mind, releasing and easing her agony. "No more pain," emerged as a thought, not as words. Yes. There would be no more of that now. I would be content to stay in—

"They say it has powers," Damor commented, sipping a glass of champagne. Haley blinked and discovered that she was still at the ball, staring again at Damor's sapphire. She looked at the champagne glass as though it were something foreign. "I'm sorry. It's just that it's so beautiful." Damor smiled at the compliment.

"Are there powers?" Haley asked, curious to know more.

"Yes. Yes, indeed," he replied, taking it off. "The power to give one a smashing headache." Another man approached and took the turban away. Haley smiled at the servant, but he did not return it, taking the turban without comment. Her eyes narrowed in curiosity; the man acted as though she wasn't even there. Damor spoke sharply to him in Hindi. The servant immediately turned and silently disappeared.

"Please forgive him," Damor offered, his charm instantly returning. "It's just that he is not used to seeing such a beautiful lady." Haley smiled, but her eyes still followed the man's stiff, mechanical movements as he moved away from them.

"I don't mean to intrude," Haley started, "but your English is so perfect. I was—"

"Harvard," he interrupted, "class of twenty-seven." He turned her toward the balcony. "My father insisted upon a classical education, and I wanted to go somewhere—anywhere—where there weren't any British." They both laughed. "My father is dead now these past four years, and his title and duties have fallen upon me."

Haley reached out and touched his arm, sadness welling up inside her for the pain that was etched across Damor's face. "I'm sorry to hear about your father." Damor smiled, placing his hand over hers.

"Not at all," he deadpanned. "He was a bastard of the first order." Damor didn't give Haley time to react to his statement;

seeing her startled expression, his fluid and easy smile returned. "So. How do you like our country, Miss Olsten?"

"It's a beautiful land. And the mystery! I've heard so many strange things about India." She stopped moving toward the balcony. "Are the stories about fakirs, and men who can climb ropes into the sky and drink snake poison, true?"

Saling turned away from her, resting his hands on the carved marble rail. "Is that all?"

It occurred to her that she was talking to the man's back, as he seemed unwilling to face her. Had she offended him in some way? Yes, she must have. She had offended a high raja of India, insinuating paganism in his people. She felt very small and stupid. Finally, Damor turned around and looked at her, his eyes penetrating and deep. Without a word, he moved her back into the great hall. She continued to look at him, wondering if he would give an answer to her question.

He stopped at the door and turned to her. "Of course these things are true—all of them. Now, if you will excuse me, I must attend to other matters."

The evening was a blur of dancing and meeting new people. By midnight, the orchestra started putting away their instruments: a signal to everyone that the night's festivities were over. Haley and many of the other guests found themselves waiting outside for their respective autos to whisk them back into the black night. Finally, Ann and Reginald joined her and they proceeded down the steps. At the bottom of the stairs, the odd man who had taken away the maharaja's turban appeared from behind a bush. He was trying to speak, but struggle as he might, no words came forth.

"Well," demanded an impatient Reginald, "spit it out, man!"

The servant looked horrified, terror racing through him, as

though he were fighting with some invisible demon which was tormenting his soul. She had seen that expression on her grandfather's face before he passed away; her heart went out to him, as it was obvious to her that he was suffering from some horrible affliction. Finally, the man's expression dimmed to what amounted to blankness; his eyes were reduced to blank, lifeless sockets of emptiness that simply looked forward—but saw nothing.

There it was, that knowing sensation, a feeling of eyes upon her back. Haley turned around. At the top of the stairs stood Saling, a dark outline against brightly lit archways, light reflecting off the sapphire in his turban. When Haley turned back around to her friends, the servant was gone.

> *Haley reached for the rose. And who could resist? It was so beautiful and fragrant, grander than all the roses in the garden. The temple could no longer be seen; instead, she found herself standing in a sea of deep red roses, delirious with their beauty. As she reached for the rose, it reached for her, becoming a snake whose fangs were open for the kill, a great hollow void where its throat should have been—a black emptiness in whose depths rose some horrible fury, consuming everything—all light, feeling, thought . . .*

Haley awoke. The rays of the sun, filtered through the leaves of a banyon tree, hit her full in the face. Her first good night's sleep in three weeks had ended in a nightmare. She rose, moving across the room to the dressing table. There, with a note, was a basket of freesias and roses—as grand a bouquet of flowers as she had ever seen before.

Dear Miss Olsten,
His Majesty, Maharaja Damor Saling, IV,
requests your presence for lunch today
at his palace at the hour of eleven.
A motorcar will be sent to collect you.
Bamda Shamoot, Secretary

Haley turned and looked at the clock sitting on the mantel of the fireplace. It was already ten in the morning. Her head tilted downward, unable to comprehend yet another engagement. "Doesn't anyone work in this city?"

Absently, she walked over to the mirror, still covered with the pillowcase. "Not now. Please, not now." Still sleepy, she walked over to the french doors and opened them. Her room was instantly awash in brilliant sunlight; the glare of the Indian sun drove her back inside.

Haley began to gather her toilet. "Zalub!"

"Yes, Miss Haley."

"I have to go out again. Can you prepare a quick bath?"

"It is not a problem, Miss Haley."

"Thanks, Zalub." Haley started toward the hallway, stopping at the nightstand. The unfinished letter to David sat there, waiting to be completed.

"Later. I *really* promise." With that, she flew down the hall.

The car bumped quickly over the road to the maharaja's palace. Everywhere Haley looked, she could see the heavy hand of poverty—mud huts and thatched dwellings, children as old as ten or twelve with no clothes on, and the emaciation of all: plants, animals, people.

All along the route, people stared. But not with a hunger for rupees or a piece of food. Mothers pulled children aside, covering them with their shawls. Dogs lowered their tails. Wherever the jet black Packard went, a way was made clear for it, no matter how dense or crowded the street. Toward the edge of the city, the car pulled up at an intersection; in the middle, two carts had collided and their contents had spilled out, their owners yelling and cursing at each other.

Then it became quiet. Quickly . . . silently . . . the two men in the road gathered up their wares and moved hastily away. Not a word was spoken. Every soul in the square turned away without a sound, making more than enough room for their passage.

Haley sat forward, rested her arms on the large, high-backed driver's seat, and tapped the driver on the shoulder. He didn't turn a centimeter in response. She was about to lean even farther out, to try to ask him a question or two, when the thought came—loud and very clear—that she shouldn't. Haley sat back and tried to busy her mind with the quickly passing scenery.

Thirty minutes later, she found herself seated in a garden patio more fantastic than anything she had ever seen or heard about. Situated in one of the many courtyards of the palace, it was surrounded by high walls on four sides with archways and doors opening onto it. In the center was a great statue of a woman, her right hand raised to the sky, as in supplication.

A table more than fifteen feet long was covered with every kind of fruit and delicacy imaginable. In the center of this arrangement were laid great covered pots made of gold, spatterings of ornate jewels embedded in their surface. The scented steam rising from their lids promised a more than wonderful repast.

A uniformed man seemed to appear out of nowhere. "His Majesty will be with you shortly and apologizes for the delay."

As was true of the others, he spoke so mechanically as to cause Haley to start. She regained her composure, smiled warmly, and thanked him. Without a word or any indication that he had understood the message, the man melted away through one of the many doors opening into the courted area. After a minute, Haley stood and walked over to the statue.

"Her name is Shiva," Damor said from some hidden place, startling her again. "The Goddess of Destruction."

Haley turned trying to find where he was. He tapped her on the shoulder, and she gasped in surprise.

"My apologies," Damor lied, enjoying himself and his little trick. "I did not mean to alarm you."

"No," Haley replied, gathering herself. "No, I'm sorry. I'm just . . . just a little skittish today."

Damor led her to the table, helping her into her seat. Immediately, four uniformed men appeared with wine, glasses, flasks, plates—and set up the table and served.

"I want to thank you for graciously inviting me to dine with you today. I know how busy a man you must be . . . and for the roses, too."

Damor smiled his smile. "Since last night, you are all I can scarce think of."

Haley smiled, shivered, then smiled again. She looked down, embarrassed and confused. Her index finger involuntarily twitched. "Damor. I must tell you now. I am spoken for."

Damor continued smiling. "So I've heard."

That stopped Haley, her face a question mark. "Your Miss Ann told me." Haley's eyes widened. "Do not worry, I seek only your friendship in a land barren of charm and beauty. Some wine?"

Haley nodded absently, taking a breath. "You see," he continued, "you Americans are so rich with new ideas, new boldness . . . new power. Really. I am just fascinated."

Haley nodded again, finding words difficult; instead she reached for a glass of water, grateful for having something to do. The idea occurred to her that she had been acting silly; after all, the man did say he wished only her friendship. And he looked so lonely, too. If his life was anything like David's, the very sword of Damocles must be hanging over his head.

"You must forgive my behavior," Haley said. "I'm still not quite used to your country's customs."

Damor smiled, but said nothing, digging instead into the salad that was placed before them. They ate in silence for a minute. The sun filtered through a thousand leaves, shadowing them from the worst of the heat. Before Haley could ask for anything, her every desire was anticipated by one of the attendants.

"You have a wonderful staff, Damor."

"Yes. They are handpicked for their ability to stay . . . focused." Damor glanced toward them; silently, they disappeared into the shadows. "And how long are you staying in Allahabad?"

"A few weeks. I am supposed to meet someone; then, I think, we are moving on."

Damor looked far into the distance before him. "Is this someone you are meeting, your betrothed?"

"Not yet. I mean, he hasn't asked yet. But he will."

"He is British?"

"Yes." Haley replied in amazement. "How did you know?"

"Lucky guess, as they say in the States."

The afternoon wore on. Haley discovered that the maharaja wanted to know every detail about her and her life; the trepidation she originally felt began to slip away by degrees with each passing hour. The more time she spent with him, the more she found she liked the man—though at times he seemed cold and distant. He showed her around his grand palace and pointed out its many mysteries and beauties. Everywhere there was something rare and distinct, like no other object in the world. The man was clearly a brilliant collector.

The Indian sun began to set against a purple sky, and she found herself still laughing and enjoying the company of Damor. Finally, she begged off, fatigue setting in. Before he would allow her to leave, however, he received from Haley a promise to come back the next day. Haley slept in the car on the way home, oblivious to the countryside and its pain.

Zalub stood on the balcony, staring out into the coming night. Miss Haley had been gone all day, and still there was no sign of her. He looked down at the garden, its beauty invisible to his worried heart. Sighing, he sat down, wishing to be of service to her . . . or Master David.

Ann appeared behind him, champagne glass in hand. "Hey, Zalub, ol' boy," she slurred, "how ya doin'?"

Zalub winced but did not face her. "I am still waiting for Miss Haley. She is not arriving so far."

Ann walked directly behind him, leaning down near to his ear. "She is not arriving so far?" she mocked his way of speaking, laughing. Unnerved, Zalub looked back at her, glaring in repugnance at a person whose heart could be so mean.

"Hang it on a nail, Zalub. Your Miss Haley's with a *new boy*."

Zalub continued to stare at her, unable to grasp her sarcasm. "No understandy?" Ann continued in a contemptuous, mocking tone. She moved directly in front of him, the stench of sweat and brandy pouring from her, producing an air of noxiousness between them. Zalub unconsciously shrank as far away from her as the wall behind him permitted, but Ann moved with him in small, uneven steps.

"See," she drawled, "you think she loves your Lord Hampton. She doesn't. Hampton doesn't stand a chance against the maharaja."

Zalub stopped, his face red with anger. "These are not truth! Master David wishes only to wed and make her most happy!"

" 'Master David wishes only to wed and make her most happy,' " Ann mocked again, laughing so hard that her glass slipped from her hand and shattered on the floor. Zalub started to leave; Ann stepped in front of him. "Now you listen to me, you filthy little bastard. There's going to be *no wedding*. Your Miss Haley is going to wed Damor Saling."

For the first time in memory, Zalub truly despised another living thing. A thought, shameful to a man whose heart was always patient and tender, flashed through his mind: Push her over the railing. Mortified with himself, he dismissed it, and instead pushed her out of his way, disappearing into the room. Ann staggered a few steps, screaming after him, "You can tell *that* to your Master David!"

Alone, the dark Indian night settling in and around her, lights in the hotel coming on, Ann lit a cigarette. "*I'm* going to marry David Hampton," she said under her breath. "And no one else."

Zalub stood in the lobby, near the front doors, a tear slowly rolling down his face. Seeing the love between his employer and Miss Haley had been the answer to a prayer for him and the whole staff at Hampton Manor. For all that Master David had done for Zalub's people, it was the least God could do for him.

Finally, the black Packard pulled up and out spilled a tired and sleepy Haley Olsten. Zalub smiled—relieved—and proceeded to help her.

She walked right by him. Not a word spoken. Nothing. Not even "hello." It was as if he wasn't there. Zalub's face wrinkled in pain, as he watched in disbelief, his heart hurt by the slight. Maybe it was as Ann said. Maybe, Haley only used him . . . and his master.

Haley disappeared into an elevator—she didn't even notice him standing right there in front of her. Zalub walked over to the registration desk. "Please to borrow a pen and paper?" His steps heavy and slow, he walked glumly over to a great armchair by the fireplace and began to write.

❧ CHAPTER 5 ❧

More Radiant Than the Sun . . .

Love, what mystery you are to us,
bearer of children, singer of songs.
Can you not lean out your endless embrace,
and carry us hither to your heights?

Well?" David Hampton asked Zalub patiently. "Where is she?"

Unable to look his employer in the eye, Zalub winced from the sharp stab of anxiety and remorse that flooded his thoughts and feelings. He was sent along to protect her and had failed. He had spent his entire life in the service of the man now demanding the whereabouts of the woman he hoped would wed him. Zalub had come to see his life as a service to a greater service: he was helping a man who helped others. A good twenty years older, Zalub had been Lord Hampton's brother, friend, sometimes father, protector, and valet from the very beginning. He had watched David the boy grow into Lord Hampton the man; with adoration and love, he then watched him grow into a great and benevolent soul.

Sobbing, Zalub fell to his knees. "I am most sorry, Master David. I thought it better to let her go, as Miss Ann—"

"Ann?" Hampton exclaimed; he closed his eyes for a second, shaking his head. He had never really liked her, try though he might to find something about Haley's friend to admire. He had shielded Haley from the knowledge that Ann tried on two occasions to seduce him, long after it was publicly known that he and Haley were an item. After her second attempt to lure him into bed, she had warned him that he would soon forget Haley and would come begging to her.

The event was still vivid in his memory.

David had turned on her. "Do you really believe a man could love such as you? A dead heart in a woman leaves you no woman at all. Did you actually think you could be attractive in your hatred of men?" Ann didn't move; she was frozen by the unexpected rebuke. Hampton wasn't finished with her. "I thought you were Haley's friend. You've no right even to stand next to her."

That parting remark had earned him a slap and the warning.

On top of these experiences with a woman he now considered to be dangerous, David remembered the nightmare he had had the night before they all left Ceylon. He'd dreamed that Ann had set fire to a house they were living in, laughing the whole while.

David turned to his servant. "*Now*. I want the whole story *now*. Leave out no detail, no matter how insignificant."

Zalub gathered himself and explained everything. The visits that became frequent. Haley's growing distance from him. The black car that arrived one day to collect her things. His letter to his master. Hampton had rushed as soon as he heard the news— but six precious weeks had passed, the mail in India being what it was.

The air in the room seemed to grow more hot and stale; even the ever-annoying presence of flies was missing. David paced nervously, trying to sort out the information to some useful end. But each new fact he wrenched from his reluctant friend and servant increased the bleakness of the scene. "And you say that happened three weeks ago?"

"Yes, Master David. They were most insistent and would not let Zalub stop them."

David turned and walked away from his shattered friend, his mind racing with worry—but clear. He walked out of the lobby of the hotel and into the gardens beyond, finally sitting next to the great lily pond. It felt good to let his hand sink into the stale and motionless water that reflected the even staler air above it. A water lily, not two inches from his fingers, drifted closer and bumped against him ever so slightly, as though Nature, ever healing, could feel his unspoken sorrow.

Something brought David around. Oh, yes . . . he was sitting in the garden. Without any reason, he found himself drawn to the water and smiled at the beautiful bloom. Then he looked up and realized he was not alone. A quick glance back over his shoulder and he immediately stood up and walked over to the hedges, stopping just at the corner.

"You've heard?" David asked him.

"Yes. Yes," a voice said, standing behind the curtain of shrubbery, out of sight.

"What shall I do?"

"Within their stronghold, nothing can be done."

David's heart sank. He had heard of Saling. In the circles of the Brotherhood, Damor Saling's reputation as a black magician was well known. How could this have happened, to his Haley of all people?

"There has been and always will be only one weapon, my brother," the hidden voice said. Hampton gave a quick glance and nodded in agreement. Sighing, he looked away toward the pond, the flowers, the sky—he didn't see them, grief overwhelming his heart.

David choked back his tears, attempting composure. "I should never have let her go."

"You could not know," the voice replied soothingly, waves of love rippling through the silence between them. "Young brother, it was destined to be. As it is with all true servers, each must be tested in the furnace of his heart. With our sister, this was her fate." A pause, awful in its silence and suffering, weighted the air between the two.

"Will . . . will I ever see her again?"

A wrinkled hand reached out and firmly took David by the arm. The hand belonged to a man who looked like a beggar, but whose deep eyes twinkled with limitless compassion. His voice rang out with such a quiet and understanding grace as to allay any apprehension. "Do not fear for her, as it will do her no good."

Emerging from the bushes, the old man—his great white beard touching his chest, a cane in one hand—escorted David down a path, sending healing into his young friend.

"It is up to love now," the old man commented.

David looked at him, attempting to understand the wisdom of his words, his mind and emotions mixed in a swirl of grief from which there seemed no escape. Hadn't he loved her? Hadn't he checked his motives to search out any false wish to serve his own interests instead of the object of that love, as he was taught? David's expression bore the questions in his mind, easily read by his Teacher.

His old friend stopped and faced him, his countenance free of care. "Thy purpose and heart are clean, young brother. Know that love demands freedom if it will grow from seed to tree." Watching him closely and with a steady eye of understanding, he reached out and gave David a firm squeeze and a smile of hope. "The key is love—it can enslave or liberate—each one decides for himself which it will be. Such is the significance of the One

Life, One Love, One Heart." As the old man outlined the meaning of human and spiritual love, a cool breeze, the first in weeks, filled the air; branches, flowers, and lilies swayed to a common rhythm. David brightened, smiled a little, and turned away with him down the quiet walkway.

❧ CHAPTER 6 ❧

Purer Than the Snow . . .

Will night gain its purpose,
to close out the light of day?
Was it not all a dream?

His hand was as old as the oldest oak or elm back
home in Boston, Haley noted. Yet it offered such kindness in the simple way it was extended to her, that her
heart felt about to break into a thousand separate pieces.
She could feel the wave of loving understanding sweep
over and through her, lifting her out of the stench of
poppies and roses so stupefying in their narcotic effect.
Looking up, she discovered to her surprise that it was
not an old man but, in fact, was her beloved David
come to rescue her.

She took the hand offered, letting it pull her out of
the garden, petals falling from her hair and shoulders.
David smiled and lifted Haley into the rapture of
compassionate love. Putting his arm around her, he
began to escort her up the walk to the great temple
doors, each step bringing the entwined couple closer

together in their hearts. Finally they stood at the foot of the marble steps. David kissed her—light playing gloriously around them, filling the universe with the glow of union.

The door remained open and inviting; Haley turned toward it, joyfully tugging on his arm. David remained on that first step. He could not go with her into the temple, he told her with a look; she would have to finish the journey alone.

An old man wearing the attire of a monk appeared at the top of the great steps, smiling at the two, bowing his greetings and blessings. David smiled and returned the bow; after raising himself, he looked at Haley with love and passion, kissing her on the cheek. With a squeeze of her hand he turned away from her and the golden temple; Haley watched him, not understanding. After walking some twenty paces, he turned around and stopped.

Haley stood midway between her one great love and the mysterious old man. Each stood in his place, glimmering in their radiance; but neither beckoned her on. It was time to make a—

"Awake! Awake!" a sharp voice commanded, stirring Haley from her sleep. Opening her eyes, she noticed one of Damor's servants standing near her. It was the one she liked, Hutar; she had met him that very first night she met Damor, when he attempted to say something to her as she was leaving. For some reason, being held captive was an experience she felt they both shared.

Haley moaned and turned back over in the bed, her head pounding from a severe headache. Burying her head deep beneath a pillow, she groaned and said, "Go away."

Her request was met with silence; she could feel his presence still near her. Haley peeked through the covers to check, though she didn't need to, each morning's ritual remaining unchanged. The man just stood there with no expression on his face, staring at her. Any effort to get rid of him was a waste of time, and she knew it. He would not go away.

Not until she drank again from the cup he was holding out to her.

The cup would take away her pain, remove her blinding headache, and make everything all right. After her fourth visit to the palace, she had fallen; the blow to her head had created some condition that could only be alleviated by one of the palace doctor's potions. If she drank, she could see; she would be all right. If not, the pain that would creep up her spine and into her head would bring her crumbling to her knees. Deep inside, where a well of sanity and balance reigns supreme in everyone, something screamed that this was all terribly wrong.

She thrust her hand out; Hutar placed the vessel in it. After a long moment of indecision, she righted herself in the bed and eagerly drank down the contents of the cup. Like a hungry wolf, she gulped; the bitter draft was soothing. Within seconds her pain began to subside as she felt the effects of the morning tea tear through her senses. The cup fell from her hands onto the bed. Haley smiled and laughed, then laughed some more.

Hutar gazed at her, seeing her but not seeing her. He had no expression on his face, no judgment, no awareness.

"Well, Hutar," Haley slurred, "don't you have some place to run off to?" Her attendant remained still, as a statue remains still—inanimate. Haley laughed out loud, then became angry—tears blending with fury. She grew quiet again. After a moment passed, she giggled.

Hutar turned his head slightly, as a dog would, having picked up something in the wind. He began to turn slowly away.

"Hutar," Haley said softly, "have the sheets changed again today as I've decided to relieve myself in bed." Either he hadn't heard her or didn't care to respond—she wasn't sure which. The servant continued toward the door. Haley began to weep softly, uttering black accusing oaths under her breath.

A cup crashed into the wall near the door Hutar was passing through. "I HATE YOU ALL!" she screamed behind him as she tumbled out onto the floor, landing in a sprawled heap.

Once outside the room, Hutar stopped, his eyes forever forward. He wavered, ever so slightly, a tear rolling down his cheek. Behind his eyes, something—some life—seemed to flicker on and off like a switch. The glaze returned, the flicker ended, and he moved on down the hall.

The sun was already setting, casting deep shadows everywhere in the courtyard. Haley sat in a chair, sagging like a bag of meal in a beautiful white evening gown, her chin sunk down on her chest. Attendants hovered around her, painting her nails, touching up her rouge, fixing her hair. Haley gave them no notice, staring off into space, occasionally glancing at someone, a sneer on her mouth. Beyond the activity, nearly out of sight, stood a dozen guards with rifles at the ready.

"Gimme something to drink!" she barked to no one in particular. Immediately, one of the guards trotted over and poured her some tea. She slapped it out of his hands. "Not that, you idiot! Something cold!"

Despite the outburst, all the attendants went about their business: a tuck here, some eyeliner there. There was no emotion or expression, only the dull performance of duty. A domestic servant appeared with a pitcher of iced tea, quickly filling a glass.

The sound of metallic heels emerging loudly in the courtyard indicated the arrival of Damor's secretary.

Bamda Shamoot was a small man with hair slicked down in the latest fashion, his eyes dark, clever, and piercing. As did all the staff at the palace, he wore a uniform; his indicated the rank of colonel. He moved to a chair directly opposite Haley's, setting his valise down in front of him. Her eyes did not indicate recognition of his presence.

"We are looking lovely today, Miss Olsten," Shamoot said sarcastically while removing some papers from the valise. Haley remained as she was, though for a moment she gave the impression of someone about to scream some vile insult. Shamoot waited for it—it didn't come—then looked thoughtfully at her. After a moment, he smiled and pushed a paper over to her, uncapped a pen, and set it on top of the paper. "Please sign this."

Haley blinked sluggishly, but did not move. "It's important," he added. Still, no movement or response from her. Bamda's voice became cold. "If you do not sign this paper, you will not get this." Shamoot placed a silver oblong box on the table, opening the lid. Haley looked down at the box, then at Shamoot.

"What am I signing?" she mumbled.

"Why, your marriage license, what else?" Shamoot smiled, pleased with himself. He thoroughly enjoyed the work given him by his prince. Haley moved forward, began to reach for the pen, then veered toward the box.

A hand intercepted hers. "First things first, my dear." Damor had arrived. She sank back into the seat. "Why?" she begged without looking at him. "Why are you doing this to me?"

Damor looked at Bamda, who got up and left, as did everyone else. Once they were alone, Damor sat down in the chair next to her, taking her hand in his.

She looked directly into his eyes. "I hate you." Damor smiled, reached into the silver box, and pulled out a small hypo. Haley licked her lips, her breath coming fast.

"You know," he started whimsically, "everyone says that at first." Without warning, he plunged the needle into her arm, emptying its contents into her. "Until they understand me." He removed the syringe, tossing it back into the box. Haley's eyes closed, fluttered, then opened again—dreamy and wistful.

"I still hate you," she slurred.

Damor sighed . . . then laughed, amazed at the depth of her endurance. "No you don't." His eyes bore into hers—focused, clear, with deep intent. Haley could not resist him, her own gaze centering on the sapphire in his turban. Within moments, every trace of life was completely gone from her eyes.

Damor smiled more deeply this time, admiring his handiwork. "You will wed me with all your heart," he said evenly, his voice metallic and hollow. Haley blinked, the struggle deep within the folds of her fast-sinking consciousness.

A cloud passed in front of the sun, cold shadows completely covered the courtyard, erasing any hint that the sun was even shining that day. Damor's eyes began to change by degrees to the shade of his blazing sapphire. "You are in love with me." Haley did not respond, her head hanging limp.

As Saling closed his eyes and uttered a few ancient words, the air about them instantly moved in icy swiftness, the light growing dimmer with each word.

"I . . . I . . . am in . . . love . . . with you," Haley repeated slowly.

Damor smiled and sat back, his voice echoing a rage from the nether worlds—boiled hate, lined with cold metal. "Sign the papers." Haley leaned forward, taking the pen into her hand. She hesitated over the paper, a tear falling down her cheek.

"NOW!"

Her hand moved swiftly upon the paper, her signature a scrawl. Haley then rammed the pen into the document, tearing it lengthwise. Damor stood there, unmoved by the act, then casually walked over to her, picking up a bamboo cane on his way.

"That!" The first blow struck its mark, and blood spurted from a gash on her forehead.

"Was!" Blow number two threw her from her seat and sent her crashing into a bed of flowers.

"Stupid!" Hitting her behind her ear, the cane snapped in two. Haley remained lifeless, facedown in a patch of petunias.

Damor snapped his fingers, and men appeared on either side of Haley. "Take the sow away." He watched as she was lifted up and carried off, then tossed the shattered cane away. Damor walked over to the table and inspected the document. It was barely ripped.

"It is done. She is ours now," a voice behind him said, as the sky grew dark and day finally became night. Damor fell to his knees in front of nothing. "I seek only to obey."

"We shall reward thee for thy efforts," the oily voice said.

"You have but to name your wishes."

"Stay the course," the voice commanded. "Watch over her and at the next new moon, we shall use her body."

Damor blinked in horror. "The incubi ritual . . . ," he muttered to himself. He waited for an answer he knew would not come, as they never told him more than was absolutely necessary. Straightening from his kneeling position, Saling stood up and sat down heavily in one of the chairs. He had witnessed the ritual only one time before; the agony that woman had gone through was beyond hell itself. It was amazing how long she had stayed alive. It didn't concern him, he realized, regaining his icy composure. She *had* to die. And after all, what did it matter how the bitch expired?

From some place deep within himself, Damor realized that whatever light was left within him had just died.

Damor looked out upon his small empire. They had given him power and wealth—more than he had ever hoped for. His dark brothers intimated that their time was coming and that those who served faithfully would share in the spoils; he brightened at the thought, a smile breaking wide upon his face. Already, in Europe, their work was going forward. Soon he would travel to Berlin and throw in his lot with the master plan now being activated all over the globe. Damor laughed in glee at the idea of global power within his reach: controlling millions, his every whim catered to. There remained only the removal of obstacles—obstacles who were forbidden by their own pedantic laws of free will to fight as he fought.

Bamda appeared instantly, responding to Damor's mental command. "Colonel," Saling ordered, "give my fiancé injections from now on, instead of the tea." Bamda's heels clicked as he nodded his obedience; he turned and left without a word.

Damor blinked, something in his eye; a light or—

He stood up and walked over to the statue of Shiva; a trick of the fading sunset reflecting off the old granite dame, no doubt. Moving around to the front, Damor stopped cold, his face frozen in disbelief. The statue was staring at him, no longer looking up to the heavens; a hand that at one time had been open to the stars now was a closed fist. Damor shivered, his mouth open, unsure of the meaning; instantly, a wave of helplessness swept through him, tearing into his dark heart.

A queer sensation gripped his senses, forcing him to see his life as if he were watching another's. For the first time in years, he saw what he had become in that terrible, awful moment of knowing and seeing—a pawn. A pawn with no soul. Struggle as he might to push away the images of ugliness and pain that flickered into his mind's eye, he found he could not. It was eerie; fear raced across his face. A pressure—an otherworldly pressure—pushed down upon him. It was as if he could feel destiny coming toward him, wild like a runaway train, bearing down on him. Obliterating him.

Four soldiers appeared instantly. "Remove the statue. Destroy it. Immediately!"

Hutar and his companions reacted without hesitation, as of one mind, one purpose, pushing with all their strength—toppling the nine-foot tribute from its marble pedestal. The ground shook as the ancient lady fell into the brickwork, part of an arm shattering into hundreds of pieces, finally resting on one side.

"Break it up. Scatter the remains into the sands of the desert." Damor turned hastily, quickly walking away. Hutar moved toward the gray monument, as his companions silently left to acquire tools and a cart.

Hutar stood faceless above the statue, his expression more blank than any stone, his eyes more dead than any rock. He could not see, in his trancelike state, the rays of love and power beaming at him from the statue. Then he blinked, wavered, and took a deep breath, letting it out slowly.

The first thing Hutar became aware of as he awakened was the palm tree in front of him. He thought to himself how beautiful palms were, able to grow anyplace where the sun was hot and bright. His smile dissipated as he looked around and realized where he was.

And who he was.

Looking down at his uniform, his polished shoes, his saber dangling at his side, Hutar shuddered. The realization of what had happened to him—the drugging and hypnotism by Damor, his slavery, his participation in those horrible activities—all descended upon him at once, ripping through and tearing up his simple, honest heart. He staggered forward, bracing himself against the statue.

Had it not all been a dream? Conscription in service to His Majesty, his life's purpose to serve without hesitation. Did he not sleep one night and there remain in that half-world between life and death, sleep and wakefulness?

"Heavens . . . ," he muttered, a feeling of guilt, dread, and hopelessness filling his entire being. Every act, every image, every indecency emerged into the clear surface of his mind, as a balloon held underwater will rise to the top when released.

He knew what to do. He would do it at once.

Then he noticed the statue. His heart went out to it, lying as it did, all broken and cracked. "I wish I could do something for you," he said to it as he began to turn away. His only thought was to get out of there as quickly as possible.

"Hutar," an elegant feminine voice said. His face twitched; a light seemed to be coming from somewhere.

"Hutar," the voice softly repeated.

Hutar shuddered and stopped moving. "Alaina?" he mumbled hoarsely.

"Yes, my beloved, I am here." Hutar looked down at his feet, his faculties slowly returning. "This cannot be real," he murmured.

Lying at his feet was his wife, smiling with all her heart. He dropped to his knees, taking her in his arms. *"Alaina!"* he cried, kissing her, "I thought you were gone forever." He held her as if holding dear life itself, a rapture of joy pouring into and through him.

He pulled away, drinking her beauty in, tears running down his face. Alaina was perfection: a dark Indian beauty with deep, radiant eyes that could calm a hurricane. How long had it been?

He neither knew nor cared; it only mattered that somehow she was here. If Alaina was here, then everything was going to be all right. Allah be praised!

Hutar came fully alive and awake, the full realization of what was happening to him coming to the surface of his consciousness. He let out a long sigh, squeezing his Alaina with every ounce of love and strength just now ebbing back to his once-empty soul. After a long silent moment, a moment shared by hearts bonded in love, he released her.

Her eyes spoke of quiet joy and long-lost simple love. What had happened to them, that such love should shatter? In an instant, he vowed silently never to abandon that love again. He knelt again, taking her hand in his. "How is this possible, Alaina?"

She smiled, ignoring his question. "You are free from the evil, but another is not."

Only one thought came to his mind: the woman from America. "What must I do?" Hutar kissed her hand, holding it against his cheek, tears washing over it. What would he not do for his love, his Alaina. From a grateful heart sprang praise to every deity he could think of. Something intruded upon his rapture. Oh yes, the woman from America.

His beautiful wife reached up and caressed his worried face. "Take her from this place of darkness and all will be well."

Hutar nodded. "I will . . . I will—"

"You must hasten," she implored him. "Every moment weighs."

Hutar stood, turned, then turned back toward Alaina. "When will I see you again? How can I find you?" Right then, when so much had happened during the years that had pushed their once-entwined hearts apart, he could not bear to leave her. No. If he did, surely they would not meet again, love again.

Alaina rose, taking Hutar by the shoulders. "Soon. We shall be together very soon." Hutar looked at her, not understanding. "But—"

"Hurry, beloved," she pleaded again, "there is no time to lose."

Hutar moved rapidly across the courtyard and opened a door. He stopped and looked back, his heart full of smiles.

Haley sat upright in bed, startled from her dream. After a moment, she eased herself onto her feet, walked over to her vanity table, and looked at herself in the mirror.

She faced the eyes that reproached, the heart that could not understand. What would possess someone to destroy such innocence? "Why have you done this to me?" the image pleaded. Her friend's eyes had lost their sparkle, shades of black rimmed them; her skin was pale and rubbery. Splashed across her dress were red streaks from the afternoon, and a bandage was taped across her swollen forehead. She reached behind her ears, her hand coming away stained with blood. The eyes that faced Haley were the eyes of hope lost.

"I'm sorry." Haley fell into the chair, weeping loudly.

How long she had been here, and in this state, she could only guess. In her stupidity she had let them take everything from her, including her dignity. And joy. When was the last time she felt joy? They kept her painted like a doll, ready to be put on display at a moment's notice. But for no reason she could understand.

How to leave? How to break the pain her body went through when the injections or the morning tea came late? Every time she thought of escape, Damor's eyes appeared in front of her, filling her with his will. And she saw his eyes now, fully in front of her, blending with and becoming part of her soul. Then she could not even remember what she was doing, or why she should ever want to leave this wonderful/horrible/beautiful place.

How pleasant it was here, abounding in roses and poppies and every nice thing. She could not imagine life away from the great and noble Raja Saling, her kind and gracious benefactor. What shame to think of betraying his love and gentle hand, after all he had done for her good and well-being. Damor was the sun, the hills in the morning, a fresh spring rain, and all things marvelous and good. She began to laugh. Laughter, ringing laughter, at her silliness. He had provided for her every want, filling her with a happiness she had never known, and now she would be his wife.

Haley absently opened the drawer in the dresser, looking for a hairbrush. To be beautiful for her Damor, only to please him and his goodness. She rummaged around, her hand striking something cold and heavy. She lifted the old navy Colt .45 out by the barrel and set it gently on top of the dresser. Looking at the gun, she could recall a man. The man was showing her how to shoot. And such a nice man, too. So insistent about the proper use of these odd inventions. Franklin. Yes, that's right. He was known as Franklin.

Memories blurred, bent, and twisted through her mind. A little girl holding a large gun, her father helping to steady her small arms. "Cock the hammer, *then* squeeze the trigger, dearest," Franklin reminded her. Haley looked up at him, smiling. "Okay, Daddy."

"Cock the hammer, *then* squeeze the trigger," Haley mumbled absently, staring into the mirror above the dresser. It was okay, her friend told her.

Free us, Haley. Free us from this while you can. Then, we can be together—and free—forever.

Haley looked down at the weapon. "Cock the hammer, *then* squeeze the trigger."

Now, we can run through the fields like the deer, never to think of school or Boston or those horrible roses.

She touched the gun. "Cock the hammer, *then* squeeze the trigger."

It is the only way. Please. Now. Do it now. He is mad, Haley, mad. They are going to torture us and turn us into monsters! Please! Now!

Haley picked it up, unconscious of its weight now. "Cock the hammer, *then* squeeze the trigger."

Yes. That's right, my self, my friend, my heart. Freedom is so close . . . so close.

The barrel felt cold against her neck. "Cock the hammer, *then* squeeze the trigger."

Her thumb on the hammer, she pulled it back. Click. Click. Now squeeze. Clack!

Hutar winced, the hammer of the gun having smashed against his thumb—jammed there to prevent it from firing. blood ran down his wrist from the puncture. He exhaled heavily, realizing how close it had been. Another moment and . . .

He stopped and looked at her. Haley stood motionless, staring into the mirror, not seeing him. Haley was mumbling something. "Freedom. Freedom."

She cocked the hammer again, freeing Hutar's hand.

"Stop!" Hutar commanded, tearing the iron weapon from her hands. Haley blinked, still staring off into the endless space before her. Hutar looked at the old percussion pistol and shoved it into his waistband.

He pulled her around in front of him, searching her listless eyes. "Wake up! Please, wake up!" Haley looked at him and smiled, seeing Damor. She wanted so to please him. Make him happy. She began to untie her lace nightgown, pulling absently at the bow.

Hutar blinked, incredulity splashing across his face. He slapped her. Haley laughed, her hand going to the second bow. He slapped her again. More laughter. Another slap—again and again, until she fainted into his arms. Struggling with her weight, he carried her over to the bed, laid her down gently, then stepped back—his mind racing. There was only one way.

It was dark. A smell invaded the nose: a pungent, sickly smell. Haley moved a little; her surroundings were vague and blurry, just becoming clear. She was lying on a dirty floor somewhere; high, arched ceilings with barred windows were very near to the top of the walls, the night air pouring in through them. The only light in the room came from the moonlight streaming in from the little windows—windows too high to be reached.

A heavy oak door on the other side of the room creaked open, a shaft of light arcing into and lighting the room. Haley sat up and looked around, unconsciously crawling away from the door. She stopped, too horrified to scream or move.

"Don't look at it!" a voice whispered. It was a warning issued in vain, as Haley could not take her eyes off of the rotting corpse lying next to her, its eyes already picked away by rats. Hands reached down and pulled her up.

"What is—" Haley started to ask, terrified.

"Do not ask," Hutar whispered, "and do not speak." Hutar helped her toward the door and peered through the slight opening. He turned to her. "We have minutes. Maybe not even that." Haley looked at him, her face a mixture of pain and puzzlement.

"We are going to leave this place," he told her simply. Haley wavered, her mind a haze. Hutar stopped, reached up, and caressed her face. "I once loved a woman who was like you." He looked away, lost in the distant past. "She was all I ever wanted. I do not know how this has happened to us, nor can I understand it." Hutar stopped, tears emerging, then continued, "I came here two years ago. . . ."

His voice trailed off again; he strained to listen, as sounds emerged in the distance. He turned to Haley. "There is no time. We must hurry or we'll die." Hutar pulled Haley's arm around his shoulder, taking her weight on him, and fled through the door, pulling it softly behind him.

Down the corridor. Stopping at a corner where stairs and a doorway met. The door, locked. Moving quickly away in another direction. Down more stairs. Through another door and quickly down a darkened hallway. Another door and then outside, into the cool night. The two sped along a wall, coming to an iron grate.

He released Haley, setting her against the wall, groaning in the realization that she had passed out completely. He stepped toward the iron gate and gripped the ancient, rusted handle with both hands. It didn't move. Again, with more effort. A creak. A little more, a little more . . . Finally, with a horrendous grinding clank, the handle moved freely, the door swinging out and away. Voices and shouts—coming closer. Now, nearby.

Hutar lifted Haley up and swung her over his shoulder, disappearing through the dark passage beyond the door and into the night, moving silently through the grass and bushes; zigzagging this way, then that. Stopping, sweat pouring everywhere, soaking his shirt. A few deep breaths. A glance backward. Fear. Terror. Then off again, into the blackness.

Hutar had been running for at least an hour, every muscle

aching and throbbing. He laid Haley down, resting her head gently on a tuft of grass. She was still out cold. How far had they come, he wondered? An hour of running . . . carrying a woman?

Lights, urgent in the distance, searching . . . Straining, he lifted her onto his shoulders, staggered, then charged off again. He could see the outline of the bluffs against the river ahead. Just a little farther, then he could rest. Just a little—

He realized what was happening, as it was happening. It was a tiger trap. A man could walk over it with ease, but not a four hundred-pound Bengal tiger. Hutar was amazed at the clarity of this knowledge all coming so swiftly to him in so short a time. He marveled at the realization that after all the drug-induced slavery to the dark one, his mind still could remain somewhat sharp. As sharp as the punji sticks that were ripping through every part of his body.

Even as the blood started to pour out of his mouth, choking him, Hutar smiled. Having had the presence of mind to push her away as he fell, he had kept her soul safe from the maharaja for the time being. Her hand dangled over the edge of the pit; she was alive. And all the darkness he had partaken in would not matter. He had saved her, had done his very best. It was enough.

Another smile, deeper. A smile of joy and tears. To think Alaina had left him all those years ago, now to find out she had been merely waiting for him. She looked so beautiful, so radiant—her eyes starry, her heart a fiery sun. He stood up, finding that he was not injured after all, so he eagerly took her hand as she led him away from the dark, barren desert into the star-filled night. Carried on wings of rapture and joy she bore him into the blazing sun of limitless love: two souls vanishing toward a star in the heavens above India.

◢ CHAPTER 7 ◣

Decisions

One day, one hour, one moment;
a time comes for each.

The sound of the biplane drew near. At first, miles off. Distant. A drone, echoing over the plains. Haley awoke—her head throbbing, her mouth dry, that damn far-off whine coming closer. She sat up and realized she was lying in brush surrounded by dense thickets and trees, near some kind of culvert or ditch.

"Ugh," she groaned, putting a hand up to her forehead. It felt sticky and wet, and a vague memory of flowers surfaced when she looked at the blood on her fingers. "What's happened to me?" Standing, unable to see anything, she took a few steps to her left, when suddenly she could feel the ground start to give way. She reeled, turning away from the disintegrating soft leaves and sticks, throwing herself in the opposite direction and back onto solid ground. She landed face first in the dirt.

"Oh!" she sputtered, spitting dirt out of her mouth. She sat up again, tears coming to her eyes. "Will someone tell me, WHAT IS GOING ON?"

Finally, it all began to come back to her in waves rolling into her mind, one overlapping the other: the escape, Hutar, the gun, running, fainting, a statue, oblivion. But where was Hutar? She stood again, looking around, hoping that maybe he had left to get water and would no doubt return in a moment or two. Then she stopped cold. Her hand moved quickly to her mouth as she shrank back in horror.

What she saw made her cringe: Hutar's blackening remains forced both the ugliness of the event and the memories of her life at the palace back to her with even greater swiftness. She recalled him from the dance and vaguely from dreamlike memories. Odd. Disjointed. Everything jumbled.

Haley stood there for a few minutes, unable to avert her gaze from him, his dead eyes staring up at her. A deep sadness washed over her, the fullness of her predicament and its causes holding her by the edge of the pit. The tears that flowed down her face were tears of compassion and pity—both for Hutar and herself.

At length, she realized that the sound she was hearing was a plane. A plane that was getting nearer. Aware that staying visible could be dangerous—fearing that the plane might be Damor—she wished her dead savior peace in eternity and disappeared through the bush.

The pilot of the small French biplane could see great distances from his altitude of five thousand feet. The air was clear and sunny and he had the sky to himself. It was rare to see another flier above the Indian plains, and when he did, he always went out of his way to swing by him and wiggle his wings hello. He loved his little open-to-the-air cockpit plane, won in a poker game in Peking.

"We are too high up!" a voice crackled in his ear. "We must go lower."

The pilot nosed the plane down and cut back the power,

gravity plunging him quickly to two thousand feet, the air speed dropping to about sixty miles an hour. "How's this?" he yelled back over his shoulder.

"Better. Much better!" his passenger bellowed over the roar of the engine.

Haley hugged a banyan tree, its great boughs and leaves spreading everywhere. The plane was very close, sounding very near above her. Then, the growl from its engine began to grow faint, finally disappearing off into the distance. She stepped back, breathing a sigh of relief.

"Ahhhhhhhhhhhhhh!" The scream came with the realization of finding hundreds of ants angrily swarming over and biting her—a maddening blanket of crawling pain. Running blindly. Screaming. Each attempt at brushing off the fierce attackers further enraged the tiny soldiers, their relentless bites growing deeper. After five agonizing minutes, she removed the last one.

Haley stopped and looked herself over. The welts stood out like blisters the size of quarters on her arms, neck, and legs and were growing scarlet and painful. She could not see from her left eye, as blood was running from the gash in her forehead. The air she gulped into her lungs was heavy with a steamy tropical wetness that made breathing difficult. She began to weep, out loud and heavily, as she started to trudge again through the brush. It was still early morning.

By noon, she made it to the stream she had seen in the distance, letting herself fall into its cool, muddy waters. The healing effects of the water roused and clarified her senses, the dull ache that rattled every joint intensifying into something sharper and deeper. Haley closed her eyes and let her body stay submerged as much as she could in the small stream. After a few minutes of delirious joy and refreshment, she dragged herself out of the water and sat down on its soft bank.

The sun's heat was unbearable even after a few seconds. Haley looked for something to cover her head. There was absolutely no sign of life or vegetation in any direction she searched.

She smiled. No matter how bad her predicament: the constant ache everywhere at once, being lost in a land that brooked no quarter, and living moment to moment with the certain sense that she was being hunted like an animal. It would be okay. It would just be a matter of following the stream one way or the other until she came to a village, road, or bridge. One of those must surely exist. If she became too hot, she would simply dip back into the water and cool off.

"Thank you." Haley whispered under her breath, realizing that a gift had been given her. Battered, bruised, bitten, and exhausted, she trudged down the stream, disappearing with it around one of its bends.

The officers' club at Allahabad, ninety miles from where she stood, would show that it was almost one o'clock and 125 degrees in the shade. The Indians and British alike knew from the hundreds of bodies that were found floating in brackish ponds or lying in roads on any summer day that it did no good to go moving about in such heat. Stay put and stay quiet was a wisdom taught by a climate that allowed no second chances at learning. It was a wisdom rarely taught to schoolgirls in Boston.

How had it all happened? she asked herself. Each attempt at understanding brought blurred confusion and images to her. Behind all this was a growing ache, deep in her joints; her spine felt as if it were collapsing, as if some great, internal pressure were crushing it, sending waves of nausea and pain shooting through her. Each step was painful. The sun—burning—boiling the air.

The pain racking every joint in her swelling body seemed to rub against nerves numbering in the billions. Even the simple act of taking a breath was accompanied by sharp stabs of agony in every muscle of her chest and throat.

Haley laughed. Of course.

The injections; the morning and evening drinks—bitter to the taste, but sending her swooning. She found herself wishing for a cup right then—no matter how small—more than anything in the world. Her laughter subsided, becoming a whimper; it occurred to her that she was addicted to some form of poppy, probably morphine.

Each step became a conscious effort, requiring every ounce of will she could bring to bear. The force of her step brought with it ragged shards of misery, ripping through the fabric of her body. Lifting a foot—pain and agony everywhere. Setting it back down—each bone brittle, as if it were about to shatter.

The eyes could no longer see, could no longer open, their puffy folds blistered by the sun's rays. Lift the foot, put it down. Boom. Lift the other foot. Boom. A cadence, horrible beyond imagination, resounding inside every cell of her brain, as each step echoed the cry of distress of a thousand, million cells of a body wasted and suffering through narcotic withdrawal, heat sickness, and dehydration.

After two hours, she fell to her knees, spent. Haley began to cry, the cry of a soul suffering in agony beyond anything she had ever imagined. The heat stood as solid weights of rigid iron, forcing everything in nature to bend low under its demanding presence. She let herself fall backwards, oblivious to the rock that struck her head and brought her out of her body, releasing her from the prison of torment.

Hours passed. Then a day. Then another. A finger twitches. Then an arm. Lips, blistered and shapeless. Open wounds and boils, angrily formed on the surface of once-soft skin. Lurching, a mass of flesh and hair curled into a ball, raised itself onto its knees. To all appearances, this writhing thing was no longer the body of a woman, but of some half corpse of knotted elbows and twisted features.

Unable to see from eyes caked with pus, Haley began to grope for the stream and its life-giving waters. She reached and scratched with her hands, her fingers—like maddened demons, hurriedly scrambling for the liquid to touch their tips—found only hardened, baked earth. Hot. Formidable. Unyielding.

Haley righted herself, resting again on her knees, forcing her eyelids open with her dirt-caked hands. Light, blinding light, sent spokes of torment through her.

"No!" she shrieked through sobs, realizing where she was. Haley had wandered into a ravine, bordered on three sides, and the heat of the midday sun turned the small wasteland into a living oven. She fell over onto her side, beginning to comprehend the magnitude of her plight. Somehow she had gotten off the track, become lost. There were no footprints to trace her way back; the earth was as hard as porcelain, baked by a merciless Indian sun.

A hawk appeared. Circling. Arcing. Weaving in a dance it knew would result in the consummation of its existence. Then another hawk. Graceful, as if some great orchestra were dictating the tempo, the measured rhythm of two dark objects crisscrossing the barren sky.

Haley continued to weep. Yet, tears no longer formed or trickled down her once-radiant, beautiful face. The cracks in her skin began to open, all moisture in her body rapidly disappearing. At length, the weeping subsided, replaced by a deep sigh. Then another. Quiet. Simple. Peaceful.

She had only her thoughts. Franklin appeared to her, laughing and full of joy, dancing in circles with some invisible woman.

"Daddy, am I dying?"

Franklin stopped and straightened his clothes. Taking measured steps, he headed over to his crumpled daughter. "Child, do you wish to die?"

Haley began to sob. "No, Daddy. I don't want to. Can't I go with you?"

Franklin extended his hand to her, bidding her to take it. She tried to stand, but found that her legs and arms no longer responded to her commands. She felt paralyzed—unable to speak or move, except in squeaks and lurches. Franklin began to fade, imploring her to stand and take his hand. She could not. Finally he vanished.

The scream echoed through the canyon. *"Daddy!"*

Delirium. The sun was high, its bristling rays penetrating anything still within its certain grasp. A lizard, curious and eager to know what was the matter here, came close by, but wisely stayed out of the burning heat. After a minute it scampered away from the twitching thing in the sun. A shadow passed over her, felt more than seen.

Her grandfather, bright in a shiny uniform, took her hand as they walked across a bridge. Lilies bloomed in the fields. Apple blossoms showered their tender grace upon all. In the middle of the bridge, he stopped, staring off into some great distance that only his eyes could pierce. Haley smiled. How wonderful it was here in Boston. She was grateful to be home again, seeing everything alive with the splendor and color of a fresh, new spring.

He started forward, Haley stepping with him. He turned, stopping her with a sharp look. "None but the strong can come."

Haley looked at him, fear rising in her stomach. "I don't understand."

The colonel glanced down at her, his gaze penetrating and fiery. "To do battle for a cause. A cause of freedom for all men, requires courage and strength of spirit." As he finished his words, he turned again, pointing across the bridge.

It was a scene from Dante's Inferno. Everywhere, by the thousands upon thousands, were the standing ranks of soldiers, officers, cannon, and horses—all screaming in the frenzy of a great battle. The great roar of hundreds of artillery shells bursting among the men; exploding limbs, flying parts of humanity; rivers of blood drenching everything. The world in front of her began to take on a crimson hue. Hoarse orders being shouted. Men, half crazed, delirious with battle, rushing into walls of flame and fire. Disappearing. Gaps, opening and closing. Stalwart men, vanishing in orange flashes of fiery explosions. The screams of animals in their death throes. The great rumbling roar of destruction, filling every part of every thing, from horizon to horizon. This horror amounted to nothing compared with what she saw next.

Blackened ghouls rushed from ear to ear, whispering madness and fury to the combatants, feeding upon the reddening frenzy that was this perfect universe of battle. All became consumed by the hand of death, forcing everything into the breach of absolute chaotic destruction.

Behind it, through it, and above it dwelt the grace of simple love, lifting all who expired into the loving embrace of compassion. Great angels, ministering to the fallen, lifted confused spirits from shattered forms. Wives, sweethearts, long-dead relatives, assisted by unseen agents of love, moved forward tenderly, in gratitude, for those who would give their lives for freedom.

Haley shrank back in horror, realizing for the first time what had happened to her grandfather and all the grandfathers of her generation. They had fought mostly a terror beyond mortal description. And they fought mostly without thanks from the millions who could live and die in the bosom of freedom.

She wept. She wept for the love these brave men had felt for an enslaved humanity. Men who had given the last, full measure of devotion for truth and liberty. Men who had walked into the arms of evil with clenched teeth and drawn swords, knowing that day to be their last.

She looked up and noticed her grandfather gazing down upon her. His eyes carried a great sadness in them; deep lines crossed his face. Weathered. Worn. His uniform was no longer bright and shiny. Instead, it was ragged, mud stained, and bloody—huge holes revealed skin and bone through the fabric.

He extended a rough and broken hand to her. "Are you coming?"

Haley could not move. The colonel continued to look upon her with love, his heart pouring through his eyes, his compassion deep from a lifetime of selfless service to humanity. He nodded in understanding and rested a loving hand upon her head. He looked down, adjusted his shoulder strap, and drew his saber— worn, the edge nicked and scratched from a dozen battles, the handle dirty.

"I have to go." Without another word, he turned and walked down the bridge that arched over the pleasant stream, where blossoms floated upon the water.

Haley watched him move forward; aching to join him, she found she could not move. Frozen by fear, she could only watch. The sounds of battle faded as he stepped into the fray—the scene vanishing—replaced by the quiet splendor of trees, grass-lined parks, and sparrows flitting gaily in the air.

Without warning, she began weeping violently—tears falling full onto her cheeks. For the first time, she saw who and what she was.

A coward.

Selfish. Living only for herself. Living only for her desires.

Her life rapidly appeared in front of her. Each moment, each minute, each feeling, thought, desire, and action instantly played in front of her. And with it came a horror deeper than the battle—a horror that spoke of the motive behind every action and decision in her life.

It was a life lived solely for her separate, selfish self.

"Oh, God," she cried out, "I am so sorry."

Haley crumpled, falling limp upon herself. She saw herself as she really was: a spoiled, selfish, and vain woman. The image of those thousands of brave men, giving their all for her and billions like her, was a mirror that made her own revelations all the more ugly.

It occurred to her that she was dead. The colonel had been dead for years and yet, here he was. She knew—how, she could not understand—that she was at the end of her life and that it was now time to move onward. Above her, resting softly in the heavens, a warm sun sent loving rays onto the flowers, birds, and all creation. She could feel the hand of some great presence in those rays, lifting all, healing all, giving equally to all.

Haley looked up at that presence, her heart shattered and broken—all stripped away in the presence of truth, nothing remaining but the simple soul that lies within each of us. "In your service, I dedicate all that I am, from this time forward."

Light, time, and space became one in an instant. Childhood, youth, friendships, her family, and finally India. Haley saw her blackening, swollen body, lying twisted in a ravine. A hawk pecked at her wrist, tearing her skin away.

It was over.

Light bent again, sucking her through some small space, tinier than a needle.

She opened an eye, the other crusted over with caked blood. She could no longer feel her body. Amazing, she thought to herself. She felt no terror, no fear. As though lying here was the most natural thing for her to be doing.

Oh, to say good-bye to David and her friend in the looking glass—we are free, dear friend, free. She felt it, that freedom which always seemed just out of reach. All the old friends' faces from home flashed into her fading mind; her family as well.

"Good-bye."

His face appeared in front of her. Old, kindly eyes, shrouded by mountains of silvery hair; a great long beard, flowing wide from his face. Haley could feel herself smile, glad that God had come for her at last. And was it not God? With those eyes that poured out limitless love. Did he not look like those old catechism books, with silver locks, majestically billowing around a loving, concerned face?

The Awakening

Never let hope shatter,
as it is the torch which beckons all.
Dreams. Let these also burn brightly
in the heart. How to move forward without
dreams?

Haley didn't understand—couldn't understand—*how* she could be looking at her feet. Yet, they were her feet; she could and did wiggle her toes. She raised her left hand—it, too, moved to her bidding. She gasped. The hand was that of an older woman, maybe thirty or forty. Scarred, weathered, with scabs scattered over its once-supple texture, the joints bony, each movement stiff and painful. She let her hand fall back on the bed she was lying on. The quilt that covered her was old and tattered, its weight cementing her to the mattress. Haley wept softly, mourning the loss of her beauty and inwardly cursing her foolish pride, the trip, and India.

Turning her head, she could make out nothing of her surroundings beyond a few feet. A banged-up oil lantern cast a sickly yellow light over the wall next to her. All else was black as pitch. The darkness and quiet of the room were as disquieting as the mystery of her mangled body.

124

It was then she realized that someone else was in the room.

"Who's there?" she asked urgently, fear creeping into her voice. A chair creaked—someone or something moved in the shadows of the poorly lit room. Haley's heart was pounding. Out on the plains, beyond the arm of safety, anyone could have found her. She tried to rise, to better see, but a flash of blinding pain joined forces with the heavy quilt, driving her back down onto the pillow. Pain coursed throughout every part of her body, sending wave after wave of nausea through her. Helpless. She was totally helpless; whatever happened now, she could neither prevent nor resist it.

A soft scent of incense crept around her head, easing and erasing her fears—calm and tranquillity replacing terror, the nausea subsiding to a dull ache. The fragrance seemed familiar; images of men and women in white robes flashed through her mind. Haley smiled, letting it happen. After another minute, the light from the crusty lantern dimmed further, and peaceful slumber overtook all thought and feeling.

David looked down at the letter. Haley's unfinished missive radiated such love and joy that he could scarcely believe the events of the last week. Haley was missing, feared dead. Damor Saling had been no assistance at all in the affair, saying only that she had left abruptly with friends. Who those friends were and where they had gone, he couldn't say. The British Home Office, unwilling to offend a maharaja, declined to pursue the matter with Saling, stating that the turbulent affairs in India and this Gandhi the press was constantly going on about were more than enough trouble for the empire. They told him to contact the Americans in Calcutta at their embassy there. The results were nearly similar, except the Americans promised to keep an "ear to the ground"—whatever that meant—and ring him the instant they knew something.

Things were a mess. Hampton shuddered, sighed, and then neatly folded the letter and put it away in his breast pocket. David sensed he would be meeting Damor again; the feeling that accompanied that thought was chilling and dark. He looked around, seeing her in his mind's eye, trying to imagine Haley's presence lighting up the otherwise stale room with her charm and joy, bringing that feeling to everyone who met her that they were someone special. He had watched it happen, watched the effect Haley had on people, and missed her all the more as he remembered it.

"Is there anything I can do for you, sahib?" Zalub asked as he quietly entered the room, a pain in his chest at the sight of his melancholy employer. David didn't answer, didn't hear him. His blank expression spoke volumes, revealing the depth of his love and concern, as well as his shattered heart. Zalub moved forward, laying a gentle hand upon David's sagging shoulder. Hampton moved his head slightly back and gave a smile that tried to say "No need to worry; everything's all right."

"Is there anything I can do for you, sahib?" Zalub gently asked again.

"No. No thanks, old man."

"Are you going up in the plane again tomorrow?" Zalub hadn't given up hope. His employer had been flying over the plains for eight straight days. David waited a minute before speaking. "We've done all we can, I think." David paused, turned, then stood, saying directly to Zalub with the strength that made so many love him, "Let's go home." Zalub tried to smile back the assurance and fortitude both knew were false. "I will arrange passage on the train?" After a moment, David nodded his assent. Zalub disappeared, eager to perform duties that would occupy his mind and his time.

David walked to the balcony and rested his hands on the railing. "I won't give up, my love. I swear it."

The next day, David and his staff settled into their cabins, ignoring the dinginess and smell of urine that wafted through the cars, and awaited the departure of the Indian Railroad's noon train out of Allahabad. It was three o'clock and the train still showed no signs of leaving.

Exhausted from the stress of the previous week, David excused himself to go to the washroom. After a scrubbing wash that reddened his face and woke him up, he reached for the towel on the rack next to the water basin. As he lifted it from its perch, he noticed something falling from it, flitting to the floor. He reached down and retrieved a folded scrap of paper.

Dearest Brother,

A disciple succeeds in spite of obstacles and mourns not the fate of others, trusting that all are cared for, knowing that all appearances are illusory. Labors await thy steady hand. The hour is urgent! Remember well, that loss is illusion, in the great reality of eternity.

With love to sustain you,

Master J.

David stared at the rough, cream-colored paper seemingly forever, drinking in its wisdom and love. "*Sapentia . . . Toujours, Sapentia . . .*" he whispered to himself, his smile emerging with the gratitude that flowed unrestrained from his heart. He could feel release from his pain, which allowed him to become himself again. Shaking his head, he laughed at the idea of the man who had entered the washroom minutes before, as if he were looking at someone else and not himself. "How could I have been so blind, so stupid?"

Then the promise he had made the day before on the balcony flashed through his mind. What to do? What if *he* were her only chance at salvation? No one else cared about her disappearance. Hampton sat down on the steel tub, buried his head in his hands, and stayed there for several minutes, searching for an answer. His head snapped up abruptly. John. Her brother would help. With his aid, they would certainly be more successful.

Lord David Hampton walked from the WC upright and joyful, heading back to a staff still weighted down by loss, reflecting his own past feelings. He determined to change that before nightfall.

She was standing on a dock, watching him go. It seemed to Haley that an eternity of lifetimes had witnessed this scene played out, over and over again. Meeting, separation, then service. It could have been any century, any country, any world. . . .

"Almost gave up on you," a voice said, shaking the dream away from her. Haley heard it as though it were not close by, but a thousand miles away, floating to her ears as if carried on a breeze. It was a gentle voice, laced with humor and joy. She struggled back to consciousness, anxious to see the face that could speak such melodies.

His features startled her. What took shape was an old man—

an Indian Santa Claus—smiling intensely, bringing a banged and battered tin cup up to her face. Overwhelmed by the force of kindness that seemed to blaze from his eyes, Haley could not take her eyes off him.

"I am not God," he offered with a quick grin.

Haley stared at him, unable to understand. "What?"

"You said I was God," he replied. "Not so." He started to turn away, stopped himself, then turned back again, sincerity and earnestness in his countenance. "Now, now, wait a minute . . . we are all God, or at least a part of God."

Haley looked at him, her expression revealing how very lost she was. He looked as old as India itself, maybe older. He was sprightly, moving as though not even thirty, but his face labeled him ninety or a hundred. But, that couldn't be. His skin was rich and unblemished, as though he hadn't a care in the world. Haley looked deeper, noticing as well that, whoever he was, he was letting her inspect him—even inviting the examination. His eyes were youthful, like a child's, but there were deep lines—lines caused by some heavy sadness that lay behind his air of sympathy and radiance. The more Haley looked at him, the more he seemed to change: not in appearance, but in expression. Each moment . . . nobler . . . wiser . . . older.

He smiled. "Don't remember? I see." He looked at her. Through her. Then said, "Etheric web still loose. Tea the best remedy . . . for now." He lifted the cup again.

Haley caught a whiff of what promised to be a wonderful drink, her mouth and stomach instantly responding, eager to down whatever was in the cup. The effort of lifting her arm to take a sip shot arrows through her; the pain was so intense that a tear formed and slowly moved down her cheek.

"Let me, little hope." He lifted the cup to her lips. She quaffed the draft in seconds. Haley released a sigh that Nature herself could not have reproduced with such an air of satisfaction and content.

"More?" he asked. Haley nodded. Unable to think clearly, spellbound by his fantastic radiance and simple speech, Haley just stared and found she did not care that she was staring. Although Haley's curiosity was strong—a thousand questions: what, who, where?—something deep inside implored her to silence. It seemed that to speak in such a stillness of purity, would be . . . irreverent.

After the second cupful, the old man moved away into the darkness. She found she could not follow him with her eyes; her neck and body were too stiff to function. Moments later, she could feel the effects of the tea course through her body. Haley stiffened, remembering Damor.

"You are among friends here," the queer hermit offered through the darkness. "There is no danger, only love and safety."

Haley turned weakly to the sound of his voice. "How did you know?"

"Tut, tut. It is better to rest now."

Haley relaxed back into the pillow. A moment later her mouth pursed, eyes narrowing. "Why did you call me 'little hope'?" Haley's mind went back to her father, her love for him greater than she had ever felt. If she could be back in Boston, never to see this cursed country again . . .

"Of all things, only the heart is measured. And those who have hearts are always the hope of mankind."

Haley looked out again, trying to find the voice. A yawn emerged, taking her unawares. She could feel her eyes growing heavy. Another yawn. Oblivion.

All was light. The Earth was fantastic to look at! It occurred to Haley that she must be miles above the planet, someplace in space. And she didn't feel alarmed in the least, as though here was exactly where she should be. Everything glowed. There was a bluish radiance that reached from the surface of the planet to someplace very high: the atmosphere! Haley remembered the science fiction writers and scientists—Jules Verne, Goddard—who said that we would one day travel in space. Thousands of others mocked these visionaries as lunatics.

Here, miles above the world, stillness permeated everything. It was a tranquillity that surpassed all previous experience. She felt that she was bound to everything through some strange, mystical connection.

Haley laughed. "I am in space." The joy and amazement of the moment were indescribable, the sensation of freedom grander than anything she had ever known. The stars were more brilliant than on any summer night in any land where she had traveled. What clarity, what . . . *beauty!* Haley reached out toward a particularly bright star, stopped herself, then laughed again. Giddiness and joy, two wonderful feelings that constantly rushed through her, were refreshing.

Haley tensed. How is this possible?

"This must be a dream."

Then she remembered lying on that horrible cot. Haley realized she was in two places at once: lying asleep in some hermit's abode and at the same time floating in space, miles and miles above the Earth. Amazing . . . and yet . . . it felt entirely . . . natural . . . common . . . right.

Something. A flicker . . . a flash . . . somewhere below. The thought of it sent her toward the planet at a blinding speed, the rush through space thrilling and terrifying; moments later, she found herself hovering over Europe and the Mediterranean. The beauty of it took her breath away. Then the physical beauty began to fade, something else replacing it. Shimmering over the land was a grayish-looking film, horrible . . . ugly . . . and full of the darkest pain and suffering—like smoke covering a valley, destroying the beauty like a festering wound. At points beneath the haze, blazes of shining, wonderful rainbows of exquisite beauty shot out into the sky. Arcing and joining with other rainbows, they created beautiful forms that rained blessings back down into the haze, burning it away. Yet as quickly as it was destroyed, the dark ugliness would rush back in, vanquishing the light as if its beauty had never existed. And on it went, until it occurred to Haley that she was witnessing a battle.

Then Haley felt it. She could feel an intelligence, an order to the process, something behind all the activity. As she watched, she realized that the covering of darkness was growing larger, spreading over the oceans. New spots of darkness emerged on their own and were connected to the original stain. She could feel the light of the planet dim, as if someone had changed a lightbulb to a lesser wattage.

And in watching the horrible thing grow more powerful, its darkness growing darker, Haley noticed some blazes shining out that did not dissipate, did not vaporize. One here, another there. Some of the lights flared out, leaving a hole in the dark web that allowed the blessing of the sun to shine through to the planet beneath. Others flickered and were swept away.

What happened next was horrible. Everything she was witnessing was accompanied by a vague sound. Faint. Distant. Powerful. It dawned on her that she was listening to the muffled roar of millions of souls, trapped—the sound of death in their voices, demanding something, begging for some one thing she could not quite make out. She began to weep from the agony of that roar. And the more she cried, the louder the roar became, filling and terrifying. . . .

"Ahh!" Haley realized that she was sitting up in bed, her breath coming in heaves, her own scream echoing in her ears.

Quiet. Alone in the darkness. Her breath rasping, sweat dripping down her face.

"You're trembling," a concerned voice observed from behind her. Haley turned around quickly, startled by its nearness. Pain shot through every part of her body. She relaxed and smiled a nervous smile. "Just a bad dream." Haley looked away, wiping her face with her quivering hands.

The old man moved in front of her, then sat on the edge of her bed. Tenderness and concern radiated so abundantly from him that Haley smiled again—this time with warmth—instantly forgetting the terror of the dream. Catching herself, she looked down at the quilt, embarrassed for having stared again. He extended his hand, taking hers gently. "No it wasn't," he stated quietly.

Haley looked at him, unsure. Finally it dawned on her what he was talking about. "I get all kinds of dreams, have ever since I can remember." He nodded with an understanding smile, but with eyes that revealed a keen perception behind Haley's facade of courage.

"Dreams," he said, looking past her, "are many things to many people." He turned his gaze upon her. "It is a reality closer to the truth than many scarce admit."

Haley smiled at the words. "You talk like Father."

"Your father is a wise man."

The tone of the statement unsettled Haley, because it was spoken as if the hermit knew him. Haley pushed away the questions that began to rise to the surface of her mind, finding them equally unsettling. Whoever he was, he disappeared again into the poorly lit room, humming some pleasant song.

Haley tried to locate him in the darkness, but soon gave up. Once she was sure he was off to the left, but then the whistling would come from somewhere over to the right, or ahead of her. "Where am I?"

No answer.

"Where is this place?"

Silence.

"I need to go . . . soon. There are people . . . people I need to see right away."

All she could hear was him whistling off in the darkness, clanking around and making noise. Haley threw back the quilt and eased her legs out onto the cool surface of the hardened earthen floor.

Looking down at her once-beautiful body, Haley froze in horror. Every visible part of her was scratched, cut, or blistered in some way. She thought of David. He wouldn't—couldn't—love her or anyone . . . anyone who looked like this. The thought of seeing her face terrified her. She could feel with her hands that it was—

"Love is based upon spirit, not form."

Haley jumped, as she had not heard him come near. He was standing next to her. Haley glared at him.

"I'm not really up to all this," she blurted out, "and you're scaring me!" She began to cry, so many things coming to the surface again: things she still did not want to face, things that didn't make sense, things that were beyond any understanding.

"My intention was not to alarm you," he said tenderly. He moved a small table in front of her and began to place dishes upon it. "We can talk over supper."

Weakened emotionally and unable to clear her mind, Haley pulled herself together, nodding in submission. In the middle of the table the hermit placed a bowl of wild rice and curry and a loaf of cracked-wheat bread, and he filled both their cups with tea. Haley started to move toward the food, when she noticed that he was standing, eyes closed, his hands extended in blessing.

She could feel it, really feel it. The room became electrified, filling her with joy. Finally, the old man opened his eyes and sat down, nodding his approval for her to eat. To Haley, it seemed as if no food anywhere had ever tasted better.

"Eat slowly," he cautioned, "you've not had solid food for three weeks."

Her fork froze in midair. How did he know when she had eaten last, when she did not? She absently took the food in her mouth, noticing the rough texture of the cutlery. "Have I been here that long?"

"It has been over sixty years since a woman has set foot in these most humble quarters." Her host had not even glanced at her, ignoring her question. "Of course," he continued with un-abated charm, "you are most welcome."

Haley felt ashamed at her lack of manners. "Thank you . . . for everything."

"Tut, tut."

Whatever his kindness, whatever he had done for her, recent events had taught Haley that what usually appeared quite normal and safe was not. Haley glanced down at the teacup and the grounds visible on the bottom, the memory of Saling's palace still very fresh.

Haley took a sip of tea, let it go down, and then crossed her arms. She waited a full minute to decide how she would deli-cately phrase what she had to say. After all, the man had looked out for her and cared for her well-being. "Who are you?" she blurted out finally.

"I am known as J," he offered without further explanation.

"Jay?"

"Yes . . . to some." His smile disarmed Haley, leaving her satisfied. Now, at least, she knew what to call him. Why was this Jay being so mysterious? What did he have to hide? He seemed more than intelligent, and how about that gift or power of his? Haley glanced quickly at J's face: definitely Indian, but with very European features. And his accent: Indian, to be sure, but there was something else . . .

"Cambridge," J said between bites. "After that, I spent many years in England and France during the war."

Haley nodded. That would explain his perfect English. "You fought the Germans?"

J stopped eating. He was looking at something far away, then something sad flashed across his face; after a few moments, he returned to his food. Seconds ticked by in the silence, becoming one long, interminable minute. Finally, he looked up at Haley, searching her face. Whatever it was he was looking for, he must have found it. "Napoleon."

Haley coughed, spilling tea on herself. Her mind moved quickly—J would have to be over 150 years old if his story were true—she knew her history. Napoleon had ruled over a conquered Europe in the early nineteenth century.

Though there were accounts of people in the Netherlands who lived as long as 120 to 130 years, science never verified those claims. Then there were stories of men in Nepal living for centuries, but no one had ever met anyone who was that old, and these tales were considered fantasy by even the most ardent believers in miracles. At least that was what she had learned in her perusal of the encyclopedia in her father's library.

Clearing her throat, Haley tried to be as casual as possible. "You look grand for a man of one hundred and fifty years." J smiled, but didn't reply.

She couldn't let go. "Did you know Napoleon, or have the chance to meet him?"

J stopped eating and looked her directly in the eye. Setting her spoon down, Haley decided to wait for some kind of explanation. A thought flashed through her mind that her tone and question were an insult in a land where insults were taken very seriously. Coupled with the thought was a rising feeling of shame, coloring her face red. "I'm sorry to intrude."

Reaching for bread, J glanced at her over his teacup. "How is your soup?"

For some reason she could not explain to herself, she found her curiosity insatiable—in spite of the better angels of her nature and their now insistent warning to knock it off. "Forgive me. I must know. You are telling me that you fought against Napoleon?" Haley waited expectantly for an answer, any answer. None came. Shaking her head, she resumed her repast, more annoyed at her behavior then J's unwillingness to indulge her prying. The idea occurred to her that an apology of sorts might be in order. She found she didn't have the courage to offer another one.

"In the West," J said slowly, studying her face, "lifetimes are short affairs. One may live to seventy or ninety years. In my country, many live double or triple that. If the work requires a long life, then the body is sustained in such a way as to remain fit for that work."

Putting down her fork laden with rice, Haley gaped at him. "Food? Food is the answer?"

J smiled at the simplicity of the question. "Food is the smallest part of the formula. The key to longevity, child, is in the purity of one's heart."

Though his countenance was one that made her feel he was a very honest and kind man, this type of information unsettled her. Might be the old boy had lost his mind. It would be wise not to tread in areas that could upset things. Haley dropped the subject, feeling very uneasy.

Her thoughts turned to David. She could hardly wait to see him, hold him close, and get married to him; visions of a life with David filled her head as they ate in silence. Children, helping out with the staff, taking him home to meet her family in Boston. Like a movie, her fondest wishes and dreams of romance began to play through her mind. Haley realized that her host was looking at her, his expression a mixture of concern and sadness. She asked the question with a look. "What's the matter?"

J didn't answer her unspoken question right away. Haley sensed there was something tremendously important in both the feeling she got from his gaze and the intense quiet that enveloped the room. After another minute, J unfolded his arms. "We took you at your word."

Now Haley could definitely feel something in the air—sense it, as if it were tangible. "I don't understand."

J's countenance could not have been more kind, or more accommodating, as if each word were a precious thing, thought out and treasured, and yet entirely simple and whole. "The oath."

Instantly, with the uttering of those two words, the energy in the room changed. She could feel a presence, otherworldly and ominous, yet full of love and joy. The tension in her chest was such that it was a struggle to get breath in and out of her lungs.

"The oath?" she responded meekly, feeling the gravity of his question as though it were a heavy book too difficult to manage.

"Yes."

There was a long silence, coupled with a power she couldn't understand. Haley cleared her throat again. Vague images of a beautiful sunrise, deeply buried in her mind like a mirage, lost from a memory that was at one time a vivid and important dream. As she pondered his words, she remembered enough to see that apparently she had forgotten something very important.

She knew at once that this oath, or whatever it was, was the reason she was alive. It was why she was here with this J person.

Haley looked at her host, searching for any clue that would help her make sense of things. This was no ordinary hermit. She had known her share of wonderful times and many magnetic people. But this one ... this one had more than personality. He had a shine to him. A shine that almost made him seem ... holy.

"I am a Sufi ascetic," J offered, reading her thoughts again.

Taken back by his unbelievable ability to read her mind, Haley nodded, not wishing to think. It was impossible. Thoughts came of their own accord and she gave them attention. Controlling her mind? An absurd proposition. She noticed the quiet peasant smiling at her discomfiture. She gave up trying.

She had heard about the Sufis. They were a highly religious order, found in every country in the East. No one had ever traced their beginnings, except for their emergence in Islam around the eighth century; it was said that the Sufis were the mystical and esoteric branch of that faith. More fascinating than that, though, were the fantastic stories of superhuman feats: rope climbing, the sleeping death, medical cures with the wave of a hand, and walking through walls. If even a tenth of the stories she had heard were true, J was someone very special indeed.

"Did you not say," J pronounced in even tones, interrupting her thoughts, "that you would dedicate your life in service to mankind?"

All at once, like a key to a puzzle, Haley remembered. Like a movie running too fast, everything rapid and hurried, she recalled in detail the vision of being with her grandfather on the bridge: the horror of it all ... as well as the beauty of a great, unseen absolution. Then she recalled her death and being lifted into a place of supreme peace. The fork that slipped from her fingers made little sound against the soft wooden table.

Haley looked at J, close to tears. "Am I dead?" Instantly, she knew the answer before he spoke it. Yet, she had died. From some place above, she could definitely recall watching hawks feeding on her rotting corpse. The memory sent shivers through her like ice. She looked up at her host, afraid and confused.

J smiled benevolently, shaking his head no to her question. Haley let out a sigh of relief.

Looking down at her hands, she stared at the cuts and bruises still healing from the ordeal. Haley remembered him, remembered him from the gulch in the plains—remembered being carried to some place of cool waters, deep, through an opening in the ground.

"Thank you for saving my life. I am in your—"

J took her hand, looking her squarely in the eyes. "There is no need to thank me. You yourself are the reason for your survival." He spoke words of such mystery that she did not understand their meaning. Surely, he had rescued her and carried her from that horrible ravine. Looking down again at her disfigured body, she almost wished she had died. A quick glance across the table verified his disapproval of her destructive feelings.

"Through your own heart have you found salvation," he continued evenly. "Truly it is said that by our own hands do we create our lives, our opportunities, and," he continued gently, "our suffering."

As he uttered the last few words, she could feel a warm peace enter into her heart: that same feeling of absolution that she remembered experiencing in the dream. All her former fears, sorrow, and remorse began to melt as though they were ice under a warm sun.

J squeezed her hand reassuringly. "Remember always that the body will age, no matter what the cause. It is what lies behind the form that matters." Haley nodded in acceptance.

"You are here because you found that which is the highest within you," he continued solemnly, as if speaking to someplace within her. "Whenever a soul discovers the jewel within the center, it steps upon the way."

Haley was transfixed. Each utterance was music, sweet and full, to her ears. She could feel something inside her warm with each word he said. "Tell me more . . . please, about this way."

He folded his hands in front of him; for a moment, Haley thought she smelled freesias and lilacs. "The path is one of discovering that which is the highest and noblest within us and living it to the best of our abilities each moment of our lives. The highest that we call forth is who we really are."

The words, though beautiful, didn't make any sense to her. "But we are who we are," Haley replied. "I am here, at this table. This is what I am."

J smiled. "Really? This is what you are? A woman in love with her pleasures? With a broken body, completely vulnerable to the elements of nature? Completely identified with a collection of bone and skin? Is it really to be believed that this is all you are?" Though stated without condemnation, his rebuke was there nonetheless.

Haley lowered her head. Unable to understand, there was little else she could do. She sensed he was a man who possessed knowledge—real knowledge—of the true state of affairs. In his presence, she all of a sudden felt small and stupid.

"Close your eyes," he said quietly, "and fear not."

Like an explosion, the blackness that comes from shutting one's eyes disappeared. She found herself floating in space next to her host, surrounded by fantastic and beautiful forms and sounds, as if she were standing in the center of heaven itself. In every direction she saw extraordinary buildings that glowed with the combined radiance of their inhabitants; she sensed, more than saw, those inside. She found that when she looked at one of the structures, she could by some strange trick of magic see inside it and hear what was going on. Some housed orchestras that were playing the most beautiful music. Some held simple gatherings of friends, talking and sharing the love that is friendship. Others contained no occupants, merely waiting to be used for some purpose not yet perceived.

Everywhere were harmony and the building of radiant forms which seemed to grow more beautiful as each moment sped by. Some appeared quite literally out of nothing—exploding into glorious shape and color, only to dissipate as quickly as they appeared. She wondered what it was she was seeing, when she found the answer to her question in her mind before she could speak it; these rapidly created and interesting forms were the myriad thoughts of humanity.

Haley turned toward J. "This is beautiful. What is this place?"

"It is where the dreams of humanity find their fulfillment. Nothing impossible here. Only the will to be and do and so it is."

As Haley watched and admired each fantastic thing, she found that her own light was increasing. She turned to J, puzzled.

"Love and appreciation of beauty, builds always the heart. As the heart grows, so do we in spiritual stature."

In front of Haley appeared the most beautiful woman she had ever—no—there was no human who could ever be this wonderful, this pure and vibrant. This was perfection beyond even the most extreme possible imagining. Beautiful streams of love were pouring from all around this grand being as if she were hiding the sun itself inside her heart, its light bursting through every place possible, radiating and illuminating the world with such brilliant hues of gold, blue, and pink as to be beyond imagination. The splendor of this angelic being's beauty was more than Haley could bear, as she found that she could not look directly at it; its beauty was too staggering for her eyes. A ray from this wondrous woman's heart seemed to illumine some small, deformed shape.

"You are seeing your Soul as it really is," J commented in her mind. "Know that the Self is the *real* that stands behind all illusion."

Haley swooned. The hideous shape was her! A perfect replica of her body, kept alive by a power that poured forth from the angel—Haley realized that the energy animating her body was mercy, divine and beautiful: a quality of love that held her, sustained her, and allowed her to exist. Compared with the wonderful being shining light upon her, she was an ugly, distorted toad. Each beam of radiance from the Godlike angel was linked to a small, flickering spark in Haley's back; that point seemed almost to have no radiance at all. It was a deep blue, with a wobbly flame that rose and fell in rhythm to an outpouring of love that constantly flowed from the angel.

Around the image of Haley, there was a dull, brassy glow—filled with objects and lumps. As Haley looked more closely, she could see that each object was some vanity, jealousy, fear, hate, lust, or like distortion—feelings she had created and identified with. Behind these thousands of floating, orbiting masses was a misty, chaotic film of boiling poison, flashing hideous colors. A thought entered Haley's mind: each filmy mass was created by some action of hers in which she had defied her conscience, disobeying its kind and all-seeing advice. Haley could see that every time she had acted for herself and in her own self-interest, she had darkened her heart and increased her own ugliness, shutting out the healing and loving rays from this magnificent being. Haley was seeing herself as she really was. In that moment, all vanity and ego shattered in her. No matter what flattery she had believed in, or how wonderful she had imagined she was, she realized that in truth, she had no real beauty, no real light. The despair that filled her was unlike anything she had ever known. Haley wanted, more than anything, not to look at herself. The only feeling that remained inside her was a yearning simply to die and exist no more.

Haley realized that the Great Angel was looking at her, a deep love pouring from her eyes. "I shan't ever abandon you," it declared from inside Haley's ears. Haley couldn't move or speak for what seemed an eternity of humiliation and sorrow; she realized that this Great Angel had always been there, guiding and loving her.

It whispered again in her ears. "Raise up thy visage and see thy own Self."

Weeping inside, where no tears could flow, she found she was able to look upon this Grand Angel; having done so, she found she couldn't take her eyes off this beautiful being. It occurred to her that there was a familiarity that she could not shake, as though she had known this creation of wonder and grace all her life.

The angel glimmered back in recognition. "I am your heart, your conscience." And after these momentous words had been uttered, in front of Haley appeared one image after another. Each scene was a moment in her life when she had responded nobly to some impulse, some portion of goodness within herself. She could see how the beautiful and radiant angel had, in fact, over-shadowed her at each of those moments by sustaining her with love and courage, and by helping her with thoughts of sacrifice and kindness.

Haley realized that never for a moment had she been alone.

"See now, thy heart," the angel's voice whispered from somewhere inside her head.

Haley saw a single point of radiance. Glowing, shimmering with small fountains of glorious colors, it stemmed from the deep blue point that was behind her shoulders. Haley's spirits began to rise. This fountain glowed with a purity unsullied by the cumulative weight of her own past selfish actions. As she looked more closely, she could see that this radiance was built by every single thought, feeling, and act that was not selfish. Each time she had given of herself freely and wholly, this radiance had grown larger—each time she thought of herself alone, it had shrunk.

Yet there was hope. Each wonderful ray from the beautiful angel encouraged this fountain; she could see its influence in her daily life, through feelings, suggestions, and conscience. Behind all this was the overpowering awareness that the angel was totally aware of all Haley's feelings, thoughts, trials, sufferings, hopes, and dreams. It was entirely concerned with Haley's welfare. Like a patient and loving mother, it loved, aided, and served its errant child. Haley began to weep with gratitude: she had always been loved.

Always.

"In the midst of sin, redemption," another voice commented. Turning, she saw J standing next to her.

Haley began to see the truth of it. Her whole life, lived for herself; it was a moment of awareness. She could remember her dream with her grandfather; more than that, she finally realized who J was.

"Forgive me."

When Haley awoke, she found she could not speak for several minutes. What she had experienced was so profound that her mind kept repeating the event to her, over and over again. Each time she reviewed what must have been a bizarre dream, the dream revealed more of itself to her, how the angel had interceded during some crisis or moment of indecision. Sitting there, Haley saw how much of her life had been looked after by this grand being.

In her loneliest moments, there it was . . . loving her, understanding her, and guiding her toward goodness, truth, and beauty. For the first time in Haley's life, she understood that there were no accidents—coincidence was an illusion as well, leaving only an ordered universe where even the smallest child's cry, the deepest sorrow of a careworn mother, and the patient desire of a dog to see its master were seen, known, and responded to.

J had gone off somewhere, relieving Haley of the burden of society. With the dream came the realization of who this J was, and Haley felt as if she had come home, that she had finally caught up with some long-lost relative. Someone she had been unconsciously searching for her whole life, someone who had also waited for her. She wanted to hold and thank this great man, to thank him for his patience and love—thank him for being something she saw that she really didn't understand, but that when understood would be more wonderful than anything her imagination could create.

The next thought that entered her mind made her heart leap. This was someone who could help her unravel the dream. Certainly, one such as he would know about such mysteries. It stood to reason that if he meant to save her life and show her a reality long suspected, then he would—*must*—be able to rid her of her nightmares.

Haley attempted to stand for the first time. She rose carefully, using the table as a support, pain shooting up her back and legs; grimacing, she moved forward, finally letting herself stand free. Haley let go of the table, a smile appearing as she found she was standing on her own. In the same moment she realized she was falling. Something prevented that.

"There, there . . . that's enough for now, child." J, appearing out of nowhere, was standing next to her, taking her weight onto his shoulder and easing her back onto the bed. He checked her pulse and found it much too rapid. "Better to remain convalescent for a time. The heart is still repairing."

Haley looked up at her host with the eyes of a newborn child. "I wanted to talk to you. To see you." Haley felt as if her heart was going to burst with the knowledge she now possessed.

"I know." J looked at her with eyes deep with compassion; Haley had witnessed the miracle of the *Angel of the Presence*. Whatever she had been, now or in lifetimes past, she would never be the same again. He noted the purity around her eyes. Innocent. Washed clean. Eager, as a child's are eager.

Tucking the quilt in around her, he sat on the edge of the bed. Haley took his hand in hers, squeezing love and affection into it. After a long minute, she spoke. But as a child would speak . . . sincere, uncontaminated, honest. "I *do want* to serve." J watched the beautiful forms created by Haley's spoken words, arcing and glowing about her head.

"It is not an easy path that you choose," he returned solemnly.

Haley did not reply quickly; she could sense a definite gravity, and warning, in J's declaration. There was something else. She could feel that some great door was about to either open or close, with her hand on its unseen, mystical latch.

"I know nothing of my fate. I don't even know who I am

anymore." Haley stopped, the immense weight of her own words echoing inside her head, as though they had been spoken by someone else—someone with wisdom. She looked directly into J's eyes. "I only know," she said haltingly, "that my heart wills that I choose this path."

J said nothing in response to her heartfelt announcement. Words must become action, to be of any value. Still, this was a sign that she was *responding*, not *reacting*, to the forces at work in her life. He would do what he could to help her. He noticed that she was still waiting for his approbation and decided to give it by reaching down and hugging her. After a moment, he stood. "Try and get some sleep. You must heal correctly. If you require anything, I will be nearby." And with that, he vanished into the darkness.

Haley could feel the weight of slumber forcing her out and away from her body. The last thing she saw was J, beaming down his kindly smile as she closed her eyes.

The next week she began the arduous task of walking again. Though the pain was often excruciating, she found that her body eventually cooperated with her will, and soon she could move around without assistance. After two more weeks, it seemed as if the whole episode at the palace and in the desert had never really happened, as though it were some bad dream made into reality only when she observed the scars still scattered over her body.

J's home was more mysterious and wonderful than anyone could ever imagine. From outside, it appeared to be a small, thatched hut, barely large enough for one person to live in. It made Haley feel cramped just standing inside the door, which she had to stoop low to pass through. There was a cot made of reeds, a small wooden table, and a fire pit against the hill that the hut was fronting. Next to the fireplace was a tapestry mounted on a wooden frame. It was arrayed with beautiful men and women engaged in some ceremony that made her smile, giving her a feeling of unexplained joy.

J showed her how easily the frame moved away from a carved-out hole. Even then, it appeared to be a place to store pots and cutlery, as it was very small. Then J moved a small wall shelf that stood against the back of the hole. Twenty feet past that, and Haley found herself in a place of wonder and beauty.

"This is fantastic!" The ceilings, some forty feet high, were punctuated with stalagmites, painted in the deepest blues and yellows, making a grand panorama of sky and color. It took her breath away.

"A chela performed this wonderful service," J offered.

The main room he had led her into was filled with rugs, magnificent low tables, statues, carvings, and bookcases. Everything was beautifully lit, as though there were lights in the ceiling she could not see. Punctuating its immense walls were small closed doors, obviously leading into other rooms. J led Haley to a door near where she was standing. "This is where you may stay," he said, opening it. Inside were a bed, a desk, a large dresser, a single bookshelf, and a very large candelabra, already lit.

J pointed to the dresser. "You will find linen there and clothes that should be suitable."

Everything was beautiful—the paintings, bed covers, even the vanity accessories on the desk—as though decorated by a woman for a woman. Haley reached over and hugged her host; J blushed. "Thank you. Thank you so much for everything!"

"Consider this your home and live as you wish."

J moved toward the door. "Am I the only person here?" Haley asked. Without turning around, he answered a simple "no."

The door closed softly behind him as he left. There was a warm feeling to the whole place and especially to this room; Haley fell back onto the more-than-comfortable bed—happy not to have to sleep on the brittle cot in the hut.

After a quick minute, she rose and walked over to the dresser. Opening the top drawer, she found several cotton dresses of the latest fashion, shorts, and other apparel. In other drawers were more simple clothes more common to India: homespun, dakas, and the like. Haley turned sharply around and faced the door, a thought entering her mind. She shook her head; no, whatever this strange and wonderful man was, he was *not* like that.

The irony, the unique parallel of the events made her smile. She had been drugged and taken hostage in one man's palace, and healed, served, and helped in another's. Haley walked to a washbasin hidden in a corner and began to peel off her ragged and torn dress, then threw it forcefully into a wastebasket near the door.

Sitting under a great oak tree, Haley watched clouds form overhead through the leaves—beautiful cirrus clouds, moving this way and that, dancing high up in the sky. Though she did not hear him come, she knew he would be joining her shortly. She could see it now; J was tutoring her. Every day he would spend a few minutes talking with her about reality, leaving her to think about their discussion, disappearing for hours at a time. And each day she came to a deeper and deeper realization that the world held secrets more mysterious and more wonderful than she had ever contemplated.

With her rejuvenation, Haley realized what a dear man J was. Never impatient, always loving and untiring in his enterprise to see her get well, J could always be counted on for his endless joy. Learning under him, seeing his composure, endless knowledge, and untiring compassion, Haley began to yearn to become what her Teacher was—a realized King Arthur: kind, loving, stern, and courageous. Never once had J exhibited the traits of ego, vanity, or megalomania. He simply seemed beyond the failings of mankind.

How had he overcome these weaknesses? What was his secret? How had someone who had seemingly mastered life, mastered his character, come to live in some buried paradise in the middle of nowhere? Why not bring his secrets to a world that was in the midst of chaos?

It occurred to Haley that what she was living through and learning was to some purpose, but why her? Why did she end up in India, enslaved and then liberated by this strange, kind, and magical old man? If someone had told her six months before that she would be lost in the deep interior of India studying under an ascetic, she would have thought the person insane. But here she was, learning about the world, nature, and the mysterious and wonderful spirit behind creation. What Haley was learning was both frightening and beautiful.

"As with the world, there are always two sides to reality, to love . . . to beingness," J observed quietly behind her. Haley didn't let on that he had startled her; he would have made a great brave in one of the Indian nations back home. Regaining some composure, she turned to him. "Why?"

J smiled. "Good! Always to ask why!" Then he walked past her, intent on something. Presently, he stopped moving, his eyes closed in deep meditation of some kind.

Watching J, Haley sensed that she had done some good thing. What that thing was, she hadn't the foggiest idea. After a moment, J moved to the base of the oak and settled down; he made no sound, though every step she had taken had crunched loudly from the thousands of dried leaves that littered the ground.

Haley stood there, her mouth open in amazement. "How do you do that?"

"It is not important . . . nor should young students be so trapped by simple phenomena." Disappointment flickered in J's eyes. "If you focus upon the things of the world—*the things of illusion*—the things of spirit and truth you will miss always!"

Haley looked down at her hands; she had no idea what was happening to her. She had already learned that J did not want her to know too much, at least for now, about his little magic tricks. Inside someplace, it occurred to her that she would learn all this one day; in the meantime, she would have to be patient. "Why do I always feel dumb when I am around you?"

J glanced affectionately at his student, sending his love to her. "Child," he began as tenderly as a mother, "when we cannot understand a thing, our first reaction is to feel inferior; this is not the attitude of the wise chela." With that, he turned back around, facing the clearing in front of them.

"What is a chela?"

J turned and scrutinized her, his gaze penetrating and fiery, an air of expectancy about him as if he were listening to something . . . or someone. Haley wasn't sure, but she thought she saw him say "thank you" under his breath.

"You." With that, he chuckled to himself in good humor, his whimsical, infectious smile returning. Haley shook her head in confusion.

Turning slightly toward her, he said, "It is a Hindu term meaning *disciple*."

Hearing the words, she nodded, slowly thinking it through . . . smiled, and nodded again; she was happy at the thought of being a disciple. Exactly what a disciple did, she had no idea. And as she thought about it, she could feel a great peace surround her, filling her with an ease and joy that she knew could only come from this more-than-amazing man.

"What does a disciple do?" Haley thought of the men who had followed Jesus around, praising and suffering, attacked by the legions of Rome; saving souls. She remembered her father talking with some friends over dinner how the state of discipleship, whatever it was, needed to be defined by the teachers of Theosophy and other groups that were bringing the teaching to humanity. When pressed about the issue further, Franklin merely said, "*At the feet of the Master*. Good a place as any to begin."

"We have been trying to repair that error for some time," J said, interrupting her thoughts. "And to answer your question," he continued, changing the subject, "a disciple serves."

J didn't let her ask the question about to escape from her lips. "Discipleship is the spontaneous and continuous outpouring of love, not just for family, not just for husband and friends—but for all of creation. Once a person knows who he is, knows beyond any doubt, there are but two realities here in this world." Haley noticed a special glow about J as he outlined the reality of being a disciple; she had to blink several times to see him clearly.

"To be a chela, or disciple, means always to live from the heart," he said, thumping his chest. "It means to labor—not because it is the right thing to do but because the heart commands it so." He stopped for a moment, a deep joy in his voice. "Love. Love is ever the foundation of service and in being one's Self."

Haley could feel it, feel the fantastic outpouring of beauty behind his words, warming her. "So I learn from you?"

"No!" J commanded . . . paused, "Yes. No." Taking a deep

breath, he gently took Haley's hand in his own; he appeared to her to be on the verge of tears. They were tears of joy. "Child, learn from *your heart*. It is the only true guide for mankind. A man may speak words, but if the heart echoes not back its confirmation, those words are *false*." J relaxed a little and sniffled as though he himself found the wisdom absolutely wonderful beyond his great understanding. Then it hit her. Joy, love, and wisdom had no limits in terms of understanding. J saw new things because there were always new comprehensions of life. She could discover for herself the same epiphany.

Though lost in her own bliss, she heard him say, "It is true you must learn about life and about the mystery of the world. In these things, I will teach you, of course, the little that I know." J stopped and lifted Haley's chin until her gaze was level with his own. "But knowledge without true love is the cornerstone of insanity, of evil, and begets tyrants." His words brought her back; she blinked and tried to pay attention to what he was saying.

J stood and walked toward the middle of the clearing. "Look at this world! Monsters now incarnated, enslaving truth. Corrupt leaders, consumed with dark passions and even darker ambitions. This is what happens when the mind develops without love!"

Her thoughts turned to David, a smile forming on her lips. His was a different love, a love that filled her in a different way.

"It is a matter of degrees," J offered, reading her unspoken thoughts.

"What?"

"Love for the dog is not love for the husband—and this is precisely the problem." A ray of sunlight had somehow slashed its way through the leaves and lit up the area where J was standing. "Love, like all things, is an energy. And being an energy, it does not know 'I must feel this or be that,' it simply is expressed and is reflected according to the beingness of the person through which it passes." J stopped, a deeper smile appearing on his upturned face, the light of the sun now reflecting off his soft features. "Love is love, pure in and of itself, no matter how it finds a way to shine."

Haley thought for a moment. "If love is pure, why does it seem so horrible at times?"

"You are confusing the instrument with the energy."

"I don't understand."

J nodded in sympathy. "It would appear that love is horrid, from time to time, but let us look clearly at the situation. Each person has a body, a mind, and emotions, yes?" Haley nodded in the affirmative, remembering her experience out of her body.

"We know that life wants us to grow through life's lessons, become good souls, and be the highest that we can realize. We know that, as souls, we have bodies that are crude and undeveloped." Haley's expression told J that he was not being understood.

"We are born into this world for what purpose?"

Haley thought for a moment. "It is as you say, 'to grow . . . and become good souls.' "

"This is so, but becoming a good soul is an effect of something," he commended. "Our body is not willing to obey the master within, the real person; our mind wanders endlessly from one thought to another, quite beyond control. The emotions"— J's face turned sour—"the emotions . . . hate, slander . . . are jealous, envious, mean, and vengeful." The air distinctly turned a few degrees cooler, Haley noticed. When the discussion centered upon truth and the real, the very forest surrounding them came alive and buzzed with energy. When the discussion turned to mankind, the energy shifted lower. Haley made a mental note to ask J about this.

"When love comes into the emotions of a woman who hates, who is selfish, who thinks only of her needs, her wants, her desires, this energy turns dark. If the woman allows love to be perverted into the darker feelings, it destroys her, burns her, and short-circuits her ability to express this energy in its higher forms. Finally, if allowed to continue in this direction without abatement, it will consume her soul and she will become a slave to her animal urges and passions."

As he was speaking, Ann came to Haley's mind. She hoped that this was not her friend's case, as she loved Ann dearly.

"Your friend will have many opportunities to break her slavery," J offered. "Life brings circumstances that allow for these chains to be broken." Haley looked at him, her concern and worry starting to fade.

"Whenever we are enslaved to the material world, no matter it be to possessions, money, dark emotions, or wrong thinking, the One Life creates circumstances that come to break the slavery."

Haley thought for a moment. "How does one become love?"

J blinked in amazement, his mouth open in joy. She had asked the question correctly, the first student to do so since the Russian woman half a century before. His eyes became moist.

Haley found herself drawn to her teacher, that mystical bond again pulling at her heart. She untied a kerchief from her neck and handed it to him.

"It may take a lifetime or moments," J said finally. "It is the only thing worth teaching or learning."

The two looked intently at each other, as though a great moment were passing, then J wiped his eyes and continued hoarsely, "The great mystery that we must all one day learn is that love is a great force"—he handed the kerchief back to Haley with a nod of thanks—"a force that runs through and through all things: from binding atoms together and holding forms in manifestation to linking a mother's heart to her son and a man's courage to his country."

J looked at his charge. She was thinking about love on entirely new levels. He smiled. "The wise chela flows with this force, becomes it, and in so doing, becomes the Self."

Haley had become lost in the implications of what her Teacher said to her. Love? More than an emotion? An energy that permeates all creation? Sustaining life ... life itself? "How?"

"Good question." J sat down, motioning for Haley to do the same. "That 'is the trick,' as they say." He stopped speaking and appeared to look beyond the sky and sun. "The first step is to love yourself."

"Love myself?"

"Yes."

Well, that was that. She was completely with him, until he threw that in. Haley sighed and shook her head. "I ... this doesn't ..." Her voice trailed off in confusion.

"If our actions are self-destructive, we do not think much of who we are. You know better than anyone the truth behind the being called man. So many people destroy what little joy that comes into their lives, thinking themselves unworthy. This lie is repeated, not by conscious words, but by unconscious actions—over and over again—until all love is erased and replaced by pain and suffering. Then, to compound a fate they have created for themselves, they say, 'See! I told you! I am no good. I get suffering because I am a sinner and will burn forever and ever.' "

J watched Haley closely. She was listening to every word, taking it all in. "There is only one way to break this self-image."

"Yes?"

"To believe, act, and exist as though you were what you really are." Silence followed for a minute. He seemed to know the answer before she spoke it, as he started to reveal his glee.

As she racked her brain, one thought kept coming to the surface, over and over again. Finally, Haley looked directly into his eyes. "God?"

"The very first words I spoke to you." J smiled in excitement; twice in one day she had hit the right door—it was as *his* Master had said. Haley was "special." J could see how she was. Usually, the little ones needed years to discover what was really a basic truth. *Usually* . . . they had to unlearn their garbage and learn to free their heart in order to discover these foundational realities.

Smiling with relief, Haley looked down and began to play with a blade of grass; then her face took on a look of concern. "Isn't that blasphemy?"

"Who would you be blaspheming?"

She thought for a moment, then said, "Why . . . um . . . the church?"

"Which church?"

"God's church."

J laughed. "You are God's church, but I know what you mean. The church is an institution put upon the Earth by men to teach humanity the science of the soul. In this, it has failed somewhat, but not completely. No, dear child, God is within, Christ—the great teacher of love—is within. It matters not what language this One God, this Self is called. This is so because the One God is a God of love. On this, all religions, all universes, all sages, and all true servants of humanity agree."

Haley was thinking deeply, when J rose. "Stand up," he commanded.

She stood, but was puzzled by the force of his command. Though not tyrannical, it struck something deep inside her. J was radiant, and something flowing through him filled Haley with a joy and sense of oneness she had never before experienced.

"Repeat after me: *'I am the Soul.'* "

As Haley started to say the words, a tremendous force filled her from someplace she could not locate. Then it hit her: it was coming from within her Self.

J's deep baritone voiced boomed. *"I am the light within."*

Haley intoned the second verse. A wave of blinding joy raged through her mind, her feelings, coursing through every fiber of her being, bringing a great smile to her face. J was beaming.

"I am Love." His voice carried so much power that the trees around them swayed as a wind suddenly came up, electrifying the hair on her arms. Haley's eyes opened wide. Around J was a bluish-rose radiance that extended for hundreds of yards, and passed through her.

Haley started to speak, "I . . . I . . . am lo—" and fell to the ground, crying. J moved toward her and swept her up into his arms, cradling her.

"That is enough for today. Let us rest in the shade for a time."

Franklin woke with a start. It was very quiet in his bedroom, the clock on the mantel chiming just two in the morning. Sarah, beautiful Sarah, lay sleeping silently next to him—thank God. The suffering she had gone through in recent weeks had been unbearable, for him as well as for her. Watching Sarah shrink into deep depression had been a dual hell for Franklin; he had watched his father suffer the same way. In his prayers, he begged God not to inflict this horror upon him again. Once in one lifetime was enough.

Sitting up, he pulled a robe from the chair next to the nightstand. Standing, he put the robe on, then walked over to the window. He used to watch Haley play with John from this window. How they laughed and chased each other, playing the games that children play. To have them both back home, safe, would be worth any price that could be paid.

Franklin's eyes turned down. After long months of worry about his children on their dangerous voyage—which he hadn't approved of—his worst fears became reality when John's telegram came informing him that Haley was missing. The cables that followed offered little hope. She was not seen anywhere. Search parties, scouts in airplanes, and even the local government could not find her. John's last telegram was cryptic.

From: Allahabad Station, Allahabad, India
John Olsten

To: Western Union, Boston, USA
Franklin Olsten

Dad. Not giving up. Stop. Local man says he will help, has information. Stop. Getting visa to Nepal. Stop. Contact you Annapurna in two months. Stop. Love, John

Sarah cried for three straight days. Finally, the doctor had to give her morphine so she could sleep. Franklin, having overcome one tragedy with his father, was determined to be strong for his wife. Only when she was asleep and the house was quiet did he allow himself the luxury of sadness and grief.

Then Franklin smiled. In the dream that woke him up, he

talked a long time with his much-loved daughter. She assured him that she was okay. She looked wonderful and radiant, bringing him flowers on the porch. They walked along the cherry tree—lined avenue toward the park. Funny, he never thought to ask Haley what was happening, he was so overjoyed to be with her and hold her hand. Finally, when they reached the bridge, she went off to the park on the other side, blowing kisses back to him as she walked away.

Franklin knew without a doubt that everything would turn out all right. He looked back at Sarah, sleeping deeply, and wondered if she, too, were dreaming of their daughter.

He prayed that she was.

CHAPTER 9

Through the Valley of the Shadow

Nay! What matters knowledge,
without application?
Divine is all that comes,
each moment brings out what we must be.

"What does it mean?" Haley yelled across the pool to J. He had taken her to a place where a stream formed a pool of clear, cool water. Shielded by trees on all sides, the pool was completely hidden. J was floating in the water on his back, his eyes closed— no doubt conjuring with the cosmos in his mind, Haley speculated. Haley started to speak again but thought better of it, not wanting to disturb him. He was the picture of peace and contentment and had begun to blend into the scenery as if he had always been here. Haley wanted that peace, desperately.

Haley *needed* that peace. She walked to a break in the trees that allowed her to look out upon the plains; the view was impressive, as she could see for miles. Although the air was stifling, there was an aura of peace that seemed to flood the region, pushing away India's harsher realities. Whatever it was, it seemed disinclined to flood her.

J was floating in a slow-moving circle, the slight and invisible eddies of the pool moving him this way and that. "The solution to your problem," J said evenly, eyes still closed, "is to decide who you are."

Haley turned back from the trees and sat down near the water, staring incredulously across it. "I don't understand *any* of this," she whimpered to herself. After all this time, she was no closer to understanding the mysteries presented to her by her Teacher than she had been when she started. She had learned a great deal about a great many things: what man's constitution was, cause and effect, and the character elements and virtues. Yet, even as she came to understand the forces at work within her and in the world, Haley found that the knowledge brought something else. With knowledge came responsibility.

"There must be some mistake," she announced, hoping to end the misery.

"Too quickly you Westerners want answers, no time given to work out the problem yourself. For the answer, you must look within."

Haley frowned. That old man and his "Look within, look within . . ." J hadn't or wouldn't let her go on with this issue; inside, she could sense the importance of unraveling this mystery. She had been struggling with this ache that she didn't understand for some time now. She asked the questions . . .

Who am I?

What am I doing?

Where am I going?

But each revelation of her nature brought only more questions. Finally it occurred to Haley that she had been dancing around the issue but not facing it. She laughed out loud.

J was already heading toward the shore. "Most good." He joined her, plopping himself down on the sand. "It is best to laugh when we begin to take ourselves too seriously."

"Your words have so many meanings to them, so many levels," Haley blurted out, tossing a small pebble into the water, "but I can't make heads or tails out of any of it."

There was a long silent stillness, punctuated by the occasional *skeeerak* of a bird in the trees. Haley turned her head to him and said flatly, "This is very hard."

"Of course it is. The greatest mystery is man—beyond any reality we can confront." J patted Haley on the shoulder. "Greatness requires great efforts. No attainment is unearned. All that we possess—our character, skills, knowledge, and beingness—comes from hard work upon ourselves."

"I've seen people sit down at a piano and play wonderfully in a very short time," Haley countered. "They do it so effortlessly, too."

"These are the fruits of previous labors, coming to the surface of their current lives. Which also explains the attraction to music or whatever the heart finds gladness in."

Haley looked down at the sand, her own heart heavy with a sadness she had never been able to understand—that damn question mark sitting in her stomach, not allowing her any peace. Everything he told her made sense, but nothing seemed to be the key she was looking for.

"Your whole life," J began in a gentle voice, his eyes focused upon something in the invisible distance, "you have believed yourself unworthy—and yet this lie is only an excuse to avoid what is inevitable."

Haley lifted her head up and turned toward him. Had he heard her? Known always about her pain? For here he was now, the doctor addressing the patient. She no longer heard the flies or the birds in the air. She watched his eyes, listened to his words.

"Dear, you see what must be, inside, here, in the heart. For lifetimes you have prepared for this, and all that is pain in your life is the rejection of a fate you yourself have created and labored toward."

"I—" Haley blurted out, unable to finish.

"Daughter, for you, there will be no family, no husband, no carefree life of idleness." J paused, then continued. "For you, there is only service to humanity. This is the source of your pain."

"How can this be? I've never, never thought about service or sacrifice. How could I be rejecting something that I haven't even dealt with consciously?"

"Did not your father talk of the Ageless Wisdom? Did he not say that the path was through giving of one's self?"

"Yes, but—"

"When he spoke of this, did you not think of something else, walk away, or change the topic of your discussion?"

"Yes, but—"

"In all these things, have you not looked at your life in those terms in which many young women certainly view a life? Marriage, love, pursuit of friendships, family, and a home with conveniences?" Haley started to speak again, but J waved her off. "For you, haven't these thoughts yielded barren fruit, creating instead anxiety and discomfort?"

For a long moment, Haley said nothing. J reached out a gentle hand, but she turned away from it, her mind in pieces.

J sighed, his compassion for her suffering reflected in his eyes and words. "The rejection of our heart is always the source of all misery. When humanity accepts its conscience and acts accordingly, suffering will cease. It will cease for you as well."

Haley staggered to her feet, tears already running down her cheeks. Every word spoken by her teacher hit with the force of a hammer. Every word of it was true. Finally, she had to confront what she had suppressed from the beginning, what she had always known, had always feared would come. Now, here in

India, she understood the purpose behind the events that brought her to this strange and wonderful man.

She understood why she had so easily fallen in love with David—*escape*.

Why she had allowed Damor to entrap her—*escape*.

Why she had not tried harder to save her own life in the desert—*escape*.

Haley had been running from her own destiny. "I don't want it!" she cried loudly, "I—"

She could feel his hand laid gently upon her shoulder. "There are millions who will suffer, will become enslaved by darkness," J said in quiet understanding. "We few who labor do so under great personal sacrifice for the many. Daughter, become who you are and find your own peace, if not for yourself, then for all mankind."

"Peace?" she roared. "This is not peace! I have never been so confused in all my life! And you call this *peace*?"

"Your conflict will NOT simply disappear because you wish it so," J said evenly. "You have pursued the path of the heart. It is the destiny of those who would climb the heart's mountain, to serve humanity."

Haley stepped away from J, her hands clenched into fists. "I've made no such commitments, other than my vow . . . to . . . serve. . . ." Her voice trailed off, the memory of a declaration once made coming back to her while she spoke. Yes. She had vowed to serve that love that poured through her as she lay dying. Haley shook her head. That was recent. She had been suffering her whole life.

J smiled. "Prior to our birth, we decide how our life will be spent. Thus, we choose our homes, parents, friends, and we choose what might happen to us."

Haley blinked in horror. "A woman would choose to be

raped and murdered? A child to be abused? A man to kill or be killed?"

J stopped her. "Yes. We must choose this, if we have the debt to pay. Murder in one life, and be murdered you must. Rape in one and be raped in another. We decide if we pay now or later; balancing all that is in the great wheel of life."

Haley crumpled to the ground, her sobs coming in heaves. J did not move to comfort her. She would have to work this out on her own. Presently she stopped, and in between sniffles said, "It's true. Every word of it. I know it. Damn it."

Finally, she stood up, wiping tears away. "Thank you." She turned and walked up to the edge of the water. "I accept my fate and destiny. Whatever it is. Come, show me how to live." The weight, that damn horrible weight, was gone. Haley started to laugh; the freedom felt exhilarating.

"I will take terrible risks and undergo horrible fates," she began hysterically.

"Naturally," he agreed. "It makes for interesting days."

Haley laughed. "I am going to die."

"Of course," J rejoined humorously.

After a minute, she stopped laughing. They were facing each other, looking into each other's eyes with dead earnestness. "Okay," Haley stated with conviction, "let's do it."

J laughed. "It, as you say, has already begun. You are just now recognizing it."

"Is it this way for everyone?"

"At one time or another, yes. During these great periods of struggle between good and evil, between right and wrong, all who live from the heart must one day tread the path of self-denial, suffering, and service for the good of all."

Turning away, she stopped in midstride. "Teacher, how long have I been gone?"

167

"You have been in my care for three months."

"That long . . ." Haley sighed with contentment; the time had flown, seeming only a few weeks.

J picked up a rock and pressed it in his hands for a few moments. "A chela will meet with your brother; your family will soon know of your well-being." He opened his hands, and the rock vanished; in its place was a beautiful golden-red ruby.

Haley's mouth dropped open. "How . . . how did you do that!?" What she had witnessed was beyond understanding. Could all these Sufis do this?

"Tut-tut," J chuckled, absently tossing the stone over his shoulder. It landed a few inches from Haley, its luster literally hurting her eyes as she picked it up. It was warm to the touch.

"No, really. How did you *do* that?" The ruby was flawless.

J turned around and looked at her. "To what purpose do you inquire?"

Haley looked down; this was a rebuke, but she felt that her question—after J had performed his sleight of hand in front of her—was more than appropriate.

"Was it magic?"

"Magic is magic except to the magician."

She looked hard at her Teacher. He never answered a question directly; it was always an answer that forced her to think.

J stood up. "When we master our bodies completely, we master the plane those bodies exist on as well." After he had spoken, the water in the pool rose up in the center and formed a shimmering, beautiful tree. Haley let out a small gasp and scurried back to the edge of the water. It was a perfect elm tree: large trunk, towering twenty feet high, with full branches and thousands of translucent swaying leaves. Then she blinked. A fish was swimming in the center of the tree, oblivious to the fact that the water had changed shape. Haley walked out into the pool until she was standing next to the tree; she shoved her hand into the massive trunk.

Her teacher grinned, and instantly the entire form crashed down upon her as though a bucket had been upturned from on high. "Oh!" she sputtered, floundering and trying to stand, finally losing her balance. Emerging from the foaming water, she turned angrily toward a laughing J. "That wasn't funny!" J doubled over; the sight of Haley staggering out of the pool, drenched, was more than he could bear. Haley walked over to him and shook herself like a dog, showering him; he continued to laugh until they both were on the ground in hysterics. After a few moments, their laughter subsided into giggling.

J produced a rag and began drying his face. "After all, this is the plane of greatest illusion. Does it matter what form the illusion takes? Does it matter the personality or the appearance of forms? Nations rise, then fall away. Birth, old age, death—all according to cycles."

Haley looked at him directly. She had learned that even his most casual-seeming remarks were meant to teach her. "What *does* matter?"

"Experience. Conscious learning," he replied, "and, of course, being yourself."

Haley thought for a moment. "Are you saying that once we connect with reality, we become masters of unreality?"

"In one sense, yes."

Haley frowned. He had said to be ourselves, decide who we are, and to become love. But how to begin? How to understand these mysteries?

"Come," J said, standing, "let us get into dry clothes."

∞

The train screeched loudly to a halt, steam hissing, forming great clouds that enveloped the swarm of humanity standing at the station. David Hampton felt uneasy standing in the swaying throng; he shouldn't be here. He belonged somewhere else, doing his work. His thoughts turned to Haley; he couldn't abandon her. David looked down. He could feel the disappointment of his Teacher in his heart, urging him to change his course. He sighed and shook his head, murmuring to himself, "I don't know what course I could have taken. I can't just let her die out there." After a few moments, the uneasiness passed.

At the final screech of the steel wheels, he moved forward—squinting into the mist, earnestly looking toward the rail cars. Then he smiled.

"Hello, David!" a voice out of sight shouted.

David stepped forward, extending his hand. "Hi, John. Have a good trip?"

Emerging out of the haze, John Olsten shrugged his shoulders. Travel in India by rail was interesting at best, at worst it was . . .

John adjusted his shoulder bag. "Have you made the arrangements?"

"Yes, but we must talk."

John nodded his agreement as they headed for the baggage car. Zalub appeared, greeting John with a warm handshake. "Master David, sir," he said with enthusiasm, "we are ready with the car. I will be most happy to assist with the luggage."

"Thanks, Zalub."

The train began to unload its human cargo in earnest. Everywhere around them, in between them, and sometimes underneath them, hundreds of people swarmed—pushing and bumping the pair. The noise level made talking nearly impossible.

"What's going on?" John inquired, noticing that David was now frowning.

"There are complications."

John stopped. "Don't tell me we didn't get our passes to the frontier?"

David touched his arm, and they continued walking. "No, nothing like that. Everything is in order, old man."

John looked at him. "Well?"

"Remember the man I told you about?"

"That Saling rascal?"

David nodded his head, then stopped John from walking, gaining his undivided attention. "I have word that he will try to kill us once we cross over into the frontier."

John stopped dead in his tracks. "What! Why?"

After a long reflective minute, they both started again toward the baggage. "We know your sister was with him when she disappeared. We're certain she is alive, somewhere, and I feel he is afraid of her going to the local governor."

"Why do you say that?"

"I've heard things about the man. Terrible things. Sex magic, white slavery . . ."

John looked ashen upon hearing the news. "What's the plan?"

"I'll tell you over lunch."

"I . . . I look like a man!" Haley observed in the mirror. From head to toe, she was dressed in peasant's clothes—torn, dirty, and oversized.

"Precisely so," J commented. "Too dangerous for a woman to travel in the north country."

It occurred to her that if she stayed in India any longer, all her femininity would vanish, but she smiled and turned around announcing, "I'm ready." Then she shrank back in horror. J was standing in front of her with a pair of scissors.

"We cannot risk exposure," he said evenly, extending the shears to her. "It would mean certain death."

"But if I tied it in a knot, then—"

"No." One of J's eyebrows arched suspiciously. "Of course, real disciples are not concerned with appearances. Besides," he continued, "the maharaja's spies are still most certainly looking for a woman, not a boy."

Haley turned back toward the mirror and began cutting. Back in Boston, her beautiful locks had been constantly admired and praised, and she had taken it upon herself to keep her hair beautiful and luxurious. *Snip . . . snip . . . snip.* Each lock fell unceremoniously on the floor, some landing on her shoulders, a few hairs still clinging. Finally, Haley laughed; she needed this. And in cutting her hair, she could feel a freedom from something inside. She looked at herself in the mirror and then began the project in earnest. Two minutes later, she was finished.

"Voilà!" she said with a flourish of the scissors as she turned around. "What?"

J handed her a bowl. "We must give you the face of a pig." Haley looked dolefully at the bowl, then slowly took it. She brought the bowl up to her nose. "This stinks of camel dung." Whatever was in the bowl, it smelled foul and was dark colored.

J smiled. "And so does a pig." He turned and started out of the room, saying over his shoulder as he left, "Put it everywhere, all over. Miss nothing."

Ten minutes later, Haley emerged. Her complexion was that of some poor soul who made his living working on a dung heap. Her clothes were tattered and colorless, her feet wrapped only in sandals.

J was fussing over a bag, his back to her. "You are finished?" Noticing she did not answer, he turned around. Then he laughed—loudly.

Haley scowled at him. "I think you enjoy humiliating me."

J was still laughing. "A more humble soul I have not seen."

"Will this wash off?"

"After several weeks, it may. Of course, anything is possible."

Haley moaned as J walked up to her. "You are a true pariah," he announced. "Here is your bag." Haley slung it over her shoulder as J had his and followed him through the tunnel to the hut. They emerged into bright sunlight.

"Where are we going?"

J pointed toward a massive peak, far off in the distance. "There." Then, without another word, he moved off in its direction. Haley stood looking at the beautiful mountains, many miles away. She was awestruck by their beauty and magnificence; she always had been. They towered over everything—even the clouds that closely hugged the great peaks appeared small. Noticing that J had already gone, she hurried after him. "Teacher. What are those mountains?"

J did not slacken his pace. "The Himalayas."

Damor glided to the window, his back to the dozen men standing in a semicircle around his desk. A few exchanged nervous glances; some shifted their feet. Finally, a captain stepped forward. "Sir, we have every approach covered, there is nothing to worry—"

Maharaja Saling slammed his fist down upon the windowsill, cutting off the man. "*I'll* decide, in *my* kingdom, whether *I* should worry or not!"

The men snapped to attention at his words, all eyes forward.

The captain's face went white. Saling sighed, then turned and faced them; his expression icy, his voice soft and even. "Hire another two hundred men. I want them alive or dead." He stepped within a few inches of the captain's face, adjusted the poor man's shoulder strap, and buttoned his tunic. "Of course, I prefer alive."

The captain snapped a salute and barked a "Yes sir!" With a nod from the captain, the men saluted and began to file from the room. Damor stopped the captain, who slowly turned and faced him, trembling.

"My humor has vanished," Damor quipped with a smile. "If I cannot have the woman and her friends, you and your men will do nicely."

The captain turned whiter than thought possible, blinked, and hurried from the room. Damor snapped a switch on a box sitting on his desk. "Send her in."

A few moments later the door opened. "Sit down, please," Damor said sweetly. He himself sat down, folding his hands pleasantly on his desk. "My dear, I am in need of your assistance, it seems."

Ann looked nervously across the desk, then cleared her throat. Despite his charm, Saling terrified her now. "What can I do?"

For the next few weeks, Haley and J slowly made their way across streams, fields, barren passes, and empty plains. They saw small villages and the occasional caravan. Although they kept up a quick pace, J seemed to know when Haley was tired and needed a rest. Out of his knapsack would come rice and wheat cakes ready for a fire. Eating simply, traveling fast, and avoiding the local populace, they kept to themselves.

Each night she would sleep under a thin blanket while J sat upright in the lotus position; each morning when she awoke, he would still be sitting there wide awake and alert.

"Don't you ever sleep?" Haley asked one morning, rubbing sleep from her eyes. J stood and stretched. "My body is at rest," he replied humorously. "That is all it needs." He picked up his goatskin bag and walked to the edge of the clearing where they had camped. Beyond the clearing was a small rise. Beyond it, a stream.

Still blinking from the deep sleep her journey had forced upon her tired body, Haley watched him. Having no real perception of distance, she estimated they must be covering twenty miles each day. At first, it was hard work, and her limbs ached by noon. Now, her body had acclimated to the pace and she felt fine by evening, though exhausted. The country she and her teacher were passing through was beautiful in a stark way. She knew she would miss this later, and she made herself a promise to try to remember as many details of it as she could; for some reason, this would be important in the future.

Then she hurriedly came to her feet; J had reached the rise and then dropped quickly to one knee. Haley dashed up behind him.

"Who are they?" she asked, starting to step forward. J's arm shot out, holding her back. "Do not let them see you," he whispered. "They are bandits." Haley dropped to the ground as he had done.

Fifty feet below, five men with British Enfield rifles huddled around a campfire. None had slept well, having passed a miserable night being attacked by water mosquitoes. Curses and oaths were being muttered under frustrated breaths.

A surly man with front teeth missing walked up to the group.

"The horses are watered," he announced to no one in particular as he joined his comrades.

The largest of the band, with a beard down to his chest, snarled, "Well, Verada? What did the woman say?"

The horse thief began to fill his cup with boiling coffee. "Malakar, she says she saw a man and a boy walking yesterday. She does not think they have gone too far."

Malakar lowered his head, swearing. "Curses to Allah! We are looking for a woman! A woman, I said!" Malakar drew his knife. The group of men shrank somewhat, all moving slightly from their violent leader.

"It is not all," Verada offered fearfully. "Old woman says boy not walk like boy."

Malakar stopped swearing, blinking intensely with interest at the man he was about to kill. "Boy not walk like boy . . . hmm." He sheathed the knife and stood up, throwing out the rest of his coffee. "Mount up. Let's find this 'boy.' "

J turned to Haley. "Get back to the camp and wait for me." Haley started to speak. "Do not argue. Do as I say . . . *now!*" Haley edged back down the ridge slowly, glancing back toward her Teacher, whose stern look informed her she should do exactly as he advised.

J turned back to the group below him, a smile wide upon his face. A quick glance informed him she was gone.

J vanished.

Verada was riding back down the stream on a skittish mare, holding a handful of reins to guide the horses behind him. A strange hum began to fill the air. The horses started to shift uneasily, pulling at their ropes. Malakar and his men looked up to see Verada fall from his horse, screaming, as the animals began to run in different directions. Mouths opened in disbelief; the group began to scurry after their fast-scattering mounts.

176

Malakar reached Verada and pulled him to his feet, blade in hand. "What is the matter with you?"

"A beast! A strange beast! There, in the marsh!" Verada was terrified, not of the blade against his throat, Malakar noticed, but of whatever it was out in the brush. He slowly put the knife away and jerked a pistol from his waistband.

Slowly scanning, Malakar looked in every direction. All was quiet, the gentle reeds barely moving in the soft wind. Finally, he threw the man to the ground. "Get your horse, you stupid fool." Verada scrambled away quickly from his angry leader, looking back once to be sure a pistol wasn't being aimed at him; death was the usual fate of those who disappointed the great warrior chief.

Cursing under his breath, Malakar shook his head, then stopped. He could sense that someone was watching him; his instincts, developed after years of spying, stealing, and killing, were working overtime. Strangely, this feeling was different, as he felt no fear. It seemed as if something was warning him, imploring him to abandon his goal of attaining the reward of fifty thousand rupees for some stupid girl. He shook off the feeling and grunted. That much money was a rare opportunity. Usually, he had to content himself with selling his skills as an assassin to some local chieftain; these jobs paid poorly and were accompanied by great risks. No, this was Allah smiling upon him. For the first time, in a long, long while, too.

Presently, his men began to return with their mounts, gathering around him, waiting for his orders. Malakar climbed into the saddle. "You idiots!" he shouted at the men still standing with reins in their hands. "What are you waiting for? Do you think this woman will wander magically into your arms?" For Malakar, it looked as if that is just what might happen.

J watched as the horsemen sped off toward the east. Waiting

another minute to be sure they were gone completely, he began his descent down the ridge toward camp where Haley would be anxiously waiting.

Knowing the direction the bandits were going, he realized that he would have to choose another route to avoid the murderous gang. Haley was holding up well and the long marches were good for her system, giving her a stamina she would need later if all went well.

J stopped at the base of the ridge and thought about the future in the quiet of the meadow. There were so many variables to consider. So much depended upon the outcome of critical events, choices, and timing—all outside his and the Brotherhood's control. What would she do when the time came? Would she have the courage to face herself and her destiny?

Would she choose wisely?

Sad and weighted with a burden he began to see as outside the range of his capabilities, J started again for his camp—then stopped, something catching his eye.

He was here.

"The gardener knows the inevitable outcome, being attentive to all things."

Beaming with unimaginable joy, J looked toward a place some ten feet in front of him. Nothing was there except a soft glow—more a reflection from the rising moon than anything else. Every living thing within sight brightened a little, absorbing the splendor of that small point of radiance. J felt a powerful wave of purity flash through every cell of his body, filling and uplifting his warrior's heart to a much-missed dimension of knowingness, love, and grace.

"I labor, my Master," he replied to the kind and loving presence, weariness etched behind his strong words, "but the child crawls more than walks."

"Which flower will bloom in the garden? Which will wither, waiting for another season to stretch forth its petals?"

J understood. And in his understanding gave thanks that such Grace would take a moment and bless his work with Its Presence. Presently, the light faded, the sun now fully set in the western sky, the lengthening shadows merging together as night stretched its blanket of darkness.

CHAPTER 10

Madness

Pursue destruction and it finds you.
As with anything,
we become what we seek . . . and fear.

Every opportunity to catch his quarry was somehow stymied; always, they slipped out of Malakar's grasp. Each time he received information about the two mysterious peasants, he found that they had just left that day, that morning, that hour. Vanished. A campfire would be still hot and smoking, but with no one in the vicinity. Tracks made the same day would lead to the middle of some open ground, and the trail would then mysteriously disappear.

Each hope, dashed. Each trail, leading nowhere. The men began to murmur among themselves about chasing ghosts.

There was something else, as well. A weird feeling. His foreboding grew stronger as the days went by, as though some great calamity were about to befall him and his band of now-frightened followers. His men felt it too, he knew, by the look in their eyes that reflected his own feelings. They looked at him as though they were about to mention what everyone was thinking:

that the bounty hunt should be abandoned. But for Malakar—a great warrior and fighter—a reputation was at stake: *his*. A stern glance, one that made women out of men, was all it took to keep them in line.

Malakar lit the cigar in his mouth. When was the last time he had really slept? Always that damn, insistent presence of danger, making him, his men, and their horses restless and irritable—a presence that didn't melt away with drink or whores.

Continuing to think about the matter with an intensity that usually had brought him solutions, it occurred even to Malakar that maybe this was the time to quit. Had not the old woman from Bangor told him last month that he would perish in unholy pursuits? She hadn't even flinched when he produced his knife and held it at her throat.

"I see no rest, in this life or the one after, for the man who would slaughter a helpless woman," she commented, full of determination and fire. With a look of spirited defiance, she dared Malakar to take action. He laughed at her as he cut her throat, blood spraying everywhere as she ran around the room like a chicken trying to stop its flow. Though he normally did not allow such things—except in *special* cases—he permitted his men to have their way with her corpse, there being no other women available at the time to enjoy.

The uneasiness settled over him again, like unseen ants—unshakable. Malakar sighed audibly; he regretted killing the old woman. From their lifeless depths, her eyes seemed to guarantee him damnation.

Well, he *would* have enough to settle down in some valley once he had finished with this job. Yes. Become a warlord of some small village, with everyone looking up to him, taking orders from him. After he killed his men, of course.

The uneasy feeling again.

He knew a challenge when he saw one, and as his whole life had been spent never backing down from these opportunities, he could not do so now. His command and control of his men depended upon it. But he promised himself that this would be the last time he would labor for another. From now on, he would kill for his purposes alone. Malakar would never bow to another man again.

Shifting his thoughts back to the problem at hand, Malakar felt sure that this stupid girl had protection; this much was certain. There must be powers at work here. Otherwise, why would Saling be involved? Yes. Sorcery. That would explain it. Malakar grunted a laugh. Sorcery, indeed! To triumph over sorcery would make the spoils all the sweeter when he succeeded in capturing Saling's elusive bitch.

Malakar grew worried as he thought the whole affair over and audibly sighed. Did anyone hear it? Glancing around the campfire, he noticed most of his men were asleep or nervously holding their rifles. No, they had not.

They could never be allowed to know his feelings—ever! If they suspected he had grown weak or soft, any one of them would kill him in his sleep and take over. Just as he had done, when he killed his old leader several years ago in Madras.

A long, low rumble in the distance stopped Haley and J. "What is it," she asked earnestly, "thunder?"

J listened intently—as though he were no longer present but had left her and his body. After a few minutes, he turned around. Haley became instantly concerned, as his usually calm and joyful countenance was now stern and grave. "Artillery." The rumble increased in volume, its freakish roar out of place in the tranquil meadow they were walking through.

Haley, picking up J's apprehension, turned toward the sound and frowned. "You mean fighting? People are fighting?"

J sighed. "Yes, fighting. A local dispute that has drawn in the services of the British and their field pieces."

The rumble rose and fell in crescendos, like ocean waves trying to crest a cliff. J smiled. "Come. It will be all right." They moved toward the angry roar, low in the distance, traveling on a worn and desolate road.

Presently the din of the cannonade was punctuated by the flat sound of distant small-arms fire. After another mile the sky became filled with black, twisting smoke that blotted out the sun and covered everything with an orange haze. To Haley, it appeared as though they were entering perdition itself, as every sound of nature had been obliterated by scattered machine-gun fire, barking howitzers, and bugle calls. She could see the arcs of shells in the distance and feel the ground tremors as they screamed into their targets.

The road they followed was deep within the confines of the valley that they had been tramping through for several days. Soon the road began to curve upward, following the natural hill in front of them. When they reached the crest, Haley gasped. Until now, she could only hear the sounds of war. Until now . . . she had never really known madness.

In the valley below raged a fierce battle. Stalwart ranks of men, standing in front of batteries of cannon belching flame and smoke, fired against a burning wall of explosions. Ranks of soldiers on one side, separated from another large body of men engaged in similar practice in the exact opposite direction. There were thousands of men, trucks, cannon, and tanks concentrated in what seemed like an area too small to accommodate so many people. From above, it looked as if some terrible vise were pushing the two sides together, each frantically attempting to merge with the other, yet resisting that awful pressure—one to join with the other in a freakish unity of destruction. In between the two forces, a fiery hell—a no-man's-land—of flame and billowing black smoke where detachments of men would rally under some officer and charge, only to disappear in the smoke, never to be seen again. Dissolved. Evaporated. Swallowed up by the strange, ghastly magic of the explosions.

In terrible fascination—too horrible to watch, yet too bizarre to turn away from—Haley stared at the grisly carnage. J appeared in front of her, blocking out the view.

Haley blinked out of her trance. "I'm sorry. I—"

He cut her off with a wave of his hand. "We must advance through this valley." For the first time since she had known him, J did not radiate his usual joy and peace; he seemed grim and determined.

Haley blinked in disbelief. "How? Surely, they will not let us pass." She could see he was serious. What was she doing here? In the middle of some civil war—with an old man—maybe a crazy old man—who was about to lead her into a place no sane person would ever go?

Shaking her head no, Haley unconsciously stepped back away from him. "We would be killed! There must be some other path. I saw a trail back in the meadow heading off through those hills." Just as she finished her plea, an errant artillery shell screeched through the air between them where she had stood moments before, knocking her backwards and to the ground.

J, acting as though nothing had happened, sighed in disappointment. "So quickly we forget to trust and believe. So easy to doubt, so easy to ignore the heart. Was it not said that 'it would be all right?' "

Haley staggered to her feet, brushing herself off. He was right. She had no basis for doubting him; in fact, a feeling of security and peace welled up from her heart as she realized she would have to go into that inferno of death. Haley slowly looked up at him and his sad eyes. He had never harmed her; instead, he always protected her. She felt humiliated and ashamed.

After a moment, she nodded her apology and began to move downward on her own. As they descended, the rumble and roar became deafening. Here and there, an angry stray bullet would whine off some rock or buzz through the air, seeming upset at not having found flesh to tear. Haley stayed close to her Teacher; when he looked in her direction, she would straighten up and attempt some composure. Whatever outward image she presented, inside she was terrified.

After twenty interminable minutes of dodging bullets and shrapnel, the pair finally reached the valley floor.

Madness was an understatement.

Everywhere at once, commanders shouted at their men to charge and fire. "Give 'em the cold steel, boys!" and "Keep up your fire! Keep up your fire!" Artillery batteries grew red hot from firing; spent seventy-millimeter shells littered the ground in every direction, testimony to the fury of the battle. Men lay dead or dying, crawling, begging for assistance. Some called for loved ones; others, for friendly hands to finish what the enemy had started. A young corporal, his left arm and leg missing, placed his service revolver into his mouth and squeezed the trigger.

Haley stood frozen, unable to move. Her dream about her grandfather had become real. A bullet whirred within two inches of her head. An explosion rocked the earth nearby, showering her with broken ground and the knee of some poor fellow. She remained as she was—transfixed by the frenzied orgy of destruction. Hands grasped her shoulders. "We must keep moving, child," a friendly concerned voice urged. Blankly, she allowed herself to be moved along the edge of death and chaos.

He appeared out of nowhere, his ear missing and his face and uniform covered with a wet scarlet stain. " 'Elp me!" his young voice begged. Haley stared at the boy's shattered face, unable to respond to his frightened plea, her eyes following him to the ground as he went down on his knees, swooning. His hand reached up in supplication. She did not see it, watching instead a spray of blood that continued to cover the ground in regular intervals. Finally, she blinked, coming around. No longer fascinated by the wound, she realized that in front of her was the same young boy, no more than eighteen or nineteen, bleeding to death, his body jerking in shock. Her look to J as she knelt to give him aid was more of a statement than asking permission. Her teacher sternly nodded in the affirmative.

Though young, the boy soldier already sported lines of weariness around his eyes. Lines of weariness and age too soon for his time. He managed a smile as she brought her goatskin bag of water to his lips. "Only a little. There. That's right," she intuitively admonished him.

The soldier looked up and stopped his spasmodic twitching, peace pouring through him, his eyes filled with gratitude. He looked around and started to laugh. "Am I dead? I must be dead—I can't feel anything."

Haley turned to J. "We must take him to a hospital." J nodded, then lifted the dying man into his arms and started off toward a tent with a large red cross on it. Noticing that Haley disappeared, he stopped and looked for her. He found her administering to some other poor soul, tying part of a rag onto his arm. A smile crept across his face as he turned back to the aid station with his charge.

And so it went. Shells bursting everywhere, men dying by the hundreds, and the roar of the cannons' incessant boom. Minutes were days, hours an eternity. Finally, as the sun began to dip into the horizon, a queer silence rose up from the battlefield. Quiet.

The battle was over.

It was a quiet unlike any someone would ever hear on this planet. And it only lasted for a single minute.

Then a new sound rose, more horrible than that of war. It was the sound made by thousands of throats too weakened by wounds to articulate their suffering. A great murmur. Deep. Insistent. Permeating everywhere at once. Punctuating this constant moan were the noises made by men staggering in random directions. Officers appeared and disappeared on horseback, shouting in strained relief. Animals and men alike screamed in their death throes.

J began his search for his missing ward, lost in the maelstrom of hell. She was easy to find: a radiant glow among a sea of hopeless black and red. He came upon her sitting alone, a bloody rag in her hand, staring off into the battlefield with its littered dead and churned, scorched earth.

He knelt in front of her. "They are so beautiful," she said without looking at him. "Those wonderful spirits."

J glanced out onto the field. Yes, they were there. They were always there after a battle. The invisible helpers who ministered to the fallen, helping them into the next world where the anger of man's stupidity and slaughter could reach them no more. It was as she said, *beautiful.* Wherever suffering raised its ugly head, these angels of compassion could be found—in a home, in a relationship, or when mankind decided its conflicts on some forgotten piece of land turned into a graveyard with weapons of war.

J uttered a prayer for the dead on both sides and then lifted Haley to a standing position. She was crying. He put her head on his shoulder. "Let us go, child. We can do no more here today." He could feel her nod of agreement as she clung to him the way a terrified youngster would cling to a parent.

"You there!" a voice barked at them from behind.

J turned around, coming face-to-face with a man with a saber in his hand. "Not you, *darky!*" he bellowed menacingly, "the other!" Haley did not hear the man; she kept her face pressed into her Teacher's tunic.

J backed away and sat Haley down, her eyes still glazed over in shock. Looking him over, J said, "Sergeant, you're wounded." The soldier was bleeding from his mangled left arm, shattered by a bullet and hanging limp. The sergeant didn't move. Ignoring J's sympathy, he demanded, "What's his problem? Deaf?"

"The boy is in shock, sahib. Let me tend to that arm." J moved forward, easing slowly in front of the red-stained saber, looking the man in the eye the whole time. The sergeant was gaunt white from loss of blood and began to crumple where he stood. J caught him as he fell.

"Wanted . . . wanted to thank him," he mumbled, losing consciousness. "Saved my brother's life, he did. Saw him. Saw him save my brother's life."

"Haley!" J commanded forcefully, shocking her back to reality. She moved quickly to J, tearing another piece of cloth from her now-torn and ragged cloak.

"Will he live?"

J looked the unconscious man over, taking the blood-soaked saber from his stiff hands. "This one will live." Haley finished with the tourniquet and stepped away while J lifted the man onto his shoulders. They began to walk toward the tents.

A jeep bore down on them, carrying three men whose eyes reflected a sick passion for destruction. J noticed that their blood was still up; they were alarmed and suspicious with weapons at the ready. "Looks like Collins, sir," one man said to the driver of the jeep.

"What the devil is going on here?" the driver demanded as the jeep screeched to a halt, blocking Haley and J's path. "Do not speak," J implored her under his breath. "A wounded man, sahib," he shouted toward the jeep. "He needs attention!"

The jeep immediately emptied. Two men took the sergeant from J as the driver walked over, never taking his eyes off J and Haley.

"What are you doing here?" he asked directly, his hand resting on his holstered revolver. "Robbing the dead? That it?" Without warning, he pulled out his gun and tore open J's tunic, mumbling an occasional "dirty buggers." The driver was obviously disappointed to discover that J was not concealing anything. Haley didn't react to the revolver pointed in her direction.

Haley's Teacher bowed with salaams. "We are traveling to the pass, sahib."

"The pass is closed," the man retorted, flipping through J's knapsack with one hand while keeping his revolver shoved in J's side, growing frustrated. "Take it off!"

J removed his knapsack, promptly setting it on the ground and stepping away. Enraged by the total courtesy of the old peasant, the driver started throwing its contents of rice, pots, and clothing onto the ground. He walked up close to J, inspecting his face. "Why didn't you go round?"

"Sahib," J replied with perfect calm, "there is no other way to Annapurna."

"Like I said, the pass is closed." He became furious, as if his words alone would discourage any attempt. The commander moved toward Haley and placed the barrel of his gun into her left nostril, obviously decided upon illustrating his intentions. She showed no alarm. Unable to believe what he was seeing, he cocked the hammer.

"Sir! Collins is slipping! We must hurry."

Upset at being interrupted in his interrogation of the two strangers, the commander growled something about spies, scowled menacingly, then walked stiffly back to the jeep. He paused for a moment, observing Haley and J. "What the devil are they doing in this unholy place?" Collins moaned, causing one of his attendants to implore again for haste. The jeep roared off, showering the area with dust and gravel.

J turned to Haley. "It is time to go." Haley nodded . . . then fainted into J's arms. Catching her in her fall, he cradled her in his arms and walked across the field.

She had braved the worst of mankind—warfare—and come out admirably, J noted. Though she was never in any real danger, she needed to learn to trust and believe—two virtues that could only be tested through the baptism of destruction.

"You sleep now, child," he said soothingly. "You have done well."

Malakar could not believe his luck. What spoils! There were rifles, pistols, wallets, and rings of all kinds. Allah was very kind to him this day. After losing the trail of his intended victims, he had followed the sound of battle to watch from above as the two forces slaughtered each other. When it was over, he and his men swooped down on the far side of the field to reap the bounty of the harvest.

"Malakar! Look here!" Malakar stuffed banknotes into his pockets, then dropped the wallet in his hands; he walked over to the shouting man. Verada held up the wrist of a dead British major. "Such a grand ring! Full of diamonds."

Bending on one knee, Malakar inspected the jewel. Truly, it was a beautiful ring that sparkled in the dying sun; he tugged on it.

"It won't come off," Verada complained, "I've tried." The dead major was already beginning to swell up from the heat, a great hole where his chest should have been. Malakar glanced around quickly. If the British found him, he would be executed on the spot. He tugged on the ring again; breaking the finger made a sickening "pop" sound, but the recalcitrant digit still kept the bauble for its rightful owner. Verada turned away, sickened.

Malakar grunted in disgust at Verada's weak stomach. "Cut off his finger." Verada winced and began the grisly task as Malakar started to rifle through the dead man's clothes.

He tossed aside a picture of the major's family, then stuffed a package of cigarettes into his own dirty shirt. He looked up and stopped his horrible pillage. Something in the distance caught his eye: something difficult to see, with the setting sun blinding him as it was. Only a vague moving shadow. Someone carrying someone else. Malakar dismissed it. Survivors, no doubt—sorry bastards.

What idiot would kill without pay? The British had contempt for everything, except their own damn officer staff and ruling elite. Malakar made more money in one robbery than a private did during his entire enlistment in Her Majesty's service. "Fools . . ."

The hairs on the back of his neck stood up. It was that damn haunting feeling again, that unknown terror. He noticed that his hand was shaking.

"We must hurry!" he shouted. "They will soon be looking for wounded."

J noticed her coming back to consciousness. She would be awake in a few moments. She had been home to see her family in her dreams. He smiled at that. After times of great crisis, the love of family is a great panacea. Haley clenched her fists and began to moan.

Haley could smell the tea's aroma in her sleep, which brought a smile to her lips. She was having tea with her friends and family in the parlor, laughing and carrying on. Someone knocked at the door. Her mother turned toward her. "Would you see who it is, dearest?" Haley kissed Sarah on the cheek and skipped to the hallway; once there, the sounds of laughter faded, replaced by a low rumbling growl. The floor shook at regular intervals, as dust fell from the ceiling. She approached the door and opened it. A young soldier, bleeding profusely, lurched over the step and grabbed her arm. "No time for tea yet, love. Much more fun to be had."

Haley woke with a start. *"Ung."*

J grabbed her by the shoulders. "It's okay, child. There is nothing to fear, now." Waking, she took in a deep breath and began to sob. He held her for a few minutes until her crying subsided.

"Tea?" J put a cup in front of her as she sat up. Haley started pushing at something invisible, screaming wildly and shaking with fear. "No. No. *Please.*"

Taking her in his arms, J kept murmuring softly, finally calming her. After another minute, she let out a long sigh. He lifted a cup for her to take. She took it and began rubbing her eyes. "Thank you." Haley drew her knees up under her and took a sip. Then another. "This tastes wonderful. Thank you again."

J filled her cup a second time. "Sometimes great stress needs an outlet. Our dreams are often a way for the mind to handle that which it cannot in our waking consciousness. If we suppress something emotionally, it almost always presents itself to us for resolution in the dream world."

Beyond conversation, she simply looked at him and nodded. She lifted the cup again to her mouth, then stopped, noticing the holes in her sleeves. She looked up at J questioningly. "Bullet holes," he commented flatly. "You never hear the one that takes your life, it is said."

"I didn't realize." Try as she might, the images of the day kept flooding back into her mind. She shivered.

"It took great courage to help those men today, daughter." J smiled, filling her cup once again.

Haley looked down. The praise was unearned—she knew she had been terrified. Even though the event seemed lifetimes in the past, the memory of it made her heart pound.

"That is incorrect," he admonished gently. "When we put our lives on the altar so that others may live, there is no greater love. And great courage can only be propelled by great love."

Haley began to cry, her sobs coming in heaves. "I was afraid. Scared! I don't think I knew *what* I was doing!"

"You? Afraid? Not in the least, little hope." J said flatly. "The feeling we call fear is not who we really are—it is the elemental that animates and sustains our bodies when they fear for their existence. It pumps its own fear of survival into the bloodstream by the various glandular systems. Remove the influence of these glands, and the man—or woman—feels no fear. These chemicals will be noted by science in the coming years."

Rubbing her sleeve against her nose, Haley blurted out,

"What are you talking about?" And to herself, "Please. Leave me alone. Enough."

Seeing that she was upset and distraught, J slowed down. He said, "Simply this: You are not the body which can be wounded or killed. Our bodies have their own defense mechanisms. These mechanisms are switched on and off by the indwelling agents we call elementals. It is the elemental that panics; and until control over the physical body is entirely secure, these elementals determine our cravings, urges, and reactions to events." J handed her a kerchief. "So you see, what we call feelings are not our selves. Any more than your hand is your soul or a thought your Identity."

Seeing that she was cold, J added some wood to the fire and uncovered a small iron pot. "Some food?"

Haley took in the delicious smell of rice and curry, her body instantly responding to its effect. "Yes, please." "My stomach is growling!"

"As it should. This is a most normal response to your body's need for fuel." J began lumping a portion into a banged-up wooden bowl for her. "See the difference here. As you notice your body's reaction to food, you can say that there is an observer which observes. This observer is somewhat the real you." Haley did not respond but chose instead to yawn, the fatigue of the day winning the battle over her body.

They ate in silence, both weighed down with thoughts of what was past and what still lay before them. After the simple repast, Haley curled back up and went to sleep, dreaming of David, John, and her family.

"This won't do at all," David yelled across the gorge. They were standing on a cliff above the Ustain rift. The break that separated

194

them from the other side of the ridge was seven thousand feet deep; such are the treacherous passes in Nepal. A man could write a letter before he hit the ground, David grimly mused. The wind whipped such a frenzy around the group that no one could hear what anyone else was yelling. Donkeys brayed. Men swore. Everyone was terrified of slipping. David noticed that the pack bearers he had hired in Lahore were huddled back away from the edge, talking in excited tones. As David turned his attention back to the pack train, sand flew in his eyes. "Damn it all!"

Between the two sides, only forty feet apart, was a small rope bridge that snapped from one side to the other. In the center of the unstable bridge stood John at the lead, a pack strapped on and a rope tied to his waist; from what David could see, the man behind him was frozen with fear and wouldn't move. David waved his cap in a vain attempt to get John's attention.

"What?" he yelled back, turning to David.

"We. Must. Find. Another. Way!" he yelled slowly, one word at a time. John still couldn't hear him and took his hand from the slender safety rope to cup an ear.

The wind snapped the bridge again, this time flipping it over.

David watched in horror as his dear friend and two other men toppled off of it and disappeared from sight. David no longer heard the wind or felt it. It grew quiet; the only audible sound was the pounding of his heart. His legs gave out beneath him as he folded to the ground, his hand clutching the rope that swung freely.

"No. Please God, no," he begged hoarsely, unable to look at the gorge, the event playing over and over again in his mind like a needle stuck on a record. David, shattered by the unbelievable, was unable to see or think of anything else.

He was just talking to John. They had joked about Hitler that morning—John doing his impression of the insane man.

David looked over at Zalub, who was staring at the rope in his hand, shaking his head.

Everything was as still as death. The wind was gone, the men, silent. David sank down even farther, his face pale in horror. A man began to wail a Hindu ritual prayer.

"This is my fault. I am to blame."

Haley woke up sharply and found to her amazement that she was crying again. A great dread filled her, as though something precious was lost, never to be found again. She let the tears flow, the horror of the battlefield mixing in with the macabre feeling pouring through her.

Feeling his eyes on her, she looked over at her Teacher and discovered that he was awake and was watching her, a solemn and grave expression shadowing his countenance. Haley sank back down into her blanket. Something had been ripped away from her heart, a great hole remaining in its place. "Something is terribly wrong, J," she said. "Something really bad has happened."

J said nothing in response to her outburst. Haley wrapped herself in her blanket and turned her back to him. In a few minutes, she was asleep.

He continued to watch her. Having kept his self-control and with no expression visible on his face, he radiated as much love and understanding as she could take in. His mind drifted away from the campfire and the hills of India to the future, where lay the inevitable struggle in which all aspirants to the flame of the heart must one day find themselves.

So much depends upon so few. How little the world knows or appreciates the grave sacrifices silently made on its behalf. Most who serve are scorned, ridiculed, and given over to the wolves.

Without the Christs and Mohammeds of the world, civilization would have ceased centuries ago.

What would *she* do, this frail creature who suffers so emotionally at the slightest trial? When the time came, would she stand forward and give all for a humanity that would happily burn her at the stake?

CHAPTER 11

Wasn't It Beautiful?

Precious are the hearts
that labor in unison.
Joyous become the heavens
when love conquers.

For the next three weeks, Haley and J continued on their journey to the Himalayas, stopping a great deal and meeting with people from villages and towns, getting food when necessary, sometimes sharing the road with the occasional passerby. Most were friendly, some were curious, others . . . But even this abundance of humanity waned over time, as each day the air grew colder. Their trek continued on and up into the passes and mountains of the northern plains. The usual swarms of humankind that were India had lessened to the point where the pair counted themselves fortunate if they saw someone—*anyone*—and then, usually in the distance. A wave to a passing caravan; smoke from a campfire where the earth meets sky.

The shock of the battle had worn off, instilling in Haley a new appreciation for the word *courage*, as well as a deeper respect for life. Waking on the morning following the battle at Sangasta Plain, she saw life with new and appreciative eyes. The grass looked different, as did the sky, and the birds who sang each morning as they went about their business of hunting food and building nests. She really heard them, and for the first time she understood their song. Sunrises and sunsets became spiritual times of bonding between herself and the world around her.

The ache in her heart remained; she didn't speak of it, not really wanting to know the cause. Someone she loved had died or was suffering in some way. Powerless, she couldn't bear to know who. One day she would be stronger, more able to face the inevitable. J had watched Haley extend her arms out on late afternoons; he saw radiant streams of love pouring from her heart. She was becoming born anew in spirit. Death does that to a soul.

There was something else. Whatever Haley believed was happening to her here, in India, learning from J, it had become clear to her that she was being prepared to do something that mattered. Her presence on the battlefield and the amazing fact that she had lived through the ordeal cinched it for her. Why would the forces of good protect a simple girl from Boston?

There was a reason; there had to be. Haley knew she would be finding out what that reason was very quickly. It was ominous and large, looming unseen in the future, all misty but beginning to take shape. Maybe days or weeks away . . . maybe moments.

Their trek had gone on for so long she had lost track of what month it was. Many times they had to sleep without a campfire—it was too dangerous, J told her. On several occasions she could hear the voices of people close to their camp at night. She and J would sit quietly in the darkness for hours. After a time the voices would fade. When she asked what was the matter, her Teacher warned her that these people were not friendly and made a livelihood from robbing the innocent traveler. India, with all its sublime beauty and high level of spirituality, was also a magnet for the worst in men's hearts. "In every saint lies the sinner, child."

Haley stood and stretched her legs, after what seemed like an eternity sitting under the billowy protection of a shrub. "And in every sinner, a saint?"

"Quite so."

Haley had not forgotten Damor. Occasionally, dreams of his palace and the wooden soldiers with soulless eyes would shatter her usually deep sleep. Certainly, she hoped, Saling had forgotten her. Every time she thought of him a chill ran up her spine, terrifying her. As time wore on, though, these sudden moments of terror started to fade as she learned to control her fears.

There was no shortage of Saling's kind during the twentieth century. In every land they were awakening the masses with promises of a better world, but in the end becoming tyrants ten times worse then the tyrannical systems they overthrew. Politics, which she had once abhorred with disdain, now became a constant in her reflections.

"Why?" she asked J as he lit a fire. "Why am I having these thoughts?"

"The birth of the heart awakens the mind to that which is not in harmony with the plan of right human relations, love, and education. These are the three essential qualities for an evolving species. Each human being can find the mind either a liberating gift from God, or a weapon of unspeakable destruction and damnation."

"As we become more in tune with the nature of our heart," she finished for him, "what was always present, we can now see."

J stood and hugged her. "I believe there is little more I can teach you, my chela."

It had become a recurring theme. Her mind was seeing

everything, questioning everything—exactly like a child, new in the world. In particular, she saw fear. Fear was now as visible to her perceptions as the color of the sky.

The more she thought about it, the more Haley realized how many of her choices and decisions were really based on some form of fear—fear of the unknown, the unseen, her future, and fear of . . . destiny. Haley believed that her decisions, all based on advice from her own heart, were the best decisions, but that did nothing to dispel the aura of disaster that seemed to hover just out of reach. She had an unsettling feeling that this would become something she would have to deal with very seriously in the future.

For now there was India's beauty. The country was filled with sights people in other lands could only imagine. Her friends back home simply would not believe the tale she could tell. What could they say? Most would not give credence to it, or understand.

Haley sighed. *She* didn't understand. She glimpsed for the very first time what all servants of humanity someday experience: the intense loneliness that comes from treading the path of illumination. The more she became in tune with nature, her heart, and the profound unity that flowed endlessly from within, the more the mundane treasures of life failed to interest her: security, appearance, and the protocols of society.

She watched her teacher walking in front of her on the trail. His radiance outshone even the splendor of the sun. Was he lonely? Or had he mastered that illusion—if that was what it was—and become so joined with reality as to banish illusions forever? Would he share the secret with her?

Haley smiled. What things she had learned! Coming to India had not only changed her outlook, it had also changed her. No more silliness and sex games, playing coy for young men and worrying about makeup and all that balderdash. She had met her Soul, her Teacher, and discovered a fountain of joy within herself that outstripped any happiness she had ever known.

Except for one thing—being with her father. Thinking of Franklin, her smile became deeper. She now understood his comments about the wheel of life, cause and effect. His discussions of freedom and choice were clear now. With a soft murmur of gladness, she decided to write him as soon as possible and thank him for that learning and those wonderful books. The knowledge she had gained from him and his library was no longer theory; it was reality. Glancing toward J, she sent him a mental thank you as well. After a moment, J turned around, then smiled and nodded.

The miles of walking were taking their toll, though. To Haley, it had become a drudgery *and* an adventure. Though she was filled with beauty and joy, walking over the endless land of the ancients was tedious . . . monotonous. They had been in the high country for at least two weeks now, she estimated. Each day the journey was becoming more difficult, the air harder to breathe.

"Don't you ever get bored?" she asked as they walked along a small stream.

J smiled and shook his head. "Boredom indicates a mind not under control, not used by its owner."

Haley frowned. "But I've thought of everything at least three times. What else can I think of?"

J stopped, looking around, his eyes narrowed; finally, he reached down and picked up a rock, rubbing the surface with his sleeve. "This rock has nothing whatever to tell us?" He handed the stone to Haley. Taking the pear-sized stone, she looked it over. It was smooth and dark colored. Just like billions of other rocks in the world.

"Teacher," she said with hesitancy and some impatience, "it's *only a rock*. It is, according to Blavatsky, just an element of the mineral kingdom. Nothing more. Nothing less." Now it was J's turn to frown; but he also smiled. Starting to speak, Haley caught herself and stopped. Her tone was disrespectful, her heart warned her. She apologized immediately, remembering how he often used mundane realities to instruct her.

Waving off her apology, J took the rock from her hand. He held one end of it in each hand and attempted to break it into two pieces. He had her full attention. She had never met someone who could crush a rock with his bare hands, she thought skeptically; she looked down, feeling embarrassed about what would surely end in failure. J was *so old*, after all. Their eyes met.

Snap.

Haley's eyebrows arched and her mouth opened. Easily separating the two pieces, J held one half up and handed it to her. The rock was hollow and filled with beautiful crystal formations—multicolored and radiant.

"It's called a geode," J offered.

Haley began to laugh. "It's beautiful!"

"And so is the world, if we would but look deeper." He tossed her the other half.

"But . . . ," she stammered, "how . . . how can I apply this to thinking?" She had not taken her eyes off the geode; she was entranced by its beauty.

"Ask always these questions when thinking upon an idea, a person, a feeling, another thought, a thing or place, or an intuition:

'Is there nothing more I can understand about it?'

'How does this relate to life?'

'Is it symbolic, or can it be?'

'How can I use my understanding of this to further my understanding of *all* creation?'

'What causes are at work here?'

'What does htis teach me about spirit and matter, truth and illusion, the real and the unreal?'

'And finally . . . *why?*' "

"Why?" Haley asked, dumbfounded.

"Yes, *why*," J replied in earnest. "The greatest question is 'why.' In the answer to 'why' lies always the truth behind the manifestation. Without 'why,' all other knowledge is empty, pointless, and illusory."

Haley nodded, thinking through his words.

J stopped talking, then stepped closer to his student. "Until we can know life and its realities, we can never know ourselves . . . and vice versa."

Haley stood there, unable to think. J grinned and continued walking. She put the two severed pieces of the geode into her haversack, running to catch up. "When?" she asked earnestly.

J continued walking, ignoring her question.

"Teacher . . . *when?*"

J stopped and sighed, his disappointment showing. "Soon. Very soon."

The pass winding down from the peak finally smoothed out into a road, easing David's and his party's retreat down the mountainside. The two men who were killed had families: fathers, sisters, wives . . . children. For David, the weight of grief on his soul was only exceeded by the knowledge that he would have to face these poor wretches, now without fathers to provide for and love them.

Now he understood what Haley meant about being responsible; her actions had meant the death of a boy, as David's actions meant the death of dear friends.

Even this guilt was overshadowed by his singular knowledge that he had lost forever someone who had come deeply into his own heart, as well as the hearts of everyone else. His men said nothing, but their feelings couldn't be hidden. David knew they blamed him; rightly so.

"God-awful mess," he mumbled aloud to no one.

Occasionally, the mental image of an old man would come to him. "Go away. Leave me alone," David would whimper, shutting his eyes in hopes of banishing the kindly visage. The likeness would always fade. After a time, the image of his Teacher began to lessen, finally never returning.

For David Hampton, son of Sir Charles Hampton, governor and envoy from the Home Office, his disgraceful antics could never be erased or removed. He was told to *"return to his labors"* by his teacher. He had never disobeyed a suggestion from his saintly guide. And the first time he had done so, he had gotten others killed. Would he be given a second chance? And if so, how could he redeem such an unredeemable failure?

He could see John in his mind: the incredulous look in his eyes the split second that he knew he was falling, powerless to stop. The eyes didn't understand, seemed full of disappointment, but also said good-bye—all in the flash of one horrible, sickening moment. Could John forgive him for the mess David had brought them all into, somewhere in the afterlife?

He already missed the debates with Haley's brother; he had loved the way they bantered back and forth over politics. What would he say to Haley? And John's father—he would have to tell him as well.

"I'll make it up to you, John. I promise."

David's thoughts turned to Haley . . . would he ever find her? What had become of her? His rage and frustration had brought him to this point of dishonor and failure. He had never desired a wife and family; it had been a test never faced. Once Haley came into his life, however, he realized how much he loved her, how empty life was without her. His talks with and labors under his Teacher seemed far away and remote, now. Like his group seeking a way out of the pass, he too was lost. Would he ever find rest?

Zalub appeared at his side, raising up a canteen. "Please to drink this most refreshing water." His faithful friend had gathered some snow earlier and melted it.

David took it. "Thanks, old man." It tasted good. After taking a pull of what seemed like the best water he had ever tasted, he stopped, noticing Zalub looking down the trail, a worried look etched across his endlessly cheerful face.

David capped the canteen. "What's the matter?"

Zalub simply pointed. David realized when he saw it why they had not noticed it on the way up through the pass. It was embedded into the hillside in such a way that it could only be seen by looking down and from the south.

Built into a sheer cliff, above a deep ravine, was a monastery—all billowy white, giving the entire mammoth structure the appearance of being made of pure alabaster. Surrounding the spires of the monastery were ephemeral wreaths of clouds, adding to its otherworldly appearance.

"Halt the men," Hampton commanded. Zalub shouted for the column to halt, his Hindi very excited-sounding.

"Maybe we can pass and not to bother them," Zalub implored urgently.

Looking at the evanescent structure, it occurred to him that maybe they hadn't missed it before—that maybe they were meant to see it now. Hampton smiled. It was too beautiful and warm-looking to be dangerous. He remarked as much to his friend.

"But I have heard the strange stories of men who raise the devil so it can hound the mountains," Zalub exclaimed quietly. "It is better to hurry on!"

Looking up at the sky, David sighed. The sun was already gone, and in another hour the temperature would be dropping some thirty degrees. There was nowhere to camp, no wood to light a fire, and the ledge was too dangerous for the horses. He and his men would have to seek shelter soon. Then there was the risk of an avalanche if someone even coughed loudly at night. "Damnable luck," David mumbled and extracted his binoculars for a better look. Everything appeared quiet.

"I shall go and inquire as to the possibility of obtaining lodgings for the night, Zalub," he announced in a way that shut off discussion.

Zalub looked up at him in disbelief; he started to speak but was waved off. "Have the men follow me down the trail." Without another word, David nudged his horse into a fast walk and set off down the road. Zalub watched him, saying prayers under his breath and shaking his head.

Ten minutes later, David found himself at the turnoff to what appeared to be the entrance. The place was a fortress, and God only knew how long ago it had been built. There were the usual figures of Shiva and Krishna adorning the outer wall, but no visible sign of a door.

Knowing that Tibetan monks liked their privacy, David approached cautiously. Though known for their kindness and generosity, they had a reputation for restricting access to their temples to members of their order. If they would just allow his group shelter in the courtyard he had seen from above, his men would have a chance of staving off the biting cold. The trail dipped into a shallow ravine, the courtyard becoming invisible behind steep walls; it occurred to him that the ravine was man-made, putting any visitor at the disadvantage of having constantly to look up the sheer walls of the monks' home.

Then he stopped, suddenly aware of many eyes watching him. Think friendship, he told himself. Be yourself. It will be all right. David waited a moment, then urged his horse forward.

Fifty yards later, he reached the impassable wall he had seen from the trail. "How?" he asked aloud, amazed that the trail would simply end at nothing. There were no signs of a door anywhere. The wall was seamless and covered with simple characters from an ancient language. His horse shifted, tossing its head slightly. It was growing dark fast. The poor animal's ears were covered with frost. "There, there," he said soothingly, patting its neck. David pulled on the reigns, turning the horse around. In the distance, he noticed his party coming down from the ridge. They would just have to face the disappointment as best they could for the night.

"You are welcome," a voice said in broken English, startling him. Turning in the saddle, he discovered a single man standing in a great square opening in the wall he had believed to be completely solid. An elephant could have passed through the opening with ease. The man standing in the middle of the gaping opening was small: probably Tibetan, by the looks of him. The small priest appeared unafraid and looked confidently into Hampton's eyes. David returned the confident gaze, allowing his inner feelings of harmlessness and friendship to come through.

David liked him. He radiated a kindness and warmth he had felt before, and which he associated with those who lived under the banner of love and service.

"Most amazing," Hampton commented to himself. Clearing his throat, he shouted through the growing wind, "I say there, could you possibly have us for the night? We've nowhere to go and the pass is quite dangerous."

The priest nodded, still smiling. He then turned and disappeared into the darkness beyond. The wall remained open.

David turned around and waved to Zalub, who had now reached the turnoff. The group started toward him. A few minutes later, Zalub pulled up alongside him.

"It's all right, Zalub," he started warmly, "the chaps look friendly."

Zalub looked into the great yawning hole in the wall. "Were they wearing red caps?" he asked quietly.

David looked at him, curious. "No. None I could see. But I only saw one of them. Why do you ask?"

Zalub leaned closer to him. "Those who wear the red cap have sold their hearts to darkness."

David turned in his saddle and looked back toward the temple, concerned about what his friend had just told him; Zalub was not given over to fears or irrational behavior. If he said it, he believed it. David looked on. To him, a place had never seemed so peaceful and serene. He turned around. "Not to worry. All's well." With that, he waved to the men to follow him into the opening.

With David in the lead, the group filed out of the blustery wind and into the quiet darkness of a tunnel. There was no sign of the monk who had welcomed him. He looked down at the pistol strapped to his leg and shook his head; no, he wouldn't be needing that. If what Zalub had said was true, he doubted that bullets would be of much use. He would have to trust and believe—but after his earlier failure, these qualities might not mean much in the end. Was he unconsciously destroying his life and anyone foolish enough to come along? What horrible fate was he invoking for himself by acting so irresponsibly?

Presently, the darkness of the tunnel began to abate somewhat, revealing a large underground courtyard. The walls inside were made of the same material as those outside, white and polished-looking. The enclosure was a huge circle, with stairs in front and on each side that formed a triangle of steps down from some upper level. It was then he realized there was a solitary figure standing at the top of the stairs; he was old and clean shaven, wearing a simple daka and a yellow robe.

David looked behind him. All his men were now inside. He noticed, too, that the outer entrance had closed behind them. Turning around, he found the man in the robe standing in front of him. David blinked, his mind racing. That's a good fifty steps from top to base; how'd he do it so quickly? Hampton smiled and nodded. "We thank you for your kind hospitality. We won't be in the way. Just plop down right here, if it's not a bother."

It was then that David noticed the old man's eyes. They were kind, full of life and fun. He had seen these eyes before . . . but where? David dismounted and bowed, saying from his heart, "*Namaste.*"

"*Namaskara*, my welcome guests," the old man replied in a thick accent. David righted himself, still unable to shake the sense of familiarity, of knowing the small man bowing before him. David started to speak.

"Leave your animals," the monk said, smiling, "and come, if you will, with me, where the air is warm for tired travelers."

"Thank you. Thank you very much. We're most grateful."

Hampton turned to Zalub and his men. "Let's go, shall we? Bet there's a hot meal in there somewhere."

Zalub glanced between David and the monk, obviously weighing something in his mind. "As you wish," he said finally, with an iota of hesitancy. Moments later, several small Tibetan men wearing yellow robes appeared behind the group.

The monk lifted a skinny, withered arm and pointed toward nothing in particular. "These men will see to the horses."

A flash of shame tore through David. "I'm terribly sorry," he gushed, extending his hand, "my name is David Hampton."

The monk's smile widened as he took the offered hand. "We know." Hampton's uneasiness started the monk and the other priests laughing in a genial way. Seeing David's blush turn a deeper red, the monk stopped chuckling. "Please to follow."

Hampton stood there with his mouth open; then he smiled. It was the same way his Teacher had greeted him, so many years ago in Ceylon, when he had first arrived from Oxford to begin his training in the diplomatic corps. He turned to Zalub. "Not to worry. All's right."

They were led into a long, low corridor which opened into another large room fitted out with several small tables without chairs. At the end of the room was a large fireplace already roaring and crackling.

The monk stopped and extended a bony finger to the room in general. "You may rest here."

David nodded his gratitude, holding his hands together as in prayer and salutation. The man smiled, turned, then walked away through an open door, closing it behind him. David turned to his men, motioning that it was okay. Some dropped where they were, others scurried to the fireplace and began to strip off their parkas. Zalub stayed next to David. "I will not sleep tonight."

David turned to him, slapping him on the shoulder and laughing. "If you don't, you won't be much good tomorrow."

Several hours later, the fire had died down and most of the men were asleep. David, watchful of his entourage, decided against his own advice to Zalub. He would remain awake and make sure there was no foul play. The memories of John and his two servants—coupled with an agonizing pain in his heart—gave him no other choice.

David noticed presently that the old man who had greeted him earlier was standing in front of him; there was a fantastic glow around him, extending fifty feet in every direction.

"I didn't see you," David apologized, getting to his feet, still amazed at the little man's radiant splendor. The man said nothing, instead motioning for him to follow. It occurred to David that he could not go; the safety of his men came first, in spite of the totally harmless atmosphere and countenance of their host. Before David could speak, the old man turned to him with a wave of his hand. "Fear not. No harm will come to you and yours while you are in our care."

Hampton could not believe what had just happened. He had clearly heard the words said to him, but the man's mouth hadn't opened. How was that possible? Again, before he could speak, the old man gestured toward David's feet. "On this plane of beingness, vocal cords, air, and lungs are not required for speech."

David looked down. Looked down at *himself lying asleep on a bedroll*.

"You are not dead," his guide answered before he could ask the question. "You are merely out of your body—as many are, each night we sleep."

As he looked around the room, he could tell which men were asleep and which were just dozing, as there was a bright radiance around those who were still in their bodies, while those who had left showed a slender, silvery white cord emanating from their hearts that extended and disappeared into the ceiling of the room. David laughed. It explained so much! Why he sometimes felt like he had traveled to distant places when he awoke in the morning, or met people he had not seen before, having that always inexplicable feeling of knowing them! It instantly elucidated the mystery of dreams that seemed too real to be just imagination.

"Man's knowledge of reality is very limited," the priest said calmly. "It will be another two hundred years before he understands the higher planes of beingness. Come."

David turned to follow. "How is this possible? I mean, how am I able to do this?"

Without turning around, the priest replied, "Your Teacher wishes it so. Please come, someone is waiting for you." The priest was already at the door. David followed, intrigued that the mere thought of following him brought him there directly—as though he had traveled the distance of thirty feet with one step. The priest disappeared through the door. With some degree of hesitance, Hampton eased up to the solid surface and extended his hand. It passed through easily, as though the door were made of steam, the act causing some tingling in his own, semitransparent hand.

Pulling his hand back, he stopped and turned around. There he was, sleeping deeply. "Most amazing."

In a flash, he found himself sitting on a dais in a brightly lit room. The light was so brilliant that he tried to shield his eyes from the glare. It occurred to him that the illumination wasn't coming from any lamp or other light source; it was coming from the gentleman seated in front of him.

"Welcome, my son," the man said. He was impressive. Long, beautiful brown locks flowed evenly about his shoulders. Deep blue eyes . . . kind and noble, with a perfect face. He radiated love, pure and simple. His demeanor was so humble and accommodating that David Hampton felt instantly at peace. Then he looked down, a feeling of smallness overcoming him. What to do with his eyes—look at him? NO. That would be disrespectful, especially of someone whose spiritual caliber was obviously very high. He decided to keep his eyes instead on the hem of the man's plain white robe.

"I am known as Termas," the gentleman said. David was taken aback by the gentleness of his voice, how melodious it was, and how full of interest and goodwill. He wanted to speak but found words difficult; there would be no point in introducing himself—the man knew who he was, of that he was certain. Inside, he could feel a peace that surpassed anything he had previously known—even that of his teacher. He knew also that he was sitting in front of his Master, something his Teacher and he had talked about before. He had known that one day this would come. And now, finally, here he was sitting in the presence of a Mahatma.

"My son," Termas began softly, interrupting his thoughts, "your path is not where you seek it."

David's eyes closed. His Teacher had warned him, and now his Master. He felt like crying. In all the times he had imagined meeting a Master of Wisdom, it had never occurred to him that his first visit with a true holy man would be one that involved his failure. It took a supreme effort of will to keep from sobbing out loud.

"Forgive me, Master." It was sincere and heartfelt. He knew the Brotherhood had only the highest intentions for humanity, and if they advised something, it was for the good of all. David had failed not only himself but also all those to whom he had dedicated his life in service.

Termas had warmth and understanding in his eyes. "Let us look to future labors, young brother, and not be confined by what is past."

David nodded. There was no condemnation or rebuke. It was as the books and his Teacher had always said; these Masters were masters of compassion and love. David never wanted to leave. If he could stay here at Termas's feet forever, he would.

Presently the old priest appeared. It was time to go. Gathering his strength to look a last time into the eyes of the One he knew had always cherished and protected him, David lifted his head. Termas was smiling his love.

And what Love!

The joy that filled David was beyond description. The stain that darkened his heart with regret and agony evaporated, replaced by an intuitive understanding that some great power was at work in his circumstances. The knowledge, wherever it came from, was deeply welcome. "Thank you."

As he was starting to rise, Termas extended his right hand and placed it over David's head. David swooned, as the energy of a thousand suns burst into his mind and heart. In the briefest flash of a moment, Lord David Charles Hampton II of Hampton Manor saw for the first time the true identity of his nature. Before he had the time to understand what had been granted to him, he found himself snapped back into his body.

"Many years hence," David heard echoing in his head as he lost consciousness, "thy giving soul will be afforded a deeper understanding of the mystery of the Self."

The next morning he awoke with the taste of honey in his mouth, and a wonderful scent of incense. Had it been a dream? So wonderful and full of joy as it was, it could not have been anything but real. He found he could remember every detail, every nuance, every word. David sat up, filled with the energy and enthusiasm of twenty men. "Thank you. Thank you. Thank you."

The others were stirring, as a group does, at first one or two, then the whole assembly.

He looked over at Zalub. Zalub was still there, in his own dream. Presently, Zalub opened his eyes, smiling, then looked over at David.

"You—?"

"Yes," he replied, cutting David off. "A most wonderful night. I shall not soon forget it."

"And the chamber?"

Zalub nodded. David smiled and embraced him. "My brother."

"Allah is too kind," Malakar announced quietly to his assembled men as they lay hidden behind a rise overlooking a shallow pass. He lifted his binoculars and peered through them one more time, smiling. Below, in the pass, wind and snow whipping around them, were two solitary figures walking slowly.

Watching a little longer, Malakar nodded his approval and lowered his glasses. "They do not see us," he whispered with glee—the effect of his happiness at finding such easy prey rippling through his men.

Malakar rested his hand upon his .308 Enfield and sighed. Damor had said he wanted the girl alive . . . if possible. Pleasing the maharaja would mean a great reward and the realization of his dream of being a raja himself.

One of his men appeared suddenly at his side; it was Serge the Armenian, who had been blinded in one eye by a ricochet in a botched robbery attempt some years earlier. Serge had a price on his head, some said, for raping a young girl and then slaughtering her family to remove the witnesses.

"Let us kill them now while we can!" Serge implored, excitement blazing in his one good eye. Malakar slapped him, knocking the man down. "Fool! Get back to your position." The man staggered to his feet, blood running freely from his mouth, and skulked back to his place on the ridge.

Malakar's eyes followed him, his hand on the dagger in his belt. Once Serge was out of sight, he looked again through the binoculars. Maybe the pair below had heard the scuffle? No. There was no sign of alarm.

Malakar sighed again. Serge was right. These two had slipped away too many times, making a fool of him. If he failed again he would have to face Saling. Fear and panic swept through Malakar, the idea of confronting that sorcerer terrifying him. He waved to the men nearest him. "When they come around that last ridge, there," he said, pointing, "fire until they move no more." The two dirty men smiled and quickly spread the word. Malakar could hear rounds being chambered and hammers cocked.

Malakar raised the glasses, but only one hand responded. The other hand burned as though a match had been lit under it. "What?" he said absently, dropping the binoculars. He couldn't believe what his eyes told him. He had only two fingers left on his right hand. How could that be? There was another burning feeling in his chest, as his shirt and coat exploded in a storm of tattered cloth. What was happening?

He turned to his left, coming face-to-face with a man who no longer possessed a mouth, the back of his head having been blown out. Then he saw it: the puffs of smoke from twenty rifles, all firing as fast as possible. Sinking, all things blurry and incoherent, Malakar fell to his knees. He could hear someone shouting about a trap. Screams—terrible sounding—ripped through the icy air.

It was then that he noticed her. There was something wrong with her throat: a horrible wound where a woman would wear a necklace. Then he remembered. She hadn't changed a bit in the twenty years since he had seen her last. She had warned him that this would come to pass and he had not listened, scoffing at her. No, instead, he had killed her for her words. Malakar looked closely at her. Her eyes were not angry; they were sad, like a parent's eyes when her child does not understand. Then she became an old woman—the woman he had butchered not one month before. "You! You infidel bitch. My blood is not yours, whore!" Like the image of the other, she expressed no hate or condemnation.

Malakar smiled, his teeth red with blood. "You have come for vengeance?" he grunted hoarsely. The woman's expression didn't change, nor did she respond to his question. Instead, she began to fade. In her place stood two men.

"Zalub, get the sergeant and his med-kit," the taller one ordered. It occurred to Malakar that the man looked familiar. Malakar coughed, blood spraying everywhere. He realized he was lying down, someone holding his head up, saying "Why were you going to kill those people? Tell me!"

It seemed like such a long time ago, chasing after that damn girl. "I almost had her, you know," he said sadly, "I could never catch her. Me, the great Malakar, could not catch a stupid girl."

Hampton's eyes blazed. "Girl? What girl?" The wounded man's eyelids fluttered as the light in his eyes went out, his head falling limp in his arms. "Damn you! What girl?"

The man fell lifeless to the ground. David stared at him for a few moments, then closed his eyes and said a prayer for the dead man's soul. After a minute, he climbed up on the embankment. The pass below was empty and unapproachable from the ridge. Whoever they were, they were gone now. He hoped they would be safe.

Zalub appeared at his side. "Three are dead. Others wounded. What do you wish?"

David did not answer right away but looked longingly down

into the pass. Finally, he turned and faced the carnage. "Let's get them bandaged up. There is a hospital at the post in Bangor. Bury the others." Zalub turned and left, shouting orders.

Having regained his composure, David knelt next to the dead bandit and closed the lids of his lifeless eyes; he felt sad for the man, his voice almost a whisper. "Why were you trying to kill those people?"

CHAPTER 12

The Initiation
of a Server

Life's purpose is to lead
the searcher within.
Learning this, a being profits.
All else is intrigue.

Haley was exhausted. She had been walking up an icy ravine for over three days, and though they'd been on the road for what seemed like an eternity, J still wouldn't say where they were heading or when they would get there.

They walked in shifts—hike two hours, rest thirty minutes. Each morning, J would produce a vial of foul-tasting liquid, saying only "It is good for the blood." Taking it, she felt no hunger or cold; but her lungs hurt, and every so often she would have to brush ice from her eyelashes. Her concern for their survival at such a high altitude, in a climate that had no forgiveness for stupidity, increased as the weather turned decidedly nasty. At times she could lean on the wind—the force of it able to hold her upright.

The trip was not without strain; it seemed that every fear, every emotion she had ever felt came to the surface to be cleansed by the spontaneous disciplines J would improvise. The more

Haley watched and learned, the more she realized how little she really knew about who she was and what made her go on.

When she felt pressured to think and act at her very best, she realized her emotions would kick in as a defense mechanism to shield her personality. She learned also that these mechanisms were the forces that kept the real woman inside her in bondage and slavery. Her father had once told her, when teaching her how to catch a baseball, to look at the ball as it came to her and not flinch and shy away. Haley had argued that it was normal to flinch—as any animal would when an object comes to it that can inflict harm. Franklin had smiled at her schoolgirl psychology. "Haley, whenever your body decides and acts of its own accord, it is master. This is why you must learn to catch the ball. It's the first step."

His words, spoken seven years ago, finally made sense to her in the icy regions of Nepal.

On the first day in the pass, J insisted that they take a detour from the main trail, though Haley protested that the path didn't seem like a path at all. With some hesitancy, she followed him up the tortuous winding ridge that sported a dizzying mountain on one side and a bottomless gorge on the other. The rock- and ice-strewn trail was steep and narrow, making progress necessarily slow. On the second day, they reached a height in the Himalayan range where the world disappeared under the canopy of clouds—it seemed as if they were walking on the ceiling of heaven itself. Even the sun made a quick appearance and disappearance—obviously not liking the locale. Its brief meridian brought little warmth or comfort to their journey.

Haley noticed it before it happened—just as she anticipated the ringing of the phone back home before it rang. Like a rippling wave, tremendous sounds—*boom-boom-boom*—of explosions flowed through and around them in the icy pass, freezing the pair in their tracks. J stopped and watched the hills, looking for something. Haley watched J.

Scanning the horizon, she couldn't see any clouds at their altitude—the rumbling had reminded her of thunderclaps in the far distance. Haley had learned to appreciate the unpredictability of nature while in India, and knew that life or death could be determined in a matter of seconds in the Himalayas. Though alarmed and ready, she did not have to act; the rumbling lasted but a few moments. Once it subsided, J moved on without saying a word. The thunder never recurred.

After two hard hours of quiet marching, Haley begged for a rest. Plopping herself down on the frozen ground, she watched her Teacher. J, always quiet and reserved, was unusually silent today. She could feel that something more than she could perceive was going on; the thought of what that something might be made her feel uneasy.

Haley scanned the trail, her eyes following the winding pass as it curved up and beyond the peak. The sun dropped behind the horizon, taking ten degrees of temperature and her hopes of having a warm fire sometime soon with it. It was only three o'clock. She sighed, realizing there were miles still to go before they would be able to leave the windswept ledge.

That's when she saw it.

A great boulder had fallen on the path not one hundred yards away. It was enormous—the size of a house. The little ledge they had been hiking on looked like a rope stretched to the breaking point, barely able to hold the great rock against the will of gravity that demanded it.

Before she could speak, J moved forward a few paces. "I see it." He was already moving swiftly when she stood up. Haley scrambled after him. Five minutes later she was standing next to a solitary slab of solid rock that appeared to have broken off somewhere in the heights above them, taking tons of earth with it as it slid down.

Upon completing his inspection of the massive obstacle, J informed her that it would be too dangerous to climb over it, as it looked as though the huge slab of granite would continue on its journey down the side of the mountain with hardly any provocation. Haley walked up to the mammoth rock and peered over the edge. It was a drop of several thousand feet, which took her breath away. She literally could not see the bottom of the gorge.

"If ever the word *abyss* was appropriate . . ." she commented quietly. Her heart sank.

They would have to backtrack the entire distance they had come since yesterday morning. Five hours of walking uphill—all to be redone. In spite of the setback, she smiled. If this trip had taught her anything, it was not to let life's problems upset her joy; so with a chuckle, her smile turned into exultation. "It's a beautiful day! I'll lead us back." She turned around.

A reflex action, beyond any control, made her shriek out loud. *"Eeeeeeeeeeeeeeee!"* Haley fell back against the mountain, her scream piercing the air, its echo booming around the peaks.

Standing squarely in front of her was a small man wearing a brightly colored yellow robe. He hadn't reacted to Haley's alarm, standing as immovable on the trail as the boulder—silent, ominous, quiet. The man was Tibetan, by the looks of him; his face was small, oblong, and very weathered from years of living high above the world. Cold, dry air does that to the skin, she remembered. Haley backed up the trail cautiously, bumping into J, who quickly stepped around her, giving salaams to the man. She relaxed, watching her Teacher and the peculiar man who had appeared out of nowhere, as they talked in short quick sentences. From time to time, the stranger would glance at Haley and smile knowingly.

"This is our guide," J said, turning around. "He will see us the rest of the way."

Haley nodded to the man and smiled, relieved—there was a way around the boulder, after all. Then she noticed that he was watching her intensely, obviously thinking something through. His eyes twinkled greetings and friendship. Haley relaxed a little more, intrigued by his curious inspection of her. Without further ado, the man turned and walked right through the sheer cliff wall, vanishing into the granite.

"Huuuuu!" Haley gasped, her hand going to her mouth in disbelief. "Did you see—"

Then J walked through after the guide, smiling at her as he too vanished into the frozen rock. Haley stood—seemingly forever—staring at the place where two people had entered the side of a mountain. Her Teacher and the Tibetan had used the rock as though a door existed for their private use, hidden from all eyes. But that couldn't be, her mind told her, reminding her that what she had just seen was completely impossible.

There was an eerie silence there on the path, a silence only heard when a person is alone and far, far away from ordinary life. A wind came up, whistling and whipping around her. "J?" she called out plaintively, the echo reverberating around the peaks and finally fading. She waited a minute in the roaring quiet. There was no answer, the mountains, gorges, and peaks silent in their knowledge. A rock fell somewhere in the distance, its *krack-krack* the only answer to her plea. Haley became frightened. She had been abandoned on a ridge overlooking a bottomless crevice, somewhere in the Himalayas.

She walked over to the place where the two men had vanished and extended her hand. The rock was icy cold. Solid. Immovable. Unyielding.

How did they do it? Didn't they know she was not advanced

like them and would need help in passing through solid rock? Touching a sheer wall that soared higher than she could see, Haley began to doubt that she had witnessed the event at all. Maybe it was just an illusion, another test for her to work out. Could be they were standing right there, right now, watching her to see what she would do. Even as she considered that possibility, her heart told her that this was not so. Haley reached out and touched the wall of rock again—no change. How? *How?*

All at once she became terrified. What if she were stranded here, with night coming on in a few hours? What if robbers were to come up the trail and find her? Haley closed her eyes; this couldn't be happening. Why? Why would J leave her like this? Fear turning into terror, reason succumbing to panic, Haley's heart and mind stopped functioning. She could no longer see clearly. Everything around her—the sky, horizon, ground, and icy snow—all seemed to mix together in the weird confusion of terror.

"Stop it. Stop it. Get a hold of yourself." After a few moments, the panic subsided. Taking a few breaths, she decided to look at the facts and then act responsibly.

One: Maybe J had been ordered to leave her like this. Maybe she hadn't passed some test.

Two: There is a way—there has to be.

Three: What? Where is the answer?

Four: Four . . . My God. There is no four. The panic began to creep back, as one wild fear after another tore into her. Haley crumpled down on the trail and started to whimper.

He appeared quite out of nowhere, walking up behind her, with jet black hair down to his shoulders, dark eyes, and an easy smile. He was definitely American and wore a zipped-up, black leather flight jacket she had seen pilots wear. "So, how long are you going to let an illusion keep you out here in this horrible weather?"

No introductions. No name. Straight and to the point.

Haley blinked in relief—saved!—what? Illusions! What . . . what was he talking about? "I have to sit down." The stranger clasped his hands behind his back, grinning.

"You are going to help me, right?" she asked. "I mean, that's why you're here."

"Maybe . . . maybe not. Depends on you, really." He was casual about it, even bored. He sat down next to her, gazing directly into her eyes.

Haley looked down at her hands. "Am I dreaming?"

The stranger stared hard at her, shrugging his shoulders. "A dream to some, to others . . ."

"A nightmare?" Haley finished, searching for some clue in the man's face. He remained as impassive as the stones around them, choosing to gaze off into the distance. It occurred to her that he was aware of her thoughts. Who was he? From the Brotherhood? He smiles at that thought, but says nothing. I'm not a mind reader like you, Mister Whoever-You-Are, so if you *are* here to help . . . then she realized she liked him. Whatever or whoever he was, he radiated goodness.

Gathering her wits and still sniffling from her crying fit, she decided to get through this with as little nonsense as possible. "My name is Haley. And you are . . . ?"

The man looked at her as if she was from another planet. "You were just going to sit out here and cry until you froze to death?" he said, ignoring her question. "I have that correct, yes?"

Haley looked away, her face slightly red. She wanted direct-ness, but this was more than she had expected.

"No wonder they called me." He picked up a piece of ice and sucked on it. "I was flying barnstormers in Ohio with a friend when I got the word. Not a minute too soon, by the look of things."

Cringing inside from the obvious insult, Haley turned to him and barked sharply, "Where is my teacher?" All at once, she realized that she was being defensive and rude. J had told her once before to watch her speech, as it would reveal just who was talking. Right then, the only thing talking was fear.

He smiled. "Sitting in front of you." The flier was dead serious, his eyes even and unblinking.

"You mean you are J?" This, Haley could not believe; she was sensitive to people's vibrations, knowing others by the way they felt to her. Again he gave her a look that said she was slow getting on the train.

"No," he said with a sigh, "I mean that, for now, *I* am your teacher." He looked around, ignoring her again. "Good a place as any, I suppose."

A roaring log fire, complete with licking flames three feet high, appeared directly in front of him—it was a good fire, too: one that had been long burning, with embers and smoking coals deep beneath the stacked wood. Haley got to her feet and stepped back, her mouth wide open.

The stranger moved close to the fire, standing and rubbing his hands over the flames, pleased with himself. "That's much better." Then he looked at her, puzzled. "Aren't you coming over to get warmed? Can't learn while you're freezing your keester off."

"How . . . how did you do that?" Haley hadn't moved.

He looked over at her with a curious expression. "Cold over there, isn't it?" The American was enjoying this, she noticed. Haley collected herself and made some attempt at composure. There was no reason to be surprised by miracles after what she had been through. She had learned a great many things—one being that members of the Brotherhood possessed powers and abilities that made them truly supermen. Still, she had not quite gotten used to the display of these endowments. One day, when she herself became advanced, she might do these things too. But, she sighed, that was probably lifetimes away.

"Load of hooey," the man offered, interrupting her thoughts.

"What?" Haley asked, moving toward the fire. The heat felt good; it was the first deep warmth she had felt in weeks. It brought a smile of relief to her face. She noticed he was watching her, a knowing grin playing on his face. It was then she saw it— the glow about him. Look for it and it wasn't there. But, it *was there* just the same. Whoever he was, he radiated a soft white glow just as J did. And something else . . . his voice; his voice was magnetic and soothing.

"Look," he started, staring deeply into the flames as though lost in them, "it's not about lifetimes, or advancement, or any of that other business." Then he looked up and straight into Haley's eyes. "It's about conviction, doubt, and self-esteem."

He had her full attention.

"You've read Besant, right?" he asked. "In one of her books, didn't she say that her Master told her once that one way to attainment was a matter of conviction and will, and that there were Arhats in existence who had achieved that exalted place of spiritual beingness by simply acting and believing as if it were so?"

"Now wait just a minute," Haley countered, "saying you are something when you are not is pure vanity and ego." She had him, Haley realized with a smile. Get out of that one, flyboy.

The American smiled with her. "True, true. If you say you are and you aren't, that is vanity. But I am not talking about illusions within illusions or diseases of the mental body. What I am talking about is walking through this wall!"

And, like the others before him, the abrupt man with black

hair turned and walked directly into a solid granite wall. Disappearing.

Haley blinked . . . then groaned, "Not again."

"See what I mean?" a voice behind her said.

Haley screamed while jumping a good two inches off the ground. "Don't . . . don't do that!"

The American who could create fires and walk through solid rock sauntered around her, laughing, finally halting next to the undiminished flames. Haley waited for him to say something, to explain. He didn't. Instead, he stared off into the flames as if she didn't exist. Bored, he whistled a soft, lilting tune: something popular, but she could not quite place what.

The flier stopped whistling. "If you insist on having limitations, limited you will be." He started the tune up again, from the beginning.

Haley looked at him sharply. "You're saying that because I don't believe I can pass through that wall, therefore I can't."

The American lit up. "Excellent. Go on."

"All right. But before I do, answer my question. If we say we are something, but we aren't, isn't that vanity and ego?"

His smile was nonstop. "Good question. The difference is this. The person lost in vanity *knows* he isn't anything, but pretends to others that he is. This is vanity and egotism—very dangerous. It's like lying to yourself. But the person who has conviction *knows* he is already divine. It's his personality that needs convincing, or training, or practice. This is attainment. Once we recognize our divine nature, once we understand what limitless creations of light, love, and power we truly are, vanity and ego dissipate—though usually not without some struggle."

He could see that Haley was thinking it over. She looked confused over certain details. That could be fixed easily. He walked up to her. "The vain person," he continued, "doesn't really know she is a divine and complete being. She thinks she is a nothing—or maybe she believes that she has acquired a few qualities that she has developed. This is why she puts on the show of attainment. Her vanity is in convincing others that she has what she, herself, believes she does not have."

Haley stared at him. The man who flew airplanes in Ohio stared back.

"Understand?"

Haley didn't answer, instead mumbling something along negative lines under her breath.

"Now it's your turn," he declared eagerly.

Haley blinked, her eyes searching. "Um . . . I forget."

"You were going to tell me about attainments and—"

"Oh yes!" Haley brightened, her thoughts becoming clear. "You said that if we believed we were limited and were unable to do something, then we couldn't. Right?"

"Loosely, yes."

"But what you really mean," she continued with some pride, "is that because of our identification with limitation, the limitation becomes real."

The flier's eyes widened. With his smile, he nodded. "Go on."

Haley was breathless with excitement. "Then, the solution is to see the problem or limitation as something other than a problem or limitation. Once seen in its true light, it can be overcome!"

He clapped quietly, nodding his approval. Haley beamed as only a learner can, doing well in the eyes of the teacher.

He took a few steps closer and folded his arms. "For example," he said.

"What?" Haley twitched nervously; he meant for her to practice what she had just preached. Then she found herself looking closely at him. He was young. Or at least young-looking. His flier's scarf was draped casually around his neck. Deep

230

behind his eyes was a sorrow. For a moment, he looked like Atlas, carrying some tremendous weight on his shoulders.

"Show me," he said, his eyes glinting mischief. "Give me a practical example of this Great Truth."

"I don't understand." Haley shot him a sideward glance—her heart pained. He recoiled from the lie, as though it were some noxious cloud floating from her to him.

"Yes you do. You do understand. And if you lie to me again . . ."

"I—"

"Don't say it!"

He was upset, she could see that, and he moved back and forth in front of the fire rolling his eyes. Instead of moving forward and growing, she wasn't doing very well here. He stopped pacing.

"If you say the *I* word in front of something, then you are telling your little universe, which comprises your body, mind, and emotions, that you *are* that thing."

Haley stared at him, her eyes wide and frightened, knowing that this man—whoever he was—was someone who knew something about the way things worked. Here was someone who was going to help her understand—in spite of the queer feeling rising up from within her, warning her to be as honest as possible. "I'm sorry for lying."

"Want to know a secret about lies?"

"Yes."

"Lies do two very unpleasant things. One: they short-circuit the brain's ability to remember detail, because every time we lie, we distort information in the areas of the brain that store things. Two: they burn the petals in your heart center, which in turn limits your Soul or Guardian Angel's ability to advise and assist you."

Haley looked ashen— the information was terrifying. Like

most people, she had told so many "white lies" that she doubted they could be counted.

The flier walked back to the fire. "Moving on. The seat of our personal identification is how we see ourselves. And in that light, we make our universe."

Haley stared at him; it made sense. J had mentioned something about placing ourselves mentally where we believed we should be.

He waved her over to the fire, and she moved closer, letting the heat fill her lungs. "How do you get to Carnegie Hall?"

This was easy, she mused, remembering the old school joke. "Practice."

"Wrong."

Unable to say anything in response to this contradiction to what was accepted reality, she waited for him to explain.

"Everyone practices. Everyone tries at something. Most fail. Why?"

A weird sensation began to rise up within her. A great truth was coming; this she knew from being with J. Whenever he taught her something that gave her a wonderful insight into human character, she felt goose bumps. "They fail because . . . because . . ."

The flier put his finger to his lips, urging her to let him finish the sentence. ". . . because they did not—at any time—believe they would ever be good enough to make it. They doubted. They had no vision. They thought so little of themselves as divine creative beings that the universe simply responded to their conviction. They believed they were average musicians, and so they were."

The flier realized he was going too fast. "Look. If we say 'I can't,' then we can't. If we say, 'I am angry,' then we are handing over our identity to a negative emotional state—anger, in this case—and saying to it, 'When you are active in me, you are master.' The emotional elemental hears this command, and says, 'Great! Now, whenever I kick in this negative emotion, I can run her life, her mind, her body, and do with it what I will!' "

He could see her mulling the information over. "It gets worse," he added quietly. She shot him a quick glance.

He started slowly, trying to let her see the words in her mind. "When we say the deeper mantras—and that is what every statement beginning with the I word is—we can either destroy or build our lives."

Haley thought about what this strange man who flew planes was saying to her. "I don't—" She stopped herself and frowned.

"Here's how to fix it." He slowed down his pace a little more. "Every time you feel lost or frustrated and are about to commit the great SIN of identifying with the illusion and not the reality, say . . ." He stopped speaking.

Haley couldn't stand the suspense. "Well?"

The flier looked off into space, grinned, then glanced at her. "I have a better idea. You say a negative identification, and I'll give you the correct opposite."

Haley stared at him. "Okay. Fine. How about . . . *I can't.*"

The stranger looked at her, accepting the challenge. "The best one, right from the start, eh?" He was smiling hugely.

"I am a supreme and divine being, with no limitation other than my karmic debts, my ignorance, and those bodies that wish to defy my spiritual divinity."

"I am tired."

"Good. Good one," he replied, happily.

"I use a body that is tired right now; it is not me. I will rest it . . . or not, as *I* see fit."

Haley thought about it. She knew she was not only a body— she had seen hers sleeping.

"It's impossible," she countered quickly.

"Impossible cannot exist for me—the wise, creative, and loving being that I AM, therefore I can do anything I wish to, whenever I wish."

He stood waiting—proud of himself—for her to do her worst. Haley glared at him, on the verge of laughing out loud, her mind racing furiously for another example. Meanwhile the flier bowed, accepting his victory.

After a minute, she sighed. "I understand now. Thanks."

"So?"

Haley looked down at the ground, closing her eyes. She knew what he wanted.

"Make it something simple, you know, for starters."

Digging her toe into the ground, she shook her head.

The flier glanced at the cloudless sky. "Rain . . . rain is good. Make it rain for us, oh-creative-being-that-you-are." Haley looked up at a sky so clear that in broad daylight the stars seemed visible. Then, she glanced at a roaring fire that fifteen minutes before did not exist.

"I see rain everywhere." Haley closed her eyes and was concentrating very hard. "It is raining very severely. Clouds are forming overhead. Rain is coming down everywhere." She opened her eyes. Not even a wisp of cloud to be seen. The flier was drinking a hot beverage of some sort and eating a sandwich. Haley's stomach growled.

"Who *are* you?" She eyed his food and contemplated asking for some.

"You may call me . . . Don." Don bowed, then looked at her suspiciously. "Whip up your own vittles—these are mine."

She pouted, her growling stomach becoming more insistent. She began to dig again into the dirt with her foot, glancing at him from time to time. He was ignoring her completely, even looking off into another direction back down the trail.

"Look in your front pocket," Don said between bites.

Reaching in, she could feel something bulky. Wrapped in wax paper was a cucumber sandwich—her favorite. "Thank you." Haley began to peel back the paper.

Don stopped eating. "Kinda dry, though, without something to drink." He was smiling. Taking his last bite and gulping down his drink, Don stood and cracked his knuckles. "Here comes that drink."

The first bite of what looked to be a wonderful lunch was ruined by no less than a total downpour of rain on Haley, completely soaking her and the ground where she stood. Within twenty seconds she was drenched, the sandwich ruined, and then, abruptly as it had started, the rain stopped. She looked at the soggy repast, which presently—no longer being held together by firm bread—fell apart to the ground. She scowled at Don, who was already laughing to the point of tears.

"Very funny." Haley began stripping off her wet parka. After a few more guffaws, Don walked over and handed her his flight jacket. "This will keep you warm—for a while—but it won't be any good come nightfall."

"Why? How could you do this and not me?"

"Simple." He began to clean his teeth with a toothpick. "You doubted it could happen, doubted your ability to create and control. Haley, you even dared me to make it happen—the whole while remaining a skeptic—here." He was pointing to his heart. "Quite frankly, since you never believed in yourself, why should Nature?" She hadn't seen him pull it from a pocket, but nevertheless, Don was puffing on a lit cigar. "Havana," he said with a smile.

Haley kicked at the remnants of her sandwich. "How come you didn't get wet?"

"What? And ruin my day?"

Haley looked at him, searching, then at the granite wall. Without another word, she marched directly over to the icy mountain and threw herself into it.

Don turned his cup over, emptying its contents onto the fire. A cloud of steam rose up, then vanished, dissipated by the wind. Wrapping his arms tightly around himself, he watched as the fire and any trace that it had existed vanished, leaving him standing alone on an isolated trail.

Don motioned to the mountain. "You can keep the jacket." A quick flash of light—too fast to be clear—and the flier from Ohio was gone.

❧ CHAPTER 13 ❧

To Be

It is often said
that there is no time like the present
for learning and being.

She was beautiful. Feminine perfection, dressed in a floor-length gown. Her blond hair was supple and luxurious, and she wore a simple gold chain around one wrist. Even more brilliant than her beauty was the soft and gentle radiance shining from her pale blue eyes.

"I am Liana."

Smiling, Haley realized how filthy she was. From what she could see of herself, every part was grimy. "Haley. Haley Olsten."

The woman nodded, then extended her hand. "I'll bet I know where we can find a hot bath and some good food."

Haley perked up. "That would be wonderful. Thank you."

Following Liana down a beautifully lit hall, Haley was not surprised to find her or this most interesting place mere feet inside a granite mountain. Its walls were covered with tapestries, a fresco here and there, with various paintings. Some of the paintings looked new, while others appeared to be centuries old. She thought she recognized some of the works.

"Yes," the woman responded to Haley's unspoken thought, "these are the originals."

They continued down the hall, reaching a T-section, and then turned left. Haley watched Liana. She smiled constantly, her eyes bright. Right then, Haley wanted to be like her. "I've never seen a woman Master before."

Without breaking stride, Liana laughed. "Well, I am doubtful you are seeing one now."

Haley looked down at her fidgeting hands. "I'm sorr-"

"No need to apologize. After what you've been through, I would think you'd want to rest after your bath." Haley was sure—she could definitely smell . . . roses! The scent seemed to be emanating from Liana.

Finally, they reached a door that *swooshed* open as they approached. Haley looked for the person who had opened the door—no one. "Marvelous!"

Liana stopped, extending her arm out for Haley to enter first. "In fifty years," she said brightly, "this will be most common in the world."

"Simply marvelous."

The room Haley walked into was nothing short of perfection—every convenience had been thought of. There were large couches, an enormous bed, and a crystal chandelier shining above the huge room, giving it a soft, warm feeling. Then, even as she admired the tasteful beauty, she found it all beginning to blur, light and form blending together. Haley realized she was losing consciousness—she headed for a divan. Liana's face appeared above her. "Poor dear, you are quite exhausted. Rest now. I'll come back later."

Haley could feel the sensation of her body begin to slip away from her. She felt sticky, dirty, and hungry beyond belief. What she wouldn't have given for one of her mother's Sunday dinners right then. Haley sat up and pulled off the leather flight jacket. The initials *D.S.* were stenciled on the inside liner in red thread. "Thanks for the jacket, Don."

The bed across the room looked inviting—big fluffy pillows, huge cotton quilt—and brought a smile to her face. Everything was so clean, so pure-looking, as though washed by the sun. To sleep on *that* bed . . . Haley smiled, her eyes already closed, and curled up on the divan, pulling the jacket over her.

J was standing in a circular room, holding out something in his hand for Haley to take. The room, shining brightly from its silvery walls, had several doors, each with some symbol on it. Each symbol radiated life— fiery and resonant. It occurred to her that this was no ordinary dream about some ordinary room. The pillars, doors, and the symbols themselves radiated an unusual living presence, as though they were not inanimate objects at all. Another thought . . . it was like standing in the combined minds of hundreds of people, whose love and power were the sole creative force that held every particle and atom of the room together.

Yes. Confirmation came from her heart. That's exactly what this was.

"Child." Haley turned toward J and noticed how intense was the love pouring from his eyes. "Passing through these twelve doors, you must learn the secret of union. Until all are accomplished, this key cannot be known by you." J closed his fingers tightly around something she wasn't able to see. Again, a thought flashed into her mind—put there by something or someone, she believed. Whatever J held, it was a part of her or represented her in some way she couldn't fathom.

Haley nodded in acceptance of his challenge. J bowed to her and led her to the first door. A great chant, as from a thousand voices, filled the room, its powerful sound coursing through her, her skin hot and burning; she could hear her heart beating—loud and insistent— until the sound of it consumed all other noise. As Haley stepped toward the door, the chant grew louder and became deafening. She reached out and touched the great golden handle.

When Haley awoke, she realized she was standing in the middle of the room with her right arm extended; she turned quickly around, thinking her body still asleep on the divan. No. She was really standing there . . . sleeping there. How long had she slept? Hours? Days?

Through an open door, she could see steam rising from a bath, fogging the room beyond. Haley walked absently to it, her body unconsciously aching to slip into the warm water, eager to rid itself of several months of grime and dirt. Without thinking, she began peeling off her clothes until the last of them fell at her feet. It felt good as she stepped down into the calm pool of scented water, the strong scent of roses soothing her and bringing a deep smile to her face.

"This is nice."

Haley's thoughts shifted to the dream; like the other dreams of her past, it now explained what was happening to her. Finally, with the dream complete, she understood that she merely remembered what she had already experienced in another time and another place. The dream was, is, and always had been a token of events to come as well as events that had already occurred. The temple she so desperately feared was nothing more than a grand university, where souls lived the science of becoming one's Self.

What would be learned in the coming days, weeks, or months was sure to be grand and exciting. The thought of that glorious future brought a sigh of joy from her.

She realized why the dream terrified her so much. She had rejected her fate, and in so doing had rejected anything associated with that future. Haley realized how that it was *she* who made the terror, not the dream or the events that unfolded in and around it.

It wasn't until her hands were wrinkled and every bit of visible soil was erased from her skin that she finally stood up from the huge tub and looked for a towel. On a small vanity table lay several large body towels, as well as a rather oversized robe. She put it on and went back into the main room.

"Hello," Liana said, pouring tea into a small cup. "I thought not to disturb you. Will this be sufficient?"

On a great wooden tray lay soup, pine-nut bread, tea, and fruits and other foods she hadn't seen since leaving Boston. Haley's stomach growled instantly. She picked up a roll and stuffed it into her mouth. Then she stopped and caught herself. "I'm sorry, I didn't mean to be rude." She walked up to Liana and wrapped her arms around her. "Yes, this is wonderful. Thank you so much for everything."

Liana returned the hug and then pointed to a large closet. "There are clothes in there for you." Liana started for the door.

"Wait!"

Liana stopped and turned. "Yes?"

"When can I see Master?"

Liana smiled, and the mysterious door opened again. "I was under the impression you had." The door closed behind her as she left, leaving Haley alone. Haley stood there for a long moment, staring at the place where Liana had stood. Sighing, she turned to the tray and began to feast.

As she finished, Haley looked around the room. "Curious

place." There appeared to be only one way in or out. No windows, hardly any furniture beyond the essentials—but plush beyond belief. Missing, too, were mirrors, pictures, or any kind of memorabilia. It was elegantly simple.

Haley walked over to the closet and pulled out clothes. Dressed in linen trousers and a shirt, she went and sat on the bed, expecting someone to come for her. Presently the door *swooshed* open again. Haley smiled. "Right on schedule." Then she rose, curious. No one came into the room. The open door held only one meaning for her.

"Okay. Time to go, I suppose."

Haley started for the door, passing the divan where she had napped. Stopping herself, she turned back and picked up the flight jacket.

Smiling at the memory of meeting Don, she hurried through the door and proceeded toward the hall of beautiful paintings and tapestries, stopping occasionally, unable to resist closely inspecting some of the magnificent works. The paintings seemed alive, as though three-dimensional. After pausing at one painting of a mountain lake with two men in a boat, she realized she was dawdling and hurried on down the hall.

Coming to an intersection in the hallway, she stopped. Branching off from the center were several corridors, each slightly different in color. The brightest, or so it seemed to her, was a deep red; all the others were less radiant. Haley closed her eyes and listened to her heart. Her heart echoed back the answer to her unspoken question.

"Yes. This one. This must be the correct one."

Upon stepping into the gaily lit hall, she felt the energy around her change in tone. Haley immediately stopped, observing the effects of the strange sensation that was overcoming all her senses. The queer feeling grew in intensity—leaving the impression she was stepping into someone else's body and leaving her own.

"Wait! I don't understand what's happening. What's going on?"

She had entered the Temple. The Teaching would begin.

CHAPTER 14

Nepal, 1935

We ask that life be lived,
in the quest for fulfillment.
Not random is our experience,
but sought out with purpose.

Two years. Had it been so long? It seemed only a short time ago that Haley's ship had landed at Ceylon. She thought of her family—what they would be doing and how they were faring. Sometimes, in dreams, she would visit them at home in Boston—laughing, taking walks in the parks, singing comic songs at the piano with her father and brother. She dreamed of the joy of family—idle happiness as it can only emerge when among loved ones. The person she saw in her memories, though, was a frightened and often terrified Haley, afraid to sleep and uneasy with her thoughts when left by herself too long. Remembering that Haley was like watching a movie about another person, or looking at the picture of someone she barely knew. The girl who had left her home and all those closest to her heart was now someone very different. Life back in Boston was death, compared with the realities she had experienced and the knowledge she had gained.

Going beyond the limits of the five senses, Haley learned to use her inner ears to discover the true meaning behind the world's ills. Now, as she met and made friends, she could feel their pain and anger, though more often than not, her new friends at the Temple possessed no such intemperate feelings. Many times, a conversation took place between eyes that beamed thoughts of care and love, sent through the invisible ethers of space between hearts tuned to realities where time and space were meaningless, words were cumbersome and unnecessary.

As she passed each test, her teachers gave her new knowledge and new understandings that she used to build her character. For Haley Olsten, now a woman in every sense of the word and in no sense of the word, the only realities were those that had their foundation within the circumference and radiance of the soul.

Each travail, as the tests were called by the silent and joyful members of the Temple she now called home, introduced her to a new and different Teacher—a person more friend than tutor. Some were young men about her age, some women, most older Masters. All her teachers brought to their eager student a perception of love where they held mastery. In the end, the tests were passed and the student moved along.

Haley learned to control the appetites of her body, the unpredictability of her emotions, and the vacillations of her mind. These attainments were the product partly of the travails and partly of the strict regimen of meditation and service, ever the hallmarks of the Brotherhood of men and women whose task it was to serve humanity at all costs. As months became years, she found within herself levels of beingness beyond mortal description.

Beyond even these great accomplishments was her growing and sensitive heart. It was a heart that for no less than two years had seen every kind of suffering, both animal and human—a heart that grew strong and compassionate, serving always the needs of the many. Haley's heart became a server's heart—thinking not of self or her own needs and wants, but of the needs and wants of all creation.

The last test was brutal, centering on nonattachment to self. Everything she held dear, even her own self-esteem, was shown to her as the illusion it was. The event, signifying an end to her studies and training, was the last challenge at the school. Its arrival spelled a joyous time of attainment and release into the world of service, as well as a grave farewell to a co-worker who would be missed.

It was Liana who broke the news to her one afternoon, mentioning simply to take no nourishment, save water, for three days and nights; on the third day, she would be taken someplace—Liana didn't say where. True to form, the morning following the third day of fasting, Liana retrieved Haley from her room and escorted her to a river that flowed in a vast place known only as the *Hall of Wisdom.*

There, after all she had been through, she was left alone among the quiet meadows and beautiful lawns with only one injunction: "Think upon thy life objectively, as truth approaches."

After Liana left, Haley immediately went into a meditative state for several hours; after a time, she sensed she was no longer alone. Opening her eyes, she saw a woman approach her.

"Sister. For your next labor, you must see yourself as you are in body and then in spirit. But, before the latter can be known, the former you must behold." The woman who spoke to Haley could not have been over fifteen years old, judging by her looks. Behind her eyes, though, was an intensity of strength and love that belied Haley's impression. Haley smiled.

"Do you accept?"

"Yes," Haley replied mentally, "I accept."

The woman stepped forward, took her by the hand, and led her down to a pool of water. Near the bank, the woman stopped. "What must be learned is for your eyes alone. Know this: What you shall see is what thy spirit sees in you and all mankind, as a reflection of its spark, as that spark is hidden among the myriad seas of the emotions, the antic states of the mind, and the dense and coarse substance that is the body. This reflection-in-bondage is the not-self, the illusion that enslaves the true soul. Once the elementals of form and matter are known, they can no longer hold the soul that would be spirit in lasting bondage."

After her guide finished speaking, a great hush came over the valley, bringing a strange and intense stillness to the solemn moment. As in other tests, it was now the moment of decision; she was given a final chance to reverse the inevitable course of destiny—ever does free will move through the gate that binds the past and the future. Move forward and face the challenge, or decline. The former held mystery and attainment. The latter, end of instruction and release back into the world.

Haley didn't hesitate.

She approached the still, quiet surface of the small pond. Bending on one knee, she peered over the edge and gazed upon the reflection looking back at her in the water.

Haley inwardly screamed at the horrible thing that now manifested itself as a living reality. All that was coarse, base, and evil in the world streamed from the reflection in the pond, enveloping her—a laughing demonic monster whose lurid and blackened eyes sought only the worst within her.

Though this was the darkest horror her gentle eyes had ever beheld, Haley did not flinch.

Beyond this unspeakable reality was the greater abomination that the Beast she observed was now aware of Haley, its attention entirely focused upon her as its foul stench reached up and seized

247

her; paralyzing her—even reaching for her from the surface of that once-still pond—the Beast no longer remained a bizarre, animated image but a living entity. Powerful . . . determined . . . vicious.

Determined to face life, no matter what the cost, she held firm. The demon sensed her resolve and exploded in a frenzied anger.

Overwhelming her mind and senses, the entity began to flood her with what it was. Every selfish act ever committed, both in this life and in lifetimes past, ripped through Haley's mind with blinding speed. Each time she had hated, that hate filled her now. All her acts of vengeance and jealousy enveloped her in all their nauseating ugliness. Within moments, it seemed to her as though every dark thought, act, and deed had descended and merged with her once-simple and loving soul. Opening her eyes against the torrent of dark and base feelings, she found the demon was starting to merge with her—a demon empowered by all that was evil in the universe.

She closed her eyes. "This is not me. I am not matter, but spirit. I am the Self—that Self am I." Remaining steadfast, Haley opened her eyes to discover the demon frozen in panic and shrinking away from her. Haley looked upon the ill-formed beast, now inches away. "You are only what you must be: a great part of the Divine Plan, created by the Great Love which guides all reality. I, too, love you, as I would love the dearest and noblest child. I know you are what I once was and am no longer—I cannot hate or reject you, that which is my own creation of myself."

A great shriek pierced the air throughout the vast expanse of the Hall of Wisdom, its evil wail echoing for several moments. The demon vanished; in its place on the surface of the water appeared a radiant, angelic woman, whose eyes shone as pure as the sun and from whose heart shone kindness and compassion. Overwhelmed at such grace, Haley fainted on the soft clover.

The memory of that experience some weeks before warmed Haley as she sauntered among the ruins of an old Tibetan lamasery, abandoned by time and history. Since that time in the Hall of Wisdom, she now knew what real peace was. Having witnessed man's pursuit of life and what it offered, she realized that the human race was living lies and was wholly blind. True contentment could be found in one place alone. Until the heart was discovered, all of life was nothing more than vain pursuits of folly and ruin. Physical beauty became dust with time. Money, an anchor of responsibility few understood or could shoulder. Passion, a fleeting moment, which brought ruination to the senses and bankruptcy to households the world over.

The world was a playground for the foolish and an exalted wonder of love and magic for the wise.

She sat down among the rubble that had once been a grand and mighty temple. She had been staying here for two weeks, sent here by her teacher after passing the Eleventh Travail. It was a desolate place, long vacated by some ancient race. The architecture contained Grecian elements, from what she could tell, in addition to a definite Arabic influence of some kind. Had the Greeks come this far north and east? Haley didn't know.

Told to rest at the ruins at Kanchenjunga, beyond Katmandu, she did what she could to make a home among the silent mountain peaks that stood as guardians over the world. To pass the time, she pored over the broken pieces that littered the windswept tableau, searching for clues about the structure. Occasionally, she would get lucky, as she did today while uncovering a half-buried column. The inscription was worn, covered with mud, and difficult to read, but after several minutes of rubbing on the ancient marble pillar, Haley was finally able to make out the Sanskrit.

Mysteries not yet born
truths not yet lived
The way to truth, within
The way to ruin, without

Haley ran her fingers over the faded relief of the letters. Who had carved these words? What could the carver tell her about them if he were here now? She smiled, passing her hand over the shattered marble. Instantly, it re-formed into its original shape— a beautiful mirror, polished and standing some twenty feet tall. The words, once difficult to see, now stood out brilliantly, the carved letters filled with gold and reflecting light from their glasslike surface.

"This must have been a very beautiful place at one time."

"I agree."

Haley turned around, beaming. Balancing on a teetering, broken slab of marble was Don. He looked exactly as he had when she'd first met him, though without his jacket. Slung over his shoulder was a knapsack.

Haley laughed. "Balance a problem?"

Don jumped off, the slab falling in the process and crumbling as it hit the ground. "Well. It can be for an advanced soul, you know."

Haley arched her eyebrows at this immodesty. "But it's not a problem for one such as you." Seeing into his clean and pure heart, she realized the statement was meant for her, as no vanity existed in his kind and watchful eyes. Haley opened her arms, squeezing and hugging him. Don began to gasp. "It's nice to see you, too, but I think I need to breathe."

Smiling, he walked over to an open archway, Haley following in his wake. "Hear you've done pretty good." They stood in the arch, looking at the valley floor, some several thousand feet below them.

Haley knew Don was here for a reason. "Even so, there must be more to learn."

He smiled and turned toward her. "Quite right. But first, lunch." From his knapsack emerged two sandwiches and a large cantcen. "If memory serves correctly, I ruined the last meal we shared together."

She took the sandwich, her mind racing in anticipation of what new knowledge or understanding he was about to unveil. Haley loved these moments of knowing, more than she loved cucumber sandwiches.

Opening up his sandwich, Don moaned. "Drat. No catsup."

Haley waved her hand over the open piece of plain bread. A thin covering of red catsup now covered the bread.

Don grinned. "Very good, oh-knowing-and-loving-child-of-the-universe." Then he grew serious, laying his hand upon her. "You can never—*NEVER*—use these siddhis for self or for personal gain."

Haley stopped eating.

"To do so," he continued, "would be to give yourself over to the dark side, forever losing your ability to gain enlightenment and aid humanity." Don gazed evenly into her eyes, then smiled. "The rule is, check with Master first, obtain permission, then act under the laws of the Brotherhood."

Haley's face screwed up. "But when I saw you last, you materialized a fire and some food." Haley faced him, hoping he would resolve this great contradiction.

Don licked his lips and grinned. "And, as you are at a place of knowing, you can give *me* the answer."

She forgot about the sandwich; a cucumber from it fell softly to the ground, unnoticed. "You were there to teach me. So, for the benefit of instruction, you materialized the fire and the food."

Don clapped his approval. "High marks." He adjusted the knapsack on his shoulder. "You can keep the canteen. I won't be needing it." Don walked over to her, wrapping his arms around her. "This isn't good-bye."

Haley returned the affection, kissing him on the cheek. "Thank you . . . *for the sandwich.*"

Don laughed and touched his finger to his head as in a salute. Before Haley could wish him a safe journey, he vanished.

The next morning, Haley rose, did her meditation and other work on the inner planes, and returned to her body just before noon.

J, not seen for two years, was waiting for her.

Their sharing of affection and love was simple, deep, and all-encompassing. Finally he sat down, indicating for her to do the same. Haley noted, for the first time, a new and dignified side to her Teacher. It occurred to her that she was seeing him as he really was, without limiting himself for the understanding of the student. J radiated a depth of tranquillity and solemnity that exceeded all experience. Around him blazed a gentle, violet glow that instantly warmed and relaxed her. His eyes, ever mysterious and full, exuded a love so pure that it seemed impossible for that grand soul ever to think an ill thought or wish harm upon any thing. More than anything, Haley wished to be like him.

J reached out and took her by the hand and held it with great affection. "I have watched you, daughter." Gone was the mien of the stern schoolmaster; in its place was kindly love and camaraderie. "We are most pleased with the progress made thus far."

Also gone was the simple peasant and his quaint words. Now, J seemed more himself. *And what a Self it was.* She truly believed she was sitting in front of a Master-of-the-Wisdom—a Great One. The other J, the provincial hermit, must have been a charade for her benefit. Then it hit her: what sacrifices these teachers make for the benefit of their students, limiting themselves in time and space, donning simple guises. Haley thought how she would feel if she had to be her old self again—in actions and deeds—it would be stepping into a rigid, plaster cast. The thought was terrifying. Then she noticed J smiling benevolently.

"I am ready for the next test, Master." There. Done with. She had called him by his true identity, the mystery finally out in the open. J did not decline the title or chastise her for using it. Haley felt a sudden relief from someplace deep inside, having always known that if all went well, she could truly address him as chela to guru.

"What remains now is to live, act, and be, as you have learned to live, act, and be." J drew a deep line in the dirt between them. "For twenty-six years," he said, his finger creating a second line, parallel to the first, "you have learned and are continuing to learn about the Self—about who you really are." His finger stopped one-third of the length of the first line. "Real attainment comes from being the Self we discover."

The Master drew a small horizontal line a third of the distance from the second line, forming a small cross. "The first seven years are spent in building up the body and integrating with it for the coming incarnation. These years should be spent in play, creative games, and in using the highest and noblest part of the imagination. This is so, because it prepares both the indwelling human soul and the emotional body for its stage of development from seven to fourteen." Haley could recall her turbulent emotional teens. She felt uncomfortable with the memory.

"The emotions develop and integrate with the body during that period. For young women, this is when their nurturing and romantic aspects come into emergence. They think of love—or more accurately—imagine their lives in romantic episodes. This refines the emotional body to some degree."

Haley could not suppress a grin—the Knight in Shining Armor. She and her girlfriends had spent countless afternoons thinking of boys as great knights, come to whisk them off into some fanciful romantic adventure, making children under moonlit skies and living happily ever after.

"After fourteen, the mind should take dominance and become the seat of intelligence, controlling the lower vehicles and aligning them to the purposes of growth, education, and goal-fitting enterprises."

Haley stopped him. "You say 'should.' Doesn't it?"

"Humanity is mostly polarized in its emotions. This can easily be noted by those things that attract the race as a whole. Drama of an emotional nature is more appealing than that which is analytical or physical. Though, we should not confuse the adventure films in the cinema as a physical reality—no—these are just vehicles to excite the lower emotions, stimulate the solar plexus, and kindle the animal passions."

He had her complete attention; her being was absorbed in his every word. After a long moment, he spoke: "In the last few years, your labor has been twofold, as it is for all disciples: one, to train the mind and elevate the emotions; the other, to develop an integration with the *Inner Guide,* the *Voice of Silence.* In these areas, much has been accomplished; much remains to be accomplished."

J smiled, then stood. "The last test is the test of life."

Haley remembered W. Somerset Maugham: "It is easy to be a wise man on a mountaintop."

Her Master nodded.

Nodding with a smile, she rose, squeezing J tightly while fighting tears. "Thank you. I will labor, I will become that Self which I am."

Haley finally released J, puzzled over something. "I have to know. Was it you?"

J looked at her, not clear about what she meant; then his perceptive consciousness revealed to his mind's eye the essence of her question. It was all he could do to keep from laughing. "Yes. I retrieved your book from the ocean and placed it on your night-stand."

Master J took her hand and patted it affectionately. "I must attend to a student in Calcutta. Accompany me on this journey; it will give us much time to talk." J glanced at the broken pieces of marble. "Great truth, that."

Haley had memorized it.

"Mysteries not yet born, truths not yet lived.

The way to truth, within. The way to ruin, without."

"What does it mean?"

J shrugged his shoulders. "Only a life lived can answer."

❧ CHAPTER 15 ❧

Forward, Bravely Forward

The true battlefield is within.
—Gandhi

Everywhere there was unrest, rioting, and plundering by tens of thousands of Sikhs, Muslims, and Hindus; opposing them were thousands of armed and menacing British troops. It was the anniversary of the 1919 massacre in Amritsar. Violating an obscure edict by the ruling British general there at that time, a group of Indians had met in a public square where they were gunned down to a man. The atrocity threw the whole of India into an uproar—and much of the world with her. Since then, oppressed Indians from all over the continent rallied each April in memory of the slain. At the spot where the machine guns were set up rested a simple plaque in honor of the dead and wounded. England and India alike mourned the tragedy.

The trip had been a long affair, with frequent stops at every city. J had disappeared twice, only to miraculously reappear on the train well after it had gotten under way. J would appear, excuse himself in some humorous way, and wouldn't mention it further; Haley loved these displays of siddhis, knowing inside she would miss them later. Aside from her Teacher's wonderful manner and superlative conversation, there was an aura of upheaval to which her heart could not help but respond.

This was not the peaceful India Haley had seen when she came up from Madras with Ann; it was a country in turmoil and rife with uncertainty. Chaos was the order of the day, now.

Their train ground to a halt, with many of the passengers spilling out onto the grassy slopes on both sides to eat or take care of their personal affairs. On an opposite track were the remains of a terrible accident, the passengers still milling around the demolished train.

Haley's hand reached out to them in sympathy but was stopped by the glass window of the train car. "Those poor people; they must be terrified."

J looked out the window at hundreds of his countrymen and women, picking through the blackened ashes of the crumpled train. "There is always an uncertainty to life—thankfully. But their hearts, though saddened by the stupidity of violence, are reassured in the knowledge that India will become a free land once again."

All over the continent, trains had been derailed and buses overturned, creating a state of martial law in most of the cities. Daily, the newspapers and radio stations reported the mounting casualties within India's borders. Departing from the stalled locomotive thirty miles outside of Calcutta, Haley found without much surprise that a car with two attendants was waiting for them.

Slowly making their way through the congested roads, they finally arrived at their destination. Haley, never having seen revolution's destructive hand at work, was overcome with grief.

Calcutta was under a virtual state of siege.

Waiting at a railhead while her Teacher went about his business, Haley stood in the hot sun for two hours. In that time, the crowd at the station had grown into a mob. There being barely enough room for her to move, she was slowly pushed and shoved, until only the wall of a building stopped her. No one was paying attention, Haley noticed gratefully, to the blond woman wearing simple Indian khadi homespun standing silently on the far side of the station.

The crowd was shouting something, raising their fists high into the air. Whatever it was, the boiling mass grew into a frenzy, becoming maddened as though they would explode at any moment if their unknown demands were not met.

One word kept coming through the din: "Bhopa. Bhopa. Bhopa." A ceramic bowl shattered against the wall near Haley's head, showering her with broken shards.

Her training had left her heart open and vulnerable; the emotions of the mob swept through Haley, weakening her. She could feel their frustration, anger, and pain. The chanting from the growing mob grew stronger and more resonant, ripping through her like a knife. The crowd began to blend into the scenery, the sun, and the color of the sky until she could no longer separate one from another.

Then everything grew silent.

Instantly, Haley recovered through sheer willpower. She looked around and noticed that the silence was not just in her mind, but everywhere at the station. No one was moving or talking.

Finally, she saw why.

At the far end of a street were several mounted policemen and hundreds of soldiers with long oak sticks. The crowd began to murmur; guns appeared from underneath tattered clothing and from bags. The murmur grew into a howl—the police started toward them in earnest, batons swinging wildly.

A small boy, not more than ten years of age, tugged at Haley's sleeve. *"Namaskara."*

Haley's heart instantly went out to the small child. He was wearing hardly any clothes, and what he did have on was in rags. From the look of things, the child had probably never known a decent meal. Behind the tatters, poverty, and grime were warm and gentle eyes.

The boy became insistent and grasped her hand. "Come to, come to please." Holding on to the boy with one hand and her travel bag with the other, she let herself be led through the fray and into the streets beyond. Her smile never faded for a moment. Nor did the boy's, as he would occasionally glance back up at his charge, his huge grin revealing rotten teeth and yellowed gums.

After several turns through small alleys and trash-strewn streets, the pair finally slowed down. They were in front of a large, whitewashed hotel, where stood some fifty men in the uniform of the Indian National Guard. Haley stopped, unwilling to be led farther. She had seen this kind of guard before; these were security people, who would not take kindly to pariahs walking past them. She had seen men and women lose their lives to the three-foot steel and oak batons these troops carried. "No. We shouldn't be here. This is very dangerous."

The boy looked up at her and laughed. "No danger here, ma'am. Come."

Before she could answer, her Master and another very small man wearing only a loincloth walked out into the sunlight. The security detail snapped to attention. J motioned for her to come over. Haley's smile returned.

Her guide tugged at her again. "See? I tell you no danger."

Haley reached down and tousled his hair. "You were right, my prince. I should always listen to angels—especially angels in a harsh world." The boy shot her a grin and blushed, taking off toward the almost tiny man in the loincloth. The little man put something in his hand, and the boy instantly disappeared down the street.

"It is a pleasure to meet you, Miss Olsten," the stranger said as Haley approached. "We have so few ladies here in India who come from America." Haley extended her hand and bowed. "You may call me Mohandas," the man said with a laugh. "It is much more suitable than the other names people give me."

Mohandas turned to J and bowed deeply. "Thank you for everything. With God's blessing, we will be free to rule ourselves." Mohandas laughed again and turned back to Haley. "The greatest blessings are always bestowed upon us by friends who serve God."

Haley watched Mohandas carefully. He radiated simplicity, strength, and humility. She liked him instantly.

J turned toward Haley. "I must attend to another matter."

Mohandas nodded. "Leave Miss Olsten with me, if you please. I do not often have such company." Haley glanced toward J, who smiled his approval.

Without another word, J turned and entered a waiting car. Mohandas's eyes followed Haley's Teacher. "He is a great Soul, our friend and brother. I have always found his wisdom to be the deepest."

Nodding in agreement, she replied, "All that I am, I owe to him." For a long moment, they stood silent, watching the plume of dust trailing from J's taxi.

Mohandas glanced at her, his smile endless. "So. Our friend tells me that you are leaving India for England." Mohandas looked at her wistfully. "I have always liked England, though its winters are much too cold for an old man." Both laughed. Mohandas touched Haley on the arm, indicating his preference to return back inside.

Along the entranceway were dozens of Hindus—all salaaming Haley and her new friend. Unable to make sense of what was happening, she let her inner sight come into operation. Haley looked closely at the man; what she saw almost blinded her.

She was literally standing next to a sun. Great rays of rose and blue streamed from his heart, penetrating everything around them. Haley quickly shut down her clairvoyance to prevent herself from swooning. Whoever Mohandas was, he was most certainly a man of great attainments. His radiance was such as few she had ever known.

Several attendants led them to a private table in the dining room. Presently, tea arrived. Haley realized she was staring, so she focused instead upon the freesias put on the table for their benefit.

Haley waited for Mohandas to drink first, out of respect. Finally, he sipped, decided it was good, then sipped some more; Mohandas set his cup down. "Our hopes are with you in the coming struggle."

Haley's eyes widened. Whoever he was, he rated knowing about the work she was to do in Europe. Mohandas smiled at her reaction to his statement. Haley cleared her throat, trying to listen to what inner advice was coming forth; her heart told her she could speak freely around him. "I do not understand it, but I will do what I can."

He gazed at her, his eyes penetrating. "Do not fear what the future holds. There is no contest that has a greater chance for success than the battle for freedom from tyranny. If the freedom is born of love, no force can oppose it. The world is sick to death of blood spilling. Our best hope lies in the knowledge that the world is seeking a way out of its miseries."

As Haley listened, she noticed a power behind the words, as though some great universal voice was uttering them and not a small, ill-clad man. Her skin tingled.

Haley cleared her throat and reached for the tea. "I will try to remember that."

Mohandas clasped his hand upon hers. "Good. Remember: a radiant and loving heart is more powerful than a thousand aimed rifles. Also, when you think you are fighting alone, the truth combined with an untiring service to a simple principle will always guide you to a successful conclusion."

"It seems an awful lot for one person."

Mohandas laughed. "That is foolishness talking, Miss Olsten. The truth of the matter is that wherever I have gone, help just seemed to pop out of the pavement."

"Were you ever afraid?"

His eyes glinted, reflecting a deep wisdom and experience. "Many times. For my family and for many innocents. It seemed always that the obstacles were greater than the achievements. But evil depends upon fear—it is a weapon that they use to suppress." Mohandas sighed. "I finally discovered that the suffering would go on in spite of my doings. My only hope was to continue on—at least in that way, there was a chance the suffering would end."

Haley started to speak but was interrupted by a man who came bursting into the room. "Bhopa! It is a miracle!"

Mohandas took off his spectacles. "Catch your breath, my young friend. What miracle are you speaking of?"

The excited man took a few deep gulps of air, perspiration running down his face. "The police, Bhopa, the police! They were about to run over us, when a great wind came up!" It was then that the urgent messenger glanced at Haley, then at the tea, whose steam was rising into his nose. He smiled politely, licking his lips.

Mohandas showed not the slightest agitation or alarm at the startling news. His only visible reaction was to smile knowingly while cleaning his glasses. "Please. Tell us more." Mohandas filled a cup with tea and handed it to the man who eagerly took it and gulped it down.

"I do not know," he continued, "but the police could not raise their arms. There was much agitation with the prefect."

Mohandas leaned forward arching his eyebrows. "This *is* something."

"There is more, Bhopa. Some in our group were going to fight back but were unable. We were both affected. Finally, the women started crying that Krishna did not want any more violence."

Mohandas was lost in thought and stopped cleaning his glasses. Wherever he was, he returned and finally stood up. "You must excuse me, Miss Olsten; it has been most pleasant. Perhaps we will meet again."

Haley rose and shook hands with her new friend, who without another word stepped quickly away with several people.

A half hour later, J appeared, taking the seat across from her. Haley's first thought was to ask about Mohandas when, absent any explanation, the thought occurred to her that she would not see J again. Her mind and heart raced at once in vain denial and the forlorn hope that her intuition was false.

J took her hand. "I am as close as your heart, Little Hope."

It was true then. Haley girded herself and struggled with a maelstrom of feelings. With a supreme effort, the raging sea inside her settled down. She was happy to show her control of her emotions to her parting friend, brother, and Teacher.

J put a small package on the table. "You will need these for your trip. Do not hesitate or be distracted until you reach London. Once you have arrived at your final destination, someone will assist you."

Haley found she could not speak the words in her heart. For three years she had labored under his love and unfailing guidance. Behind every event had stood the protective arm of J. It was a moment of sublime knowing and transition. She was leaving forever the Haley she had known, to labor into the future with the Haley she now was. J's eyes radiated a love and compassion that made it even more difficult for her to remain composed. She loved him as she did her own father.

She reached across the table and retrieved the parcel. "I—"

J cut her off. "I can always be found in your dreams. At the Temple." Haley looked away; a single tear began its slow descent down her cheek.

"Go now. Peace be with you."

Haley rose and started away. After a few paces, she ran back and threw her arms around J. "Thank you. I'll do my best." And with that, she turned and fled down the hall, leaving him.

J sighed, pleased with all events. She had made it. In each life, whether friend, brother, daughter, or student, that which controlled the affairs of the world kept Haley and her Master close. J smiled at her success.

One danger was now passed, the Dark Brothers failing in their enterprise. She would now join the ranks of the New Group of World Servers for the first time—a front-line warrior—dedicated in life and death to the betterment of the planet.

As she graduated from her probation to true discipleship, whatever gains she made on behalf of humanity were entirely up to her now. One final labor remained: a labor and service that had been almost two thousand years in the making. She stood out from the rest of her brothers and sisters as humanity's last best hope in the critical years to come. In each century, all the players in the divine drama had labored diligently, each in his own karmic situation, in the development of their virtues and capacities to love. Soon, very soon, the forces would array themselves upon the physical plane in consummation of this cosmic conflict.

It now remained the task of his European brothers and sisters to guide and aid her where possible. His part in the divine drama was over. All eyes were upon the young American woman who, in a very short time, would be sailing into the fire of the battle itself in Europe. If she was successful, the powers of darkness now coalescing in Germany and Asia would be defeated, until they rose one final time at the end of the century. That battle would take place in America. A soul yet to be would carry humanity's banner then, as Haley carried it now.

If she performed as expected, she would be allowed one more contact with her Teachers during this incarnation.

The clerk at the American embassy looked bored, even angry. They had been coming in by the hundreds, on the hour, every hour—day after day. *"Visa to U.S.! Visa to U.S.!"* He needn't look up. He could tell by the homespun she was another of the dark-skinned lower class.

"I need to phone home. Who should I speak with?"

The clerk's head shot up. Dark yes, but from the sun . . . what radiant blue eyes! She was the most beautiful woman he had ever seen. "Yes, well. That would be me of course. You are American?" A smile now, to charm—but not too much. The clerk smiled at his good fortune; after all, he wasn't bad-looking and there were so few Americans worth bothering about.

"Yes. My name is Haley Olsten."

His mouth opened in disbelief. "Did you say *Haley Olsten?*"

"Yes."

Absentmindedly dropping his pen, he blurted out, "Wait here one moment, please." He stepped a few paces from the table. "Don't leave, now." Passing through a door at the end of the room, he glanced back one final time to assure himself she was remaining.

Haley looked around the embassy, heavily guarded by Marines in their dress uniforms. She smiled. It had been years since she had seen so many Americans in one place.

"Miss Olsten?"

Haley turned, coming face-to-face with no fewer than six people. "Yes?"

"I'm the ambassador. Could you come inside with me, please?"

Saling Palace,
Allahabad

What lies behind a civilization
is directly related to the good or evil of its
people. Thus, are the gods summoned.

Ann explained what had happened. After receiving the telegram from Damor that said Haley was in Calcutta, she hurried there to meet her at the train. Yes, she had the revolver his man in Calcutta had given her. After waiting and searching for over an hour, Ann finally found her standing next to a wall wearing the clothes of a pariah. No, it had never occurred to her that she would be dressed like that.

Damor picked up the letter opener and started sifting through his mail. "Get on with it. What happened then?"

Ann shifted in her seat and wiped her hands on her dress. "Of course I started for her, but there were so many people there, all making a fuss about something."

Damor stopped halfway through opening his third letter and glanced at her. "Go on." Eager to hear the rest of the details, he got up and sat in the chair next to her. "More champagne?" Ann let him fill her glass, and she gulped down the champagne. Damor was being more than cheerful. It frightened her.

True to his word, he had connected her with a viceroy to whom she was now engaged; though he was not all that handsome, he was considered one of the wealthiest men in the East. Gone was that tedious bore Reginald and his paltry captain's wages; once she had waltzed into a play with her new beau on her arm, he had never called on her again.

True to *her* word . . .

"Well," she began, "the ruckus was so bad that I couldn't approach her. Then she just up and disappeared. One minute I was looking right at her—someone shoved me—then she was gone."

Damor's mouth opened in disbelief. "Do you mean to say she escaped?"

"Yes, but—"

Damor slapped her. "Do you know why I asked this of you?"

"Well, I—"

He slapped her again, drawing blood from her nose and nearly unseating her; Ann began to sob, mascara streaking down in almost perfect vertical lines. He grabbed her by the throat. "It was because you could get close, you idiotic American bitch! You are her friend, is this not so?!"

Damor stood and straightened his tunic—adjusting a medal and rebuttoning. "Do you know what night it is this Friday?" Ann, crying and cringing in the big velvet chair, slowly shook her head no. "It is a new moon. A special time each month for friends of mine, such as yourself. Of course, you will attend this 'party.' " He reached over to his desk and pushed a button.

Presently, Bamda appeared. "Yes, Your Excellency?"

Smiling, Damor walked over and helped Ann up from her chair. She was relieved that the ordeal was over. She smiled too, though for different reasons. She was alive, never to come back again as long as she lived—good-bye, Saling, and go quite to hell.

Damor's grip on her arm tightened. "Miss Rolingford will be staying with us for a time."

Ann froze in terror, then tried to put on her best face. "I really can't, you see. So much to do—but of course I won't miss your party."

Saling smiled and shoved her toward Bamda. "There'll be much to do *here*." Ann started to scream but found that Shamoot's tight grip over her mouth prevented that.

"Rape her. Often. Drug her." Ann's eyes opened wide in frenzy, muffled screams emerging between Bamda's laughter. "If she tries to escape, cut off a finger or a hand. I do not care which."

Ann's screams continued even as she was dragged from the room. A door slammed down the hall, silencing her wails. Tasting her pleasures in the few remaining days before the weekend would provide some much needed diversion from his more serious duties and the work that remained to be done. Damor was fair in all his bargains, and she would now pay for her failures.

The room, bright from the streaming rays of the sun, suddenly darkened—the air becoming decidedly cold. The solid-oak door to his office slammed shut, its bolts and locks turning. Even though he had been a standing member of the Dark Brothers for his entire adult life, he had never quite gotten used to his chief's presence.

In fact, Damor was terrified beyond imagination.

He had an intimate knowledge of the fate of those who displeased the Doppelgänger. Damor bowed to the unseen presence; his only reply was a stench of decaying flesh filling the room.

A soft pulsating red glow formed in the center of the room,

not human. Several voices, blended into one freakish chorus of black horror, began to speak. "The time draws nigh."

Saling went down on his knees. "I seek only to do thy bidding."

The glow increased. "Take the woman to the lake in Switzerland, no later than the equinox. Prepare her."

"It will be done."

"Proceed from there to Berlin and complete your destiny. Once you have done this, you shall be rewarded."

When Damor opened his eyes, the sun's light had again returned, the odor and the harsh ugliness of his master gone. He walked over to a small table and poured a double brandy, taking the drink in a single gulp.

❦ CHAPTER 17 ❧

Berlin, 1936

Tend thy garden,
O child who seeks.
Clear it of weeds,
lest they strangle thy buds.

The long, low whistle of the train's engine announced the arrival of the train from Hamburg. Haley had been ordered to meet her contact, Rudy Stein, who would be traveling under the name Herman Brauchner. She found herself in what appeared to be a major nerve center in the very heart of Nazi Germany. India, as a colony of Great Britain, had troops in every city— but they were almost unnoticeable unless looked for. Here, the opposite was true, as it seemed every man wore a uniform of some kind.

Though not officially at war, the city and the station itself maintained a well-armed guard at every gate, entrance, or causeway. On every corner she noticed new construction of bunkers, large-caliber antiaircraft apparatus, and other things she didn't really understand. Since she left the car from Düsseldorf, her identity papers had been checked and rechecked some eleven times. She had memorized as much German as she could on her trip from India, and she was blond and blue eyed; not many of the angry men in the pitch black uniforms bothered her.

Haley could not help noticing the stark contrast between this rail station in the heartland of Germany and the hundreds of such stations she had seen when traveling through the East. Every person seemed to cower, with some urgent business to be elsewhere. There was an aura of orderliness to the perfect suits and dresses, and glares from those few either arrogant or brave enough to look another person in the eye.

She had heard the stories, listened to the tales from exiled Jews, but this firsthand experience left her chilled. The stories *were* true, after all. Every so often, the sharp report of a nine-millimeter Luger pistol could be heard echoing through the streets, and Haley would stop to see where the shot came from. After the third time, she noticed that she was the only one bothering about the gunfire. They noticed her noticing, so she stopped paying attention, kept her nose in a newspaper, and waited for the train, trying to remain calm and casual.

She couldn't understand what made the German people bent on creating a war society. The Germans back home were fresh and hearty, always ready with a quick smile or an intelligent remark. Her father had sought out their company on many occasions. Glancing from time to time at the scared faces of the men and women around her, she couldn't help but wonder if this was normal or the product of the new Nazi regime.

"Frau Olsten?"

Slowly lowering the newspaper, Haley found herself face-to-face with a kindly-looking man whose sharp, piercing blue eyes twinkled with warmth and hidden generosity. In contrast to the men milling around him, he carried himself easily, with an air of expecting something good in the wind. His expression was that of a scientist impatient to be getting on with his thinking, upset at being interrupted by the mundane world. His iron black hair sported gray streaks above both temples, which hid the steel rims of his almost invisible glasses. One hand was extended toward her in greeting, the other carried a suitcase that was bulging at the seams.

Haley folded the paper under her arm and cleared her throat. One mistake, and she knew that she would never leave Berlin alive. She didn't have to wait long for her answer.

"I am Herman Brauchner." Then he leaned closer and spoke at nearly a whisper. "Though my friends call me Rudy."

Relieved, Haley let out the breath she had been holding, took Herman's hand, and shook it vigorously. "I have no idea of where to go. I have never been in Germany before."

Rudy Stein had found refuge in Switzerland after discovering that Hitler had personally put a price on his head and declared him "the enemy of the Third Reich." This visit, under the cover of an alias, was more than a desire to see his homeland one last time. This trip would bring meaning to a life lived in service to the ideals he and many like him felt were the best hope of mankind.

For now, though, the best course of action was to remain as anonymous as possible while traveling through a country gearing up for war. No one was safe as long as the Gestapo had free reign to operate throughout the countryside.

No one.

The Gestapo depended upon the element of fear in finding its prey. Stay calm, be confident, and all would be well, he reminded himself. Stein leaned close again, hugging her like a sister. "Do not speak in public, if it can be helped. The SS have men everywhere. Speak only German. Leave everything to me and follow my lead."

He released her, and, matching the pace of those around

them, they hurriedly left the station. When confronted by the endless waves of security men that seemed literally to "pop out of the ground," she noticed that this Dr. Stein changed his tone and demeanor to reflect the sharp tone of the explicit questions the policemen posed. His answers were direct, to the point, and very gruff, with a flavor of impatient outrage at being so bothered. Once out of range, he resumed his easy way and casual speech.

Dr. Stein hailed a cab and bustled them inside, barking to the driver, "Four-eleven Mairlanch Strasse. Bitte." He put his finger to his lips, as if to say "Do not speak." Haley noticed the cabby glancing back and forth in the mirror, studying their faces. It occurred to her that even the cabdrivers had been conscripted as spies for the Nazi intelligence community—probably against their will.

The cab halted in front of a dreary flophouse, where two prostitutes lounged on the concrete steps going up into the three-story building. Dr. Stein declined the driver's help with the bags and paid the fare. Haley started toward the building, which automatically triggered the prostitutes into descending the steps. A hand pulled her back toward the street. It was Stein. "Kommen Sie, Frau Olsten."

Taking her by the arm, he hurried her across the street and into the starless night, zigzagging down this street and that. "Never take a motorcar to where it is you are going. Always go a few blocks from your intended destination. This way, if you are reported, they will come to the wrong house."

After twenty minutes, the quality of the neighborhoods began to improve until finally she found herself entering the side door of a very large Tudor-style building on a prominent boulevard. The entranceway was dark, but Dr. Stein seemed to know exactly where he was going; with a firm grip on her hand, he led her up a flight of stairs. After a few more turns she could hear a key entering a lock. Cold air met her face, as did a musty smell from a room not lived in for some time.

"The man who owns this apartment hates the Nazis," he offered by way of explanation. After lighting a few candles, Dr. Stein wrenched the pipes of the heater on and cleared off the sheets covering the chairs and couches. The room was large, with huge windows facing out to the street below, a kitchen off to the left, and two bedrooms on the right. Presently he retrieved her from the foyer and led her to the windows, where he pulled back the curtains. Not five hundred yards away stood a huge, brightly lit building with massive red flags snapping in the wind. Haley recognized the symbols of the Third Reich. The sight of the building—cold, stark, and powerful—unconsciously pushed her back a few steps.

Stein moved to her side. "Yes. There the wolves gather." He knew the question before she asked it. "Oh, it's quite safe, I assure you. We have used this flat many times to observe their comings and goings."

Haley turned to him in amazement. His voice had changed. Though still sharp and precise in his fluent German, his speech had taken on a decidedly British accent. He seemed to be able to read her thoughts as well.

"British Intelligence. Special attaché to the PM." He retrieved a cigarette from a silver case and lit it, waiting for her to speak. In the darkened room, barely illuminated by a few weak candles, she noticed the glow about him. It was the same glow she saw around J, Don, Liana, and her other co-workers. There was no need for passwords, when each member of that select band of servers could easily be identified by the radiance of love that emanated from the environs of their hearts.

"What is wished of me?"

She noticed that he was watching her intently, obviously

thinking about the issue. Haley had the impression that he was deciding something. After another long minute of silence, he put out his cigarette and walked over to the window.

"Something very terrible is about to take place. If this event comes to pass, humanity will stand powerless against the evil that will be unleashed against it."

Haley stared at him. The room seemed to grow cold again, everything in an awful quiet of suspense. Dr. Stein walked away from the window and sat next to her. "If I could take your place—if any of us could—we would do so without hesitation."

Haley remembered a long-ago conversation with her Master. They had joked about her undergoing some horrible fate. It occurred to her that the memory of that discussion coming back to her was no coincidence. She nodded for him to continue.

Dr. Stein spent the next half hour outlining the fate of the world in grave and quiet tones. In addition to sketching the forces at work at this critical moment in the affairs of humanity, he informed her in exact detail what her role was to be. Haley's face turned ashen when she heard her assignment.

"I see."

Patting her hand in encouragement, Dr. Stein tried to remain cheerful. "So. Let us get you something to eat and a good night's rest. In my suitcase are food and some clothing—should be your size. Wear them; they are German made."

As bad as it was, he hadn't told her everything—he couldn't. Some things were best learned only when they were needed. Bidding her a good evening, as well as warning her not to answer the door under any circumstances, he left with a promise to return in the morning at ten A.M. sharp. He would let himself in.

As the door clicked shut softly, Haley turned and went to the window. The government building was four city blocks long and several stories high. From where she stood she could see at least two hundred guards and several tanks. Occasionally she saw someone light a cigarette on one of its rooftops. Security men; probably they were snipers, the ones Rudy mentioned. Haley curled up on the couch, deciding against the dust-covered beds in the other rooms. Even at this late hour, shots still rang out here and there within the city, punctuating the stillness of her thoughts in the dark room.

"It would have been nice to say good-bye to my friends, while I could."

Haley rose with the morning sun. Stiff from the cold, she hobbled into the washroom for a quick bath. No hot water. Gritting her teeth she got her bath over with, and dressed. In the suitcase were several loaves of bread and a chunk of cheese, with a few plain cotton dresses. The shoes were too small—she would have to wear her sandals.

The audible click in the lock informed her that Dr. Stein was arriving a few minutes early; Rudy stepped through the door with a package cradled under his arm. "Brought some hot tea. Care for a cup?"

Haley eagerly sat down, her throat dry from a deep-seated foreboding that she couldn't shake off. "Yes. Thank you."

While preparing breakfast, Dr. Stein chatted casually, about his confidence regarding the overthrow of Hitler and his minions. Haley listened in silence. Rudy was not a very good liar.

He stopped cutting a slice of cheese and looked her dead in the eye. "I know it's a slim proposition, beating the Nazis, but if one thinks about it, it's really humanity that's the problem." Rudy put the plate of food in front of Haley.

"Humanity won't face its bigotry and separatism on inner levels, so it—as a collective whole—must overcome its obstacles on the physical plane. Wars do that. Wars are humanity's desperate act of growth and advancement." Shaking his head, he added,

"Quite frankly, it's the stupidest method of learning we've managed to embrace. You've been selected for this, for some reason no one will tell me. They also tell me that you have the highest qualifications. I believe it."

Haley thought the implied question a fair one. "May I ask, first, how the prime minister of England and British intelligence are involved in this affair?"

Popping a piece of cheese into his mouth, Dr. Stein thought about his answer before speaking. "I have for some time now been special adviser to the PM on the occult aspects of Hitler."

Haley's eyes widened in surprise.

"Oh, yes. The governments of the world are very knowledgeable about these things. You see, I knew Hitler in Vienna while he was undergoing his training—much like yours—to take his place as the vehicle for evil in the world. He chose to serve involution instead of evolution, creating a path of madness the world might not escape from. You see, the war was inevitable, but the evil wasn't. That's the other unspoken danger. Disiciples close their eyes to evil and so evil grows in power. In the future, I'm told, disciples will come who will expose evil through their books. Once exposed, darkness will fade in the sunlight."

Haley sank back in her seat. Though the story might have sounded fantastic, it didn't when compared with her own experiences. Also, having been taught the method of discerning a falsehood when she was at the Temple, she knew he was now telling the truth. She understood; he felt in his heart that she had no chance whatsoever and would probably be killed. He lied as parents lie to their children—to put them at ease. His motive was noble.

"Please. Go on."

"Well, I studied under the Brotherhood as you did for several years. When we knew Hitler planned to invade England, I offered my services to Churchill. Turns out, the man is familiar with certain Masters in Great Britain. He hired me, and, well, I've been spying on the Ahnenerbe ever since."

"The what?"

Stein stared out the window, obviously weighed down with knowledge of a dark nature. "The Ahnenerbe—the Nazi Occult Bureau . . . created by Himmler and Hitler for the purposes of unlocking the dark powers in their quest for world domination. These are heartless people, Frau Olsten—"

"Please, call me Haley."

"—Haley. Very heartless. I have witnessed things no man should know about. I thought I'd seen the worst in humanity during my service in the Great War. I realize now that there are agencies in this world beyond imagination, whose entire purpose it is to destroy the planet."

Dr. Stein stopped speaking and took a breath, listening as Haley was to the traffic in the street below. Haley noticed a change in his demeanor—a wave of sadness emanating from him. "This will be my last trip. They know who I am and are looking for me—both here and in England." He grabbed her hand, unconsciously telegraphing his worry to her sensitive nature. "These people. They are monsters! Never underestimate them—even for a moment. If you do, it will be your undoing." Without saying it, they both knew what the consequences would be if he was ever caught. She wouldn't fare any better.

"So when do we start?"

"Haley . . . whenever you are ready."

She gently set her cup down, gazing directly into Dr. Stein's eyes. "I am ready." Rudy nodded in approval, obviously relieved at her choice.

"Before we start, may I ask why I was chosen?"

Smiling, he closed his eyes and asked to be told. The information was whispered clairaudiently into his ear from across the thousands of miles that lay between Germany and Nepal. After a long minute, Stein spoke: "He who would bring the vessel of antispirit to the West, you know. For many lives, your path and his have crossed, each opposite the other on the great road of redemption. . . ."

As Dr. Stein talked, images flashed through Haley's mind, taking her breath away. A girl, young and pretty, a concubine and slave to a rich landowner in some long-dead civilization. Then a woman, oracle to a Temple, murdered by a warlord as she prophesied the end of their city. Yet another life, a simple woman in love with a prince—*David*—both slain and their lands burned when he refused fealty to the new and barbarous king, Henry the Fowler.

In each successive life, she found that in some way she and David remained close. Once as brother and sister, then as father and daughter, many times as man and wife. Overshadowing this happy discovery was an ugly specter of darkness, personified through Damor Saling, who for countless lives had stood in the way of their happiness.

Haley was in tears—half joy and half sorrow. It explained everything: the discomfiture and agony, the endless misery that surrounded halcyon times. Her unconscious memory knew that darkness would follow her for as long as she lived.

As long as *Damor* lived.

"I see." Haley stopped crying, and looked up to find that Rudy's eyes were moist as well. She reached over and hugged him. "Let's end this. Can we start right away?"

Sniffling and embarrassed at himself, Dr. Stein tried to appear strong. "You must excuse an old romantic." Haley looked at him, curious.

"I couldn't help but notice your lives—how wonderful is your love with this man."

Lowering her head, she smiled her "thank you."

Dr. Stein grew serious. "Close your eyes."

Haley did as instructed, her inner sight filling with the soft, radiant glows of both their hearts. She smiled, watching the interplay of brotherly affection that bound the two servers.

"Now, turn your thoughts outward, into the world. Seek the place where darkness reigns."

Instantly, Haley found herself floating some fifty feet above the Katzmeinnen Gaulenplatte, a few blocks from where her body was safely being guarded by Dr. Stein. Looking around, she noticed the etheric spires above the buildings in the area, each reflecting the feelings and consciousness of its inhabitants.

What she saw was unbelievable to behold.

The spires, extending several meters above the buildings, radiated a gray mist bounded with concentric rings of brown beneath the surface. These "auras" clearly indicated a city of millions entirely afraid for their personal existence. Behind this overwhelming panorama of fear, she could see that some buildings had no radiance whatsoever, instead emanating a brassy, dull shadow that prevented any light from passing through. These would be the Nazis: those ardent followers of Hitler's program of global genocide.

Then Haley remembered. She had seen this before. And with the recollection, she knew when—the time she first met J in his little mud hut. "So, this *was* ordained." The realization sank in; she should have known, given the details and the clues, right from the first.

Laughing as she wavered above the rooftops, Haley announced to the ether: "I should listen better to my Teachers."

Finally, resolved to remain focused, she let herself flow with the idea of finding Rudy's man. Damor would not be difficult to locate, his dark vibration and stench known to her. As she relaxed, she found that the mere thought of him hurled her off toward eastern Berlin; the buildings flew by at such a speed that they became blurry, the ground swooshing silently by.

After only two or three seconds, she found herself slowing down and descending into the ground near a river. As her spirit entered the soil she realized that she was entering an underground building. The emanations from the site nauseated her almost to the point of losing consciouness.

Think Rudy, Haley. Think about Dr. Stein.

Haley opened her eyes and found herself sitting in the apartment, with Rudy handing her a cup of steaming tea.

"I know where he is. I found him."

CHAPTER 18

The Sun Also Rises

The aspiration to be the receptacle
of divine will,
is, in essence, no less than
performance of duty.

W e wait until night," Rudy whispered, bringing a hot cup of
tea to his lips. Haley nodded in agreement, trying to remain
obscure and anonymous in the small, Bavarian-style coffeehouse
on Heighlin Strasse. Filled at all hours with loud and boisterous
troops, tired factory workers, and the watchful eyes of the SS, the
small café afforded the only place for the pair to find the right
moment to act. Like their adversaries, they remained watchful. It
was only four o'clock.

Across the street stood the Meinhof Library; now closed by
order of the state, it served as an entrance to a series of underground tunnels used by the Nazis for military purposes. Though
its existence was not meant to be public knowledge, a constant
stream of overloaded trucks, full cars, and all the immense mate-
riel of war making were driven into its yawning driveway. They
left later, very empty.

The traffic was a common conversation topic in the neighborhood and a source of much derision in the privacy of bed-rooms and parlors. The official word was "remodeling." Each time trucks went down the street, someone would remark, "There go more books!" or "We have the grandest library in all of Germany that no one has ever seen," and all would laugh.

A waiter came over and filled their cups for the twentieth time, eyeing them suspiciously, though grateful for the coin pressed into his expectant hand. "Danke, Mein Herr." This time, though, the man lingered, taking special pains to look at anything he could make note of on their table: two cups, an ashtray, a silver cigarette case with the initials *R.S.* An indignant glance from Dr. Stein sent the man scurrying.

Watching to make sure the man was out of earshot, Rudy leaned close to Haley. "If we stay here much longer, someone is bound to say something."

As he spoke, Haley noticed that the waiter had stopped to speak to a man at the bar, pointing with a quick finger over his shoulder toward them. The man spoken to leaned out and away from the bar, his hard eyes going from Stein to Haley. Haley looked away, quietly calling Stein's attention to his accurate prediction. Rudy showed no reaction to her comments and instead chose to sip his tea. Setting his cup down carefully, he straightened himself and stood. Before Haley could ask him what was on his mind, Dr. Stein began singing in a loud voice, *"Deutschland, Deutschland, über alles . . . !"*

Instantly, the entire clientele of the café jumped to their feet to join him in the national song, tears coming to cold hearts. At the second verse, Haley felt his hand pulling her to her feet and leading her out the door. Even after the door was closed behind them, the full chorus of two hundred voices reverberated through the streets, stopping pedestrians everywhere. Men saluted, women stood still, and small boys placed their hands over their hearts. At the same moment, Haley realized how intensely strong the nationalism of the country was; these were people committed and dedicated to whatever direction they were being led. Sadly, she realized that direction would not be a good one.

She could feel it. Intuition is more than knowledge, and truth comes pure from the heart. Haley turned her head in time to see three large black sedans pull up to the underground driveway of the library. Her thoughts focused on the second car.

He was here.

Dr. Stein was already pulling her down the street, muttering about finding another meetingplace and "too bad . . . this was such a good location."

"He's here, Rudy."

As she spoke, Stein turned in the direction of the library, his eyes instantly drawn to the sleek black cars. Haley looked up at him, realizing that he was using all his consciousness to test the accuracy of her senses. Finally taking a breath, Stein took her by the arm as couples in love would and started them off in the opposite direction. "Let's go toward them from another direction. We are being watched by security people from the café." Haley did not need to look to verify the accuracy of his statement; she could feel the icy stares of the Gestapo on her back.

It was cold and cloudy, but their brisk pace started to take the chill away. Dr. Stein pointed out various landmarks in the famous city, from this century and from centuries long past. As Haley watched and listened, she realized that this would be a wonderful place to stay, to learn from the great minds that staffed the universities; the German reputation for higher learning was clearly indisputable. Under different circumstances, spending a summer here would be wonderful for the mind.

Under different circumstances.

Prewar Berlin was beautiful, Rudy said, full of interesting

architecture and with students bent on the pursuit of their intellectual studies of civilization; they were quite different from their counterparts in Paris, whose intentions were to understand man from a more philosophical and artistic viewpoint. Each country had its place in the world scheme, bringing their special brand of learning, knowledge, and understanding of life for the welfare of the entire planet. When the world as a whole grew beyond the limits of national borders, the human race would advance a thousand years upon its path.

Soon they found themselves at the entrance to a park; wasting no time, Rudy led her inside and found a bench for them to sit on. Watching several mothers tend their children as they played, Haley was grateful to find some humanity in a city that seemed destined to collide with the rest of the world. It was beautiful to behold.

Young boys and girls played, ran, and bounced around with an enthusiasm and energy that can only come from being a child. Haley noticed that there were several tree sprites zipping in and out among the little ones, immensely enjoying the frolic, adding their own spirit of mischief. Only a few inches tall, these translucent beings shone with the purity of Nature's love, which can only be found among those humans whose hearts are as Nature's— pure, unfettered, and joyful. Rudy laughed from time to time, clearly enraptured by the wholesome scene. It occurred to Haley that as men and women became more their true selves, they would naturally become more in tune with all that was wonderful and beautiful in Nature.

Suddenly, the fairies stopped in midair, their radiant little auras shrinking. Like a bomb exploding, they instantly scattered in every direction—no trace was left that they had ever been there. The children, no longer infused by their magical spirit, slowed down, a few of them stopping to catch their breath or to linger on the grass. Haley turned toward her left and discovered the reason for the abrupt end of joy and beauty. Two security agents from the local SS office had entered the park, unaware that their arrival had killed the only spark of real life Haley had witnessed in the two days since she had arrived.

Rudy leaned over to her and shook his head. "They carry an air of death with them wherever they go." Regaining his composure, he pulled out his case and lit a cigarette. "If we leave now, they will surely question us." He threw away his smoking match. "They are trained as hunters and would notice any movement precipitated by an action of theirs. This Himmler is a very cunning man."

Consciously or unconsciously—probably because they were drawn by Haley and Rudy's radiance—the SS men began walking in their direction. Without warning or explanation, Haley grabbed Rudy's hand and led him directly to a group of children playing on some swings. Rudy smiled at the genius. They stopped a few feet from four siblings vying to see who could go highest. Encouraging the boys and girls, Haley and Rudy clapped as new heights were reached, joining them in laughter. Eager to please two adults who seemed interested in their game, the children shouted for Haley and Rudy to push them higher. They indulged the children's requests, looking like a happy family group.

Twenty minutes later, with darkness approaching, the languid agents of the Führer moved on, silently smoking their cigarettes and lost in their own conversation. Saying their goodbyes to the children, who were sad to see their new friends depart, Haley and Rudy started back for the library. They stopped across the street again, the café's patrons ignorant of their presence outside. Rudy lit a cigarette and engaged in loud demonstrations of loyalty to the cause of the Reich whenever someone walked by.

"How will we get in?"

Dr. Stein smiled but did not answer, instead gazing thoughtfully at the well-guarded library. "You must trust me, Frau Olsten. Follow me." Flicking his spent cigarette into the gutter, he stepped off the curb and into the street, heading directly toward the library. Haley did trust him. She knew that trust was a foundation that could not be shaken in a heart empowered with knowledge of life's true realities. In the presence of such courage as her new friend continuously displayed, trust was easy. Haley followed in his wake.

The guards, as if on cue, all turned toward the large, determined-looking man who was walking in their direction. Stiffening to attention—the man might be a colonel or a general in the Gestapo—the lieutenant at the main double doors started down the steps to greet him. As Dr. Stein reached the sidewalk, the lieutenant snapped off a brisk salute. "Heil Hitler!"

Dr. Stein assumed his well-rehearsed role, merely raising his hand slightly and mumbling a "Ja, ja," reflecting the indifferent contempt and boredom displayed by the Prussian aristocracy that populated the German High Command. Without waiting to be asked, he produced a large leather wallet with an embossed swastika on the outside.

Rudy took the offensive and never let up.

"We have important work, lieutnant. My assistant and I are urgently required inside. Do not delay us unnecessarily."

The lieutenant's eyes widened as he scanned the identification credentials of the impatient man standing before him.

Reich Vice Marshall Herman Brauchner,
Ahnenerbe Grüppenführer
Totenkopf SS, Sicherheitsdienst
Nürnberg

Deciding that to obey such a distinguished man would be the wisest course of action for a simple guard, the young lieutenant snapped off a second salute, handed back the wallet, and raced up the steps to open the door. As Haley and Dr. Stein passed the trembling officer, Stein glared at him as though to say, "Remember, now, who I am for the next time, if you want to remain in Berlin and not at the front."

Securing the doors behind them, the guard let out an audible sigh and lit a cigarette. Yes, the vice marshal's face was familiar—he should have recognized him more quickly. But it did not occur to him that the familiarity of that face was in fact based on circulars sent out the previous week on known spies and enemies of the Reich.

The room Haley and Dr. Stein came upon was actually the large center chamber of one of the sections of the library. In the center of the circle, which had a two-tiered rotunda completely surrounding it, stood an enormous round table at least thirty feet in diameter. Seated at this table were the leaders of Nazi Germany's secret political branches of the realm of occultism—the Ahnenerbe and the Thulists. Here, Horst Wessel, Otto Strasser, Karl Holz, Willi Liebel, and many others sat holding the fate not only of their own darkened souls, but those of all humanity. All were seated, except one man who stood out from the others not only in clothing and in manner but also in a singular aura of chilling power.

Damor looked around the table, filled with contempt for every man in the room, save himself. These were fools who knew nothing. *Nothing!* He would show them real mastery. Their brutish guns and tanks were as toys played with by children, ignorant of anything else.

A large man, fifty pounds heavier than his small frame could support, started the meeting by reflecting the attitudes of the dark assemblage. His position in the Reich was high, and he had been fully responsible for the building up of the Ahnenerbe to a full-fledged department. This being the case, his taste for little boys under the age of ten went without comment from his superiors; that taste was satisfied as he required it from the thousands of Poles in the many camps now ringing the Fatherland.

"Prince Saling," the corpulent leader began, polishing off a brandy, "we have heard much about your connection with the Ahrimac center in Tibet. Before we start, we are interested to know whether your reputation could be supported by some demonstration."

The group murmured its approval, its appetite whetted in anticipation of real power. For twenty years they had struggled with small success in their search for true access to the dark arts. However hard they might look, something was always missing—some key that they needed to use as an advantage in their perverted quests. The heavy man smiled at the obvious approval of his associates. His request could not be refused, except on pain of instant death. Either way, the evening would not be a total loss.

Damor glared at him, thinking the same thing.

All eyes were upon Damor as he snapped his fingers. The vague, shadowy figure of Bamda Shamoot moved from the obscurity of the library walls and bent near his master. After a moment, Bamda nodded and left the room, his metal boot heels echoing and fading as he walked away.

Damor stood again, his grin sinister, his voice sarcastic. "No art of magic can ever be of true value unless the mantra is powered by the blood of woman." Many heads nodded in irritable consensus—this was nothing new, as this information could be found in any book on the subject. Damor sneered, shaking his head. The impudent pigs had no idea what was coming; they thought they knew everything! He would show them. They would worship him once tonight was over. He would sit on the high council of the new world.

After tonight.

The sound of scuffling and muffled screams interrupted all conversation at the table. Moments later, Bamda and two SS agents half dragged and half carried a bound and gagged woman into the room.

Haley, seated in the gallery above, now understood why she had to be here at this time and place. Damor could have been stopped at any moment, but this meeting brought all the dark heads of the hydra into one place at one time. As his karmic equal, it was her task and hers alone to bring this dark cycle to its conclusion. If this meeting succeeded, if she failed, the world would never recover from the stain of evil that would surely envelop it. Once loosed from their prison of matter within the bowels of the Earth, the dark prince and his minions would wreak havoc on the planet's inhabitants on a scale beyond imagination.

The hand that rested on her shoulder in comfort was a hand no less determined to aid her in her enterprise. She reached up, placed her hand over his, and smiled in grim expectancy. "I think I know what needs to be done."

Dr. Stein, her friend, co-worker, and brother in humanity, simply nodded for her to take the lead.

Haley's attention was drawn down onto the floor of the chamber, where the conversation of men had stopped. Why was the woman tied up? A hostage? Haley leaned over to Rudy and whispered, "I must get closer." He reluctantly agreed.

Silently, the pair eased back from the railing of the second tier and disappeared into the dark recesses of the upper rotunda. Slipping down a flight of stairs unseen, they found their way behind a bookcase on the floor of the chamber itself. Though they could no longer see the group, they could now hear everything clearly. If they could remain undetected, it would merely be a matter of waiting for the right moment.

From a place deep within her consciousness Haley knew—as athletes and great soldiers know—that the moment of truth was fast approaching. And, like all those who are tested through deed, she found that the waiting ... the interminable tedium and anxiety of waiting—became itself a test. She looked up and saw her friend beaming his confidence in her abilities in the faint light.

Haley smiled at him, sending her gratitude in a thought: "Thank you. Thank you for believing."

Bamda finally had the woman strapped onto a metal frame which they hoisted onto the table, laying it flat. Her eyes searched the grinning, leering faces of the men now bending eagerly forward, like so many wolves about to pounce on an injured rabbit. With obvious glee, Bamda busied himself with his task, putting large red candles into a geometric configuration around the woman—obviously having done this before—while Damor rattled on about energy flows, celestial alignments, and other secrets of the lower regions. From a large mahogany case, Bamda withdrew several surgical instruments and oddly shaped glass bottles and placed the items near the feet of the now-frantic woman, who watched in horror. She realized that something very, very bad was about to happen to her.

After Damor finished inspecting the layout and condition of the paraphernalia, he returned to his place, every eye on him in dark fascination and curiosity. "Remove her gag and chloroform the sow."

Bamda moved in and removed the terrified woman's gag.

She began to scream immediately. "Please. Please don't do this, I beg of you! Please!"

Damor, cold and clinical as a professor in a mathematics class, went on with his lecture. "You can see by her condition that she is infusing her blood with the animal passion of fear, a most necessary ingredient. Notice also that her pulse and respiration are greatly enhanced, increasing the size of the etheric envelope; this is most essential for the creation of the Incubus."

A few feet away, behind the bookcases, Haley and the ever-stolid Dr. Stein crouched in silence, horrified at the icy fashion in which the demonic group was about to dispatch that poor suffering woman. Beyond her disbelief that a human being could ever deserve such a fate, Haley was reminded of what she had learned about the law of cause and effect—no person suffered a fate unless she had been responsible for creating that same fate somewhere in her past, no matter how distant that past might have been. The hostage's frightened voice, echoing through the empty shelves that once had contained the greatest literature in the world, was the voice of a soul acutely aware of what was about to happen to it.

Haley steeled her sensitive heart to the sounds of suffering; she had work to do, work that might put an end to the madness. Optimistic that she might save the woman, she tried to send her thoughts of peace. Whoever she was, she was immune to Haley's subtle psychic suggestions of patience and fortitude.

"Please! Stop! I'll do anything you ask—anything!"

Haley's ears perked up, her face alarmed. "It's Ann!"

Damor moved directly over Ann so she could see him clearly, cold in the face of her hysteria. "How does it feel to have betrayed our bargain? Hmm? You stupid American bitch—take your medicine with some dignity." Before she could respond, Bamda placed the heavily doused cloth of chloroform over her mouth. Seconds later, her body fell limp.

Haley shrank back another inch behind the shelf. Ann. Damor had somehow gotten hold of Ann. It explained everything: the rumors, her mysterious disappearance . . .

. . . much like her own.

Before Rudy could stop her, Haley walked around the edge of the case, heading directly toward the large table. She smiled as she took her resigned steps toward destruction—they didn't hear or see her coming, so rapt were the snakes in anticipation of consuming their prey. By her inner sight, she saw that a lurid scarlet glow flickered about the inhuman faces, surrounding and enveloping the table and its occupants. The room, once a beautiful place for higher learning, now glowed darkly from the light of the blackened, red candles adding to the inner stain of vile passions swarming through the dark assemblage.

Damor continued with his details and intricacies about the destruction of the human temple, the body. Then he stopped, his eyes riveted on the soft glowing form of purity approaching his enclave. He could not believe his luck.

Haley Olsten—alive and well and now within his grasp, never to escape again. He gently set down the scalpel he was holding. "Gentlemen, please meet Miss Olsten, from America and points east."

Every eye in the room went to Haley, who radiated complete peace, and whose countenance was that of simple human dignity. The men nearer to Haley shrank from her, as though they smelled something offensive. Haley continued to smile confidently.

The bloated leader of the Ahnenerbe stood up, his face red with rage. "What is she doing here? This spoils everything!"

Damor glanced at Bamda, their knowing smiles to one

another reflecting their awareness of the unbelievable good change in fortune. "On the contrary; Miss Olsten will be of great assistance to us."

Bamda began to move casually around the table toward Haley, picking up the chloroform-soaked rag on the way, his metal heels *click-clicking,* adding to the freakish hollow emptiness of the still room.

Haley, totally aware of everything around her, remained steadfast in the face of the dragon, her courage powered by a conviction not based on theory, but on fact.

Rudy watched and admired her courage—the Brothers of Love had chosen their warrior well. He wished he had had more time to know her and learn of this great courage which she so easily displayed. Well, there was always time after she was gone . . . if permitted by his Teacher. Right then, he wanted more than anything to study from Haley and learn to be the things that made her so grand. What bravado, what fearlessness.

Haley closed her eyes, calling up all the beauty, love, and compassion that only an Initiate could command from the Higher Realms of Spirit. Shutting out the room and centering her thoughts within her heart, she called upon Him whom she knew would aid and assist. This was His battle alone, though He acted always through the vehicle of a soul dedicated in service to humanity. "Thou, who called me to the path of labor . . ."

Bamda stopped a few feet away and raised the rag as though to give it to her. "It is past that time. Pray as you wish . . . we laugh at you." True to his words, he started to laugh.

Haley continued, her voice trembling with power and love. ". . . accept my ableness and my desire. Accept my labor, O Lord."

At the pronunciation of the last words, a great hum began to fill the room. The dark men pressed their hands to their ears, trying to shut it out. The lights flickered and, one by one, began to extinguish as the volume of the hum increased.

Damor, frozen in disbelief over the unexpected turn of events, began to chant his black words of darkness—but no sound came from his mouth. Within seconds he began to change in form; gone were his handsome face and smooth skin, now replaced with small red eyes, his skin covered with open sores. Even the black magicians in attendance could not believe what their eyes showed them. He had done it. The prince from India was everything he had said he was.

Within moments, a gargantuan beast—half human, half animal—stood where Saling had stood moments before, emitting the foul stench of decaying flesh. Several of the weaker members fainted or cowered with their hands covering their heads; the vicious and strong hissed cheers at the long-awaited arrival of their true master.

As the scene continued in frenzied hysteria and madness, Haley continued to intone the sacred mantra ". . . because by day and by night, Thou beholdest me. Manifest thy hand, O Lord."

To the amazement of Rudy and every person in that room, Haley started to glow in a different fashion—strange, wonderfully eerie, and luminescent, a soft silvery light shone from her in every direction. As each moment passed, Haley's radiance and splendor increased, until the intensity of her shining heart became so bright that every person in the room had to shield his eyes from it.

The low hum, which sounded like a swarm of bees in the distance, grew in volume. The sound became more distinguishable; instead of a warm and soothing hum, it became clear all at once that the sound was in fact an angelic chorus of thousands of souls, bonded in a unity of love, from the Higher Realms. The once-darkened library was now lit up brilliantly with flashing rainbow colors of such intensity as to blind every heart not purified by love.

Bamda screamed, his hands covering his eyes. "I can't see! Why can't I see? Someone help me, help me!"

Haley finished the final phrase, her voice growing deeper with power. ". . . Great is the darkness, *I follow thee!*"

As the last syllables of the words faded, a Great Presence appeared, at first unformed in a shadowy orb but resplendent in the sheer enormity of its pulsing grandeur which penetrated every single creature in the room with its streamers of love. Haley remained immovable, her eyes closed in intense meditation, with pink and blue rays of light streaming out of her heart and into the center of what now appeared to be a flaming star.

The fiery celestial body began to coalesce and define into a very clear outline, first of an Angel, then, unmistakably, of the Master. Slowly, He descended from the air above Haley and entered her. The room, now brilliant as with the light of the sun itself, contained no shadow or hint of darkness. It was as though every angle had some fantastic light source shining upon it, seemingly reflecting light from within itself, joined as it were with the absolute light of life itself.

Haley— no longer Haley—gazed at them, the supreme essence of benevolent love emanating from eyes borrowed by The Great One. The alignment was completed. Slowly and with a great and shining smile, He looked at the body He was wearing and the little lives around Him—ever so important to His heart. "My children, thou art lost in thy ways. Turn within the folds of thy loving heart, lest harm befall thy destiny."

As cockroaches will when a light is turned on, many of the Nazis scampered away, unable to bear the proximity of such an august Presence. The remaining members started to growl and hiss, their dark hearts recoiling from the words of a Great One.

297

Dr. Stein blinked. Unable to comprehend what he was witnessing, he started to weep in shame, slowly emerging from the safety of the shelves. Languorously, he trudged toward what he had wished for his entire lifetime. Now, dream beyond dream, hope beyond hope, his wish was granted. He lowered his eyes, the weight of his unworthiness staining the supreme joy at finally meeting the Master.

The Master turned toward him and smiled. "You have labored well, your life given freely for your brothers. You are sinless." The sweetness of the words, coupled with the power of divine compassion, had the immediate effect of prostrating Dr. Stein. The Master glided a few silent steps to his young brother and gently lifted him up. "A selfless heart is the only treasure a man can possess that has true value in the higher worlds."

The Great Soul began to move among the men, touching them one at a time and speaking words only they could hear. Some screamed, driven instantly mad by their rejection of the divine love being poured into their hearts. Some wept, the ray of compassion burning away the chains that had fettered their souls in matter. Others fainted, overwhelmed by the sublime power that healed and uplifted them. Bamda, rather than be touched by a hand that would force full awareness of his dark deeds, ran blindly from the room and into the streets of Berlin. He would be found in the city dump, slumped over a heap of refuse, the revolver he had used to end his life still wedged into his mouth.

A grotesque snapping animal some eight feet high now stood alone in defiance of the Great Prince of Peace. Its minions healed or scattered to the winds, it growled in hatred of the Master who would stand as sole agent against his plans. A thousand lost voices, blended into one horrible screeching sound, bellowed, "There is another one, and another time. This isn't finished."

Filled with anguish, it let loose a wail of hatred and anger that was never forgotten by anyone who heard it that night.

As the Beast uttered these words, it vanished in a screaming shriek, consumed by a blaze of exploding fire. Moments later, the dead and smoldering body of Damor Saling, maharaja of India, lay still on the ground.

As the last echoes of the now-vanished demon faded, so too vanished the supreme light of the One who suffers all for humanity's sake. What remained in the awful silence were the former damned souls, now redeemed. They sat stiffly now, looking around the table, wondering what they were to do. Horrified at their lives, many just stared blankly into the stillness of the room.

Haley, now herself, walked over to the table, joined by her friend and brother. She reached for Ann's wrist and lifted it, noticing that she was missing several fingers on her left hand. "She is still alive. We must get her out of here." Rudy remained speechless in his awe of Haley: someone who could be so pure as to be a vehicle for such a sublime spirit of love. All he could muster was a simple and choked "Yes . . . of course."

They turned to find a large man—too big for his clothes—standing before them. "I have lived my whole life in pursuit of power," he began in earnest remorse. "What could I . . . never knowing love. Please, do not hate me." The rumpled ex-Nazi started to sob. Haley stepped forward and took the sobbing man in her arms. "You are forgiven. Not by me, but through the power of love you released yourself in the simple act of turning to your own heart."

Regaining something of his composure, he stood. "I can help you get the woman and yourselves out of here. There is nothing here for me now—they will surely execute me once they discover that I will no longer head their department of political assassinations. But where can we go?"

Dr. Stein stepped forward. "I know a place. Out of Germany. Can you get us to the English Channel?"

The man smiled, relieved. "My name is Heinrich Muechinzer." Haley and Rudy introduced themselves, handshakes passed as among family and old friends. Heinrich glanced at his pocket watch. "We must hurry, as others will be arriving shortly."

Rudy untied Ann and then started to pick her up. The hand of their new friend stopped him. "Let me carry the girl." And without allowing anyone to assist him, he swept the still-unconscious Ann up off the table and into his arms. "Follow me. I have a car."

Without another word, the small party of warriors moved quickly toward an elevator that led to an underground parking garage. In it were several armed soldiers and chauffeurs standing next to some two dozen large sedans.

"Let me handle the SS."

Effortlessly, their new friend dispatched his driver and bodyguard on some pretext; minutes later, they were gliding on the autobahn out of Berlin.

Dunkirk was forbidding in the fog-shrouded night. Haley watched her friends waiting anxiously near the shore for their passage across the English Channel. None of them had slept in the three days since their race out of Berlin to the French coastline. Had it not been for their new friend, they would never have left Germany alive. True to his word, he got their party passed at every checkpoint and station, by virtue of his position in the secret ranks of the Third Reich. Haley thanked the hidden stars above for his presence. Noticing that Heinrich was lighting his thirteenth cigarette in a row, she reached over and took his hand. "I have never thanked you for your bravery, my friend."

Heinrich dropped the cigarette. "No, Fraulein, it is I who thank you. I never knew how dark my heart was until it was filled with love." Haley reached over and hugged the large man.

Dr. Stein turned to the pair, cradling Ann in his arms. She did not see him and was unaware of her surroundings, still deep in shock. "They are late. They should have been here two hours ago."

"This is not good," Heinrich replied uneasily. "German troops patrol these shorelines with great frequency. If we are discovered, there will be no excuse to explain our presence here."

Haley, lost in her inward thoughts, raised her hand to stop the conversation. "Signal again with the flashlight."

Rudy pulled the flashlight out from his coat and clicked out *blink . . . blink, blink, blink . . . blink.*

Off in the smoky distance, a yellow light, barely visible, flickered back in response. A thrill of relief went through the group. Five minutes later, a small raft *scurched* against the sand, and they heard the unmistakable sound of Britain's finest gently hallooing to where the tired group sat. Haley blinked. This couldn't be. Impossible.

Without regard to stealth or secrecy she ran to the shore, tears streaming from her eyes. Oh, to shout out such love! To let the dams of joy burst forth in rapture! Haley could not hold it in any longer.

"David!"

The man in the raft stood up straight and turned toward the shout. A moment later, recognition sinking in, he lurched from the small craft and began to run up the sandy beach.

Without breaking stride, the two lovers flew into each other's arms, weeping with hysterical joy. "How?" Haley exclaimed, "I don't understand?" David Hampton, unable to answer, did the only thing he knew to do—he kissed her.

"Captain?" a nervous sergeant exclaimed, "best be movin' on, sir. The Jerrys might a 'erd you."

David released his fiancée and held her at arm's length, still amazed with disbelief. "C'mon, darling. We've a boat to catch."

Moments later, the small raft disappeared into the fog, leaving Germany and its future in the capable hands of destiny.

The beginning.